My Brother's Keeper

Donna Malane

My Brother's Keeper

Minotaur Books

A Thomas Dunne Book
New York

A THOMAS DUNNE BOOK FOR MINOTAUR BOOKS.
An imprint of St. Martin's Press.

MY BROTHER'S KEEPER. Copyright © 2013 by Donna Malane. All rights reserved. Printed in the United States of America. For information, address St. Martin's Press, 175 Fifth Avenue, New York, N.Y. 10010.

www.thomasdunnebooks.com
www.minotaurbooks.com

Library of Congress Cataloging-in-Publication Data

Names: Malane, Donna, author.
Title: My brother's keeper : a mystery / Donna Malane.
Description: First U.S. edition. | New York : Minotaur Books / A Thomas Dunne Book, 2017. | "First published in New Zealand by HarperCollinsPublishers (New Zealand) Limited" [2013] — Verso title page.
Identifiers: LCCN 2017025693 | ISBN 9781250111340 (hardcover) | ISBN 9781250111357 (ebook)
Subjects: LCSH: Women private investigators—Fiction. | Women ex-convicts—Fiction. | Missing children—Fiction. | Mothers and daughters—Fiction. | Innocence (Psychology)—Fiction. | Psychological fiction. | GSAFD: Mystery fiction.
Classification: LCC PR9619.4.M342 M9 2017 | DDC 823/.92—dc23
LC record available at https://lccn.loc.gov/2017025693

Our books may be purchased in bulk for promotional, educational, or business use. Please contact your local bookseller or the Macmillan Corporate and Premium Sales Department at 1-800-221-7945, extension 5442, or by email at MacmillanSpecialMarkets@macmillan.com.

First published in New Zealand by
HarperCollins*Publishers (New Zealand) Limited*

First U.S. Edition: December 2017

10 9 8 7 6 5 4 3 2 1

To my parents, Colleen and George Reid.
I couldn't have been luckier.

CHAPTER 1

The strips of crimson decorations dangling from the light fittings reminded me of intestines. Clearly, I was not in a festive mood. But at least I'd swum my fifty lengths. Okay, widths. My hand was already on the exit door when the intercom announced two minutes' silence to mark the anniversary of the Pike River mine disaster. Twenty-nine men dead. Two minutes' silence. It didn't seem a lot to ask. I waited, self-consciously clutching my takeaway coffee with raisin scone balanced precariously on top. Toddlers in the kids' pool squatted, saveloy bums dipping the water, as they peered into their parents' suddenly still faces. The splashing, squealing group had become a facsimile of the dead miners. Slumped. Unplugged from the grid.

In that hypnotic once-in-a-lifetime vacuum of silence my bloody phone rang.

Which is why I came to be waiting for Karen Mackie in Deluxe Café. She needn't have worn what she'd referred to as her 'kimono-style' pink blouse. I'd have recognised her anyway. No amount of exotic garb could disguise the institutional grey of her skin. That's not fair. Her skin wasn't grey. A bit worn maybe, but living in skin for thirty-odd years does that. I don't normally have an attitude towards former prison inmates, but there was good reason for my prejudice against this one. On the phone Karen had introduced herself as Vex's ex-cellmate. Vex was serving time for procuring the murder of a young prostitute called Niki. Niki was my little sister.

Karen started right in, giving me no chance to set the ground rules. 'I want to hire you to find my daughter, Sunny. That's Sunny spelt with a "U". For sunshine,' she added with a shy smile. 'Her father was granted custody when I went away.'

'Went away', huh? So we were going to talk in euphemisms.

'I've already done a basic internet search but couldn't find much. Justin probably changed his name. Changed their name, I mean.' A plastic bag bulging with papers and photographs sat on the little wooden table between us. I let it lie there. 'I want you to make sure she's safe.'

Okay. That got my attention. 'You think he's molesting her?'

She lifted her shoulders but that was all the answer she gave.

'Have you told the police?'

Again the shrug. 'They don't take much notice of anything I have to say.' She stared at the plastic bag, willing me to pick it up. 'It's all in there. Names, photos, contact details.' She flicked a look at me and then dropped her eyes to the bag again. 'I haven't seen Sunny since the day I was arrested. She was seven. She'll be fourteen now.'

She saw me do the calculation. In New Zealand, that kind of time is reserved for the very worst crimes. Her body straightened and she clutched at the handbag in her lap.

'I'll pay you, of course.'

I thought about it for a full five seconds. That's how long it took me to calculate my fiscal position. Since we were in the game of euphemisms I'd describe my present bank balance as 'lean'.

'These are my terms: if I find the person you're looking for but they don't want to be found, I won't tell you where they are. But you still pay me.' She thought about it, then nodded. Once. 'It's not because you've been in prison.' I needed her to know that. 'They're the terms I have for everyone.'

She nodded again. 'Okay.'

I slid a prepared one-page agreement across the table to her, the same one I use for all my clients, and she reached for the pen and signed without reading a word of it. Her hand was shaking but I could see she was elated, excited as a child. Grateful. The page was pushed back across the table. I spun it around to face me. Her signature was back-sloping but that wasn't the only sign Karen lacked confidence. Her nails were bitten. She had trouble looking me in the eye and somewhere along the line she'd picked up an odd blinking mannerism.

'Sunny won't want to see me but that's okay. It's not why I'm doing this. I just need to know she's okay, that's all.'

I let some of my attitude go but I was struggling with how

she had heard about me. The spectre of Vex stood between us.

'Look, Karen, I have to ask about your …' I hunted for a non-judgmental word to describe her relationship with my sister's killer, 'your association with Vex.'

Karen shrugged, but it was more a 'lost for words' shrug than a 'I don't give a shit' shrug, so I didn't take offence. 'I told her I needed someone to search for Sunny and she said she knew a woman who specialised in finding missing people.' She must have taken my habitual frown personally because she added, 'You don't get much choice of roommate in prison.'

We sat in silence. I was thinking I had no right to judge her. I had no idea what was going through her head. Maybe there was nothing. Seven years in prison you might learn how to do that. I was the first to speak. 'Okay. I'll do some preliminary work. See what I can find out about where your ex might be living. I can't promise anything but I'll give it a go.'

'Thank you.' She sniffed loudly. No doubt wiping away tears is a no-no in prison. I felt my attitude thawing and thought it wouldn't hurt to give her something. Some little fragment of hope.

'Your daughter might want to get to know you now that you're out of prison. You can never tell with fourteen-year-olds. Don't rule it out.'

I saw her slam a door on the gift I'd offered. 'There's something you need to know,' she said, straightening her back. 'I tried to hurt her.' For the first time she looked me in the eyes. 'That's what I went away for. I tried to kill my daughter.'

I think I said 'Oh'.

The two women sitting at the table beside us had gone very

still. Deluxe is a tiny café and I was pretty sure they'd heard her. I made a mental note not to choose this place again for meetings with clients. Karen kept her eyes on me but didn't drop her voice. She knew they were listening.

'My excuse back then was that I had a heavy P habit. Half the time I was off my face, the rest of the time I was doing everything I could to get that way. But that wasn't what it was. I was empty.' She stared directly at me. 'That was before I found God. Before He found me.' I didn't even try to hide my scepticism but she lifted her face as if to take the blow full on. 'He gives us all His love, you know,' she said, dry as a desert storm. 'The kids were making a racket. I took the handbrake off and let the car roll into Lake Pupuke. There was a man feeding the swans in the next bay round who saw it. He dived in and managed to get Sunny's seat belt undone. He pulled her to the surface and gave her mouth to mouth. He saved her.'

There was nothing, absolutely nothing I could say. But she didn't need me to respond.

'Thank God,' she added, in that different way Christians say it. 'The judge gave me some credit for telling the truth. For not pretending it was an accident.' I saw the blotches of red bloom across her neck, saw the internal struggle as she forced the confession out of herself like some kind of exorcism. I wouldn't have been surprised if her head had spun around 360 degrees. Well, okay, maybe a little surprised. 'I tried to kill her. I tried to kill my beautiful little girl.' The air seemed to have gone out of her. Her whole body slumped, deflated. She wasn't the only one. We both needed a minute. So did the two women beside us. They stared bug-eyed at each other and hadn't said a word or moved a muscle since Karen's confession began. I was struggling with how to ask the question when she answered it unprompted.

'There's no answer to "why". No excuse.' She hitched the shrug that I already recognised as habitual. 'Sure, I was an addict.' Her voice broke but she brought it back under control. 'But I knew what I was doing.'

We went over a few details of how I liked to work, she wrote me a down-payment cheque, I punched her number into my mobile. All the time I was trying to think of some way to get out of this deal. The signed agreement on the table was like a rebuke. Call me picky, but I didn't want to work for a woman who tried to kill her own child. I gathered up the bag of documents, still trying to think of a way out of the deal when she unexpectedly clutched at my shoulders and pulled me into an awkward embrace. I felt the fragile bones beneath her skin.

'I'm not that person any more. I would never harm …' She held me at arm's length, her palms damp on my shoulders. 'Just find Sunny and make sure she's okay. That's all I ask.'

For the first time since she entered the café, Karen smiled. It looked genuine to me, but what do I know? Moments before she'd told me of her attempt to murder her daughter I'd been warming to this woman. I didn't speak until we reached the door. Something was bothering me. I had to fight against the Wellington wind to be heard.

'Seven years is a long time to serve, even for the attempted murder of a child.'

Karen stalled with her back to me. 'I had two children,' she said. She turned her head but kept her body facing away. 'It was Falcon's fifth birthday. He thought we were going to The Warehouse to buy a PlayStation.'

She walked away down Cambridge Terrace in the direction of the Basin Reserve. Her heels made the lightest of clicks on the pavement.

CHAPTER 2

EASTER 2005

Sunny

Dad puts his key in the lock and pushes the door open with his shoulder. It makes the same screech it always makes but inside the house is bigger than it was before. Like a house we've visited but not lived in. The furniture is placed perfectly like in a TV programme. Falcon's toys are still on the mat. Pearl looks like someone else's budgie. Even though I know she likes it when I make kissy sounds through the bars, I don't do it. Dad puts the jug on. I don't know what Mum does. I go straight to bed without asking if I can watch TV. Dad says he'll come in later and tuck me in and then Mum says goodnight but she isn't looking at me when she says it.

My room isn't my room any more either, even though Baby Bear is still on the pillow exactly where I'd put him. Mum says I'm too old to be taking a teddy bear with me everywhere, but I don't take him everywhere, not to school, anyway. The night is very dark and it goes on forever. I can't stop shivering from the cold of the sheets. I feel as if I'm drowning in the darkness.

In the morning it's still the weekend so I don't have to get dressed for school. The house is very quiet like its holding its breath under water. My feet are huge with cold but I stand in the same place, not moving, just listening. Whiskey is waiting to see what I do before she moves her fat bum off the warm place she's made for herself. She's a lazy arse. I only tell her she's a lazy arse when Mum can't hear me or she would smack my bum for swearing. When I pull my old jersey over the top of my pyjamas my skin feels crumpled and itchy but I stop shivering. My feet are still freezing. There are no socks in the undies drawer but it doesn't matter. The flappy slippers from the hospital wait for me beside the bed. Dad must have put them like that when he tucked me in. It can't have been Mum. She would have put Whiskey out the window and shut it again tight so the rain wouldn't leak in and fill up the whole room.

Mum is staring out the kitchen window with her arms crossed under her titties, making them stick up like an advertisement for a chicken going into the oven. Dad is drinking his tea from the yellow mug with the happy face on it that someone from work gave him. Falcon's favourite red chair is pushed up against the wall beside the fridge. His T-shirt with the plastic pony on the front is scrunched up on it. There are globs of banana from yesterday on the seat and the sparkly rainbow sticker on the leg from when he was just a baby. I wonder what it will feel like to miss him. Will the feeling go on forever?

Dad says some things while I'm eating my cornflakes. He only says them so it's not so quiet. Mum doesn't turn around. My cornflakes taste funny. When I have to stand beside Mum to put my bowl in the sink she slides her eyes sideways at me. My stomach feels sick. I go outside to play the 'knife in the grass' game but it doesn't really work with one person and, anyway, I know I'm cheating because I always throw it into the grass where I know my foot can reach. The lawn is muddy because of the rain and the knife goes in fast and squishy. Then the policemen arrive, only one's a lady and she doesn't have a police uniform on but she does have a badge and she shows it to Mum.

They bring all the cold air from outside into the kitchen and they sit at the table. The lady policeman has her knees tight together under her skirt but the policeman sits at the corner of the table with one knee on each side of the table leg. The lady policeman takes out a yellow notebook with a spiral at the top and puts it on the table but she doesn't open it yet. No one says anything except for the tap that drips into the sink: *plonk, plonk, plonk*. Then Dad scrapes his chair back and says to Mum she should do it and get it over with. She looks at him with her lips tight and I think she's going to cry but she doesn't. The policeman has a bit of bogey sticking out his nose but it doesn't make me want to laugh.

The police car is parked in the driveway with its front just touching the towbar of Dad's car, which Mum says is the love of his life. Mum's car was a piece of shit. I try saying it like her —

piece of shit — and then I say shit again three times just to hear what it sounds like coming out of my mouth. The intercom in the police car is talking as if it doesn't know the people aren't in there. I see myself in the police car window. I look scared. I wonder if Mum's new car will be a piece of shit too. There'll be plenty of room for me in the back now without Falcon's booster seat.

The sky is weird. It hurts my eyes. In some places it's blue, like the sky should be, but where it meets the land there are clouds all hunched up. They look like the mushroom clouds atom bombs make. They're eating the sky right up and God knows what will happen then. I want to find a big tree to lie under but the grass will be too wet. My stomach hurts.

Dad comes out of the house and waves his hand at me like I'm very far away, but I'm standing right in front of him. Dad must be feeling the weirdness, too. Whiskey winds herself around Dad's leg. Her back is arched right up and her tail is like a toetoe, only it's golden and black. She's rubbing against Dad but she's looking at me.

Dad says, 'Come inside. The police want to have a word.'

'I don't want to,' I say.

'Just tell them what you remember, love,' he says.

He holds the door open for me with his arm stretched out and I go in underneath it like I'm playing Oranges and Lemons, but I'm not.

Dad sits me on his knee like when I was little but my feet touch the floor now. My bony arse must hurt him but he doesn't say anything. Mum doesn't look at me. She has a tissue bunched up in her fist and her sleeves are fat with the ones she's already used. The notebook with the spiral is open on the table. The lady policeman has written enough to cover the whole page. There's an empty space at the bottom. I guess that's for writing down what I say.

'Sunny?' she says, making my name a question. 'Can you tell me what happened in the car yesterday?'

I don't know if I can so I don't say anything. Mum takes her glass to the sink and fills it from the tap. She fills it right to the top so that some spills over the edge and all over her hand but she doesn't drink any.

The policeman coughs. When Dad and the lady policeman look at him he smiles at me and says, 'How old are you, Sunny?'

'Seven,' I say. Then I say, 'Just,' because he's a policeman and I want to tell the whole truth. 'I'm two years older than Falcon and it was his birthday yesterday.'

Dad makes a harrumphing noise and his leg jigs up and down making me wobble but he's not playing 'bronco riding'. He stops jiggling and turns the harrumphing into a cough.

'That's why Mum was taking us to The Warehouse.' I don't say anything else while she writes it down in her notebook. I don't want to have to keep saying it. I want to say it once and get it over with like Mum did.

'To get your brother a birthday present?' I nod because my throat feels tight like Whiskey's belly when she's full of kittens.

Mum puts her glass of water in the sink and then turns around to face the table. Her arms hang down her sides like she's forgotten about them. She's looking at the policeman holding Falcon's Robot Man. His hands are between his knees like the Robot Man is heavy but he's not. He's just plastic. He makes Robot Man's arms go up and down like he's marching. Robot Man probably has Falcon's slobber all over him because Falcon's always putting him in his mouth.

'Your mum was driving, and you and your little brother were in the car,' the lady policeman says. I don't know what I'm supposed to say. I look at Dad and he nods at me without smiling, so I nod my head at her. She writes something down even though I didn't say anything. The policeman makes Robot Man's head turn right around. I look at the buttons on the lady policeman's jacket.

She puts the pen down and looks right at me. She says, 'Do you remember Mum stopping the car?' She's not her mum and I want to say that, but I don't. I just look at the buttons. 'Do you remember the car stopping?'

'Yes,' I say, because I do remember. 'There's heaps of swans there.'

The policeman looks up when I say that. He puts Robot Man on the table and then because we're all looking at it he picks him up again. Then he doesn't know what to do with him.

'You and Falcon were making a lot of noise,' the police lady says.

Out the window behind Mum's head, the sky is white. Sometimes a sparrow flies past, its little wings beating fast, chirruping like mad. Every time it happens Pearl chirrups back but she has to stay in her cage. I can't see Mum's face because of the white sky.

I try to explain to the lady policeman but the words don't work properly. 'Falcon wanted Mum to take us to The Warehouse but Mum was fed up with us making all that racket,'

I say. 'She had the yips.' I look at Mum to make sure it's okay to say that but she turns around to look out the window again. I can't see what her hands are doing.

The lady policeman writes it all down and doesn't look up at me. 'You and Falcon were making a racket and your mum got out of the car.' She looks at me like she wants me to answer a question but I don't know what it is. Then she does ask a question. 'Do you know what a handbrake is?' I know the answer and nod. I hope she'll smile at me for answering right but she doesn't. 'And do you know where the handbrake is in your mum's car?'

This time I say 'Yes,' out loud but just watch her hand write down the words. My bony arse is sore from sitting on Dad's leg. The sky around Mum's head hurts my eyes. A seagull flies past the window. It disappears into Mum's head like she's eaten it, then it comes out the other side crying and flies off safe.

'Do you remember your mum doing anything to the handbrake, Sunny?' She's wearing pink lipstick but it's rubbed off a bit. 'Before she got out of the car?' She's looking at me like she wants me to say yes and get it over with like Mum did. My hair sticks to my neck where it's hot. I wish I'd taken my pyjamas off and not just put my sweater on top. Dad lifts me off his knee but keeps his hands there so I'll know he's not angry with me. His hands are hot and his fingers squeeze into my stomach but he doesn't mean to hurt me. I tell him I need to pee and he lets me go. I walk straight out the door without looking back at him or the policeman with Robot Man or the lady policeman with the notebook. Mum has the tips of her fingers on her lips like she is trying to stop them from saying something.

Outside, the white clouds have taken over all of the sky. A blackbird with a bright orange beak jumps across the grass. It pokes its beak into the squishy mud looking for a worm to kill. Whiskey doesn't look at me even when I make the special food-time call, 'Whis whis whis.' My voice sounds funny and then Dad comes and takes me back inside.

Mum isn't there. She must be lying down. The policeman is leaning against the fridge door. He's jumbled all the letters up and they don't spell Falcon's name any more. I'll have to fix it when he goes. The lady policeman is still sitting at the table with the notebook in front of her. Dad's hand is on my shoulder. 'It's okay, love,' he says, 'nearly there,' as if we were on a trip in the car. A green letter C is on the floor next to the policeman's big black shoe. My stomach feels funny but I don't know if it's hungry or sick. Dad pulls out the chair beside the lady policeman and I sit on it because that's what I'm supposed to do. I don't mind because it means I can't see the weird white sky where Mum was standing.

'No one is angry with you,' the lady policeman says, and smiles her lips to show me she's lying. She has dark hairs on her lip but she's a lady.

I don't know what to say to make it better so I say, 'I'm sorry, Dad,' but he doesn't look at me. The way that he's sitting there like he's broken, with his big Adam's apple going up and down, he looks like someone else's father, not my dad.

'Look at me,' the lady policeman says, and I look at her eyes, which have freckles in them. 'You and Falcon were in the car making a racket and your mum got angry with you because she had the yips,' she says, and then she stops talking but she nods her head up and down so I nod, too. 'Good girl,' she says but she doesn't smile. 'And then your mum took the handbrake off and got out of the car and the car rolled into the water.'

The policeman's foot makes a glucky sound on the lino where Falcon's juice tipped over. He closes the door softly behind him. He must be going to check on Mum. The blue F for Falcon has fallen under the fridge door and Whiskey's hair is all stuck to it. I guess Mum will have to throw it in the rubbish. The lady policeman is still looking at me, so I nod. I hope Mum has her drugs so she doesn't have the yips with the policeman. Then the lady policeman asks me if I remember the man rescuing me from under the water, but she doesn't ask about Falcon and I don't tell her about him crying when the car filled up with water. She stops writing and draws a line under her last words like it's The End.

I don't like the part of the hallway that goes past Mum's bedroom. The door is open and I hope Mum is lying down asleep, but she isn't. She's sitting on the little stool in front of her dresser where the round butterfly box with all of her make-up is. I'm not allowed to touch Mum's butterfly box. She's staring at the mirror so I see two of her, two mums looking at each other. I've gone all the way past her door and I'm nearly at mine when she says, 'Sunny,' and I stop, but she doesn't say anything else so I have to walk back to the doorway. The policeman is in the room with her. He's got his arms folded and he's staring at the back of her head like he's waiting for her to hurry up. I put my hand up to hold on to the door. I don't know which mum I should be looking at, but they're not looking at me anyway. It's only six steps from here to my room. I want to lie in my bed with the duvet pulled up over my head and make a tent for Baby Bear and me. I don't want the white sky looking in my window and making me sick.

Then Mum slides her eyes at me, but she doesn't move her head, and I have to press my feet hard into the floor so I don't fall over. My stomach feels like it's got runny poos.

'I'm going away for a while, Sunny.' She watches me but she doesn't move. 'It's for the best.' She just watches, as the big white clouds eat the sky behind her and again in the mirror where that other mum is watching me, too.

CHAPTER 3

Wolf was performing his habitual morning tap-dance routine around the dog bowl when Sean gave a perfunctory knock and pushed the door open. From the way Wolf behaved you'd think my ex-husband was the love of his life, returning from the battlefield years after being declared missing in action. Maybe it was like that for Wolf. For all I knew he was still waiting for Sean to come home. I'm not projecting. Sean was wearing a charcoal suit which looked really good on him.

'How's the baby?' I asked, reminding myself.

'Good. Good,' he repeated, squinting at me as if my question was other than innocent. As if. 'Not so much a baby any more though.' He reached for the little coffee pot that used to be his.

I took it off him. 'You could knock, you know.'

'I did,' he said.

This little exchange pretty much sums up our relationship now: both right, both saying the complete opposite. I started the coffee-making routine while he hunkered down and ruffled Wolf's neck fur. It wasn't so much the suit that looked good, but him in it. He'd lost a bit of weight around the midriff and muscled up in the thighs and biceps. I thought men were supposed to go to seed when they had babies. Oh no, that's right: it's us, the dumb sex, who do that. I shifted my focus back to the coffee-making but not before noticing his shoulders had muscled up, too.

'How's Robbie?' he asked, as if sensing my appraisal.

He was always good at reading me. I didn't want to discuss my lover with my ex, even if they had buddied up. Especially now they'd buddied up. I put his coffee on the table and took up a defensive position against the sink bench.

'To what do I owe the pleasure of this early morning visit?'

He brushed dog hairs off that good suit and watched Wolf shovel biscuits into his mouth. It was Sean's way of avoiding eye contact. I can still read him pretty well too.

'I want to talk to you about selling the house.' He looked around the room as if seeing it for the first time. 'With Patrick and all, it's time Sylvie and I bought a bigger place. Together, that is. Her place is tiny and anyway, it's time I put in my share.'

I bit the tongue that wanted to say he'd obviously put his share in already, which is why they'd gone from being a twosome to being a happy little family threesome. Instead I poured myself a coffee and kept silent. It wasn't Sean's fault he'd left me and taken up with a little pixie of a woman he worked with at Police HQ. Well, it was his fault. But on my grown-up days I accepted some of the responsibility. When my little sister Niki was murdered I'd become obsessed with finding the person responsible. It didn't help that Sean was a cop; in fact, it made things worse. I was on at him all day, every day about it. There was no room in my life for anything else. Sean was great at first but weeks turned into months and I kept hounding him all day and closing him out all night. Eventually he gave up on me. Some months before that I'd pretty much given up on myself. We separated. It was my idea. By the time I was ready to find my way back to him it was too late. He'd gone and found someone who was the complete opposite of me. I'm a rangy uncouth tomboy with a mean mouth and a habitual frown. Sylvie the pixie is friendly, feminine, finessed and fucking my husband. Okay, ex-husband, but still. Obviously this wasn't one of my grown-up days.

'Sell the house. Right,' I said. 'I'll get on to it. Anything else?'

'Diane ...'

I waited for him to say more. He didn't. He just looked at his cup and let my name hang in the air between us. Oversensitive as always, Wolf slunk under the table and dropped his head on Sean's regulation polished shoes. I refused to take that as a declaration of whose side he was on.

'It'll be tough letting the place go. Tough for both of us. I know that. But can we please try and not make it harder than it needs to be?'

At least he hadn't said selling our house would be good for me.

'You're right,' I said. 'We need to sell. It'll free us both up.'

I hadn't meant the words to sound so heavy with meaning. 'Money-wise,' I added. That still wasn't right but I didn't trust my voice to say more.

I told him I'd contact an agent and promised to keep him in touch with how it went. We made small talk and finished our coffee. Sean lovingly stroked Wolf's ears and gave my shoulder an awkward pat as he left. Of all the things we imagined when we were together, I'm sure neither of us imagined this. I watched him walk down the path.

His new butt looked good in that suit too.

While my resolve was still clear and before I could mull too much I phoned a real-estate agency. There's good mulling and bad mulling and I was pretty sure selling our marital home so Sean could buy a place for his new family would fit in the bad mulling basket. The receptionist was enthusiastic; an agent was free to come to appraise the property later in the afternoon.

'Good for her,' I said, and then into the uneasy silence added, 'thanks. That'll work for me too.' No need to take my churlishness out on her. That done, I put it out of my mind, wrung a third cup of coffee out of Sean's pot and took it through to the office. Wolf followed, climbed onto his sofa and prepared himself for a hard morning's work of lucid dreaming, punctuated by orchestral farting.

I started with the bulging plastic bag Karen had given me. She'd arranged the file roughly in chronological order, which gave me an easy overview of how events had unfolded. Opening a new file on my computer I dutifully copied down the dates of marriage, divorce and the births of their two children. Karen and Justin married shortly before Sunny was born, followed two years later by the arrival of their second child, Falcon. I flicked through the jumble of baby and little kid stuff: vaccination cards, first crayon scribblings and illustrated lists of milestones that all bore Sunny's name.

There wasn't much evidence of Falcon's arrival. Not a single photo of either parent holding the new baby boy. Occasionally he appeared propped up on a sofa in the back of a shot and in one photo Sunny was lying with him asleep on a play mat, but there were no proudly dated drawings or finger paintings as Falcon stumbled into toddlerhood.

The few family photos from that time showed a rake-thin Karen with dark rings under her eyes. It was pretty obvious this was when she had started using. Justin was thin, too, with no sign of the narcissistic body building he would take up after the death of his son. In photos close to the time of the killing, Sunny was often on the edge of frame as if she was trying to get as far away from her parents as possible. I warned myself against reading too much into this. At six or seven she was at an age when trying to escape parents' clutches is the norm.

Further down the pile I found a kindergarten photo of four-year-old Falcon, squinting suspiciously at the camera. He was small for his age. A tight, pinched little face and sandy-haired like his father, he wore a grubby woollen jersey that was unravelling at the neck. I copied the scribbled date on the back and then flicked forward through the documents to find the date he had died. Karen had killed him less than a month after the photo was taken.

I carefully returned the photo to the pile and then put the

whole lot back in the bag. I couldn't rid myself of the memory of that photo of Falcon, the last image of him alive. Did Karen carry it with her? Was it pinned up on the wall of her cell for those seven years? The son she had murdered. The little five-year-old boy who thought his mother was taking him to The Warehouse to buy a PlayStation.

Tracking Justin on the net turned out to be simple enough. After half an hour googling I knew Justin Alexander Bachelor was now married to a woman called Salena Kosovov. Salena owned and managed an 'exclusive' gym, Apricot, in Herne Bay, Auckland. From googled photos of the couple at charity and media events it was obvious both made use of the gym. Justin was pumped and polished and Salena had augmented the toned, bronzed body with expensive teeth, Botox and a boob job, which had miraculously failed to completely destroy her natural beauty.

I tracked back to find earlier photos of Justin. In the twelve months following Karen's sentencing, Justin pumped himself up to body builder size, met and married Salena and sired another son they called Neo. In the past couple of years Justin had deflated back down again to a more normal size, so maybe men do lose their bodies when they have kids after all. He was still a big guy, but nothing like what he was six years earlier. On his Facebook page he listed fourteen-year-old Sunny and five-year-old Neo as family members. Salena made no such 'family' claim to Sunny, not even the unfriendly sounding 'stepdaughter'.

Neo had the high cheekboned beauty of his mother, but not the same discipline with calories. A computer boy rather than a gym boy was my guess. A couple more minutes' searching and I found a photo of the whole family outside Salena's gym the first morning it opened. Sunny was in school uniform, which made it a simple enough match to search. Within five minutes I had the address of the private school she attended in St Mary's Bay and a quick click to the white pages gave the family's listed home address. The internet makes tracking people frighteningly easy.

I threw a Frisbee down the back yard for Wolf and thought about all this. Even allowing for the fact that Karen had only just got out of prison, where she'd been for the last seven years, she could probably have found this information herself. It occurred to me that Karen might not have hired me to find her daughter or even to check she was okay, but to make the first contact for her. It would be pretty hard to turn up unannounced on your teenage daughter's doorstep seven years after you tried to kill her; seven years after you'd successfully murdered her little brother.

As much as I wanted to convince myself it was okay to contact Sunny directly, I knew it wasn't. Plus I was pretty sure the police, who I liked to keep vaguely on the right side of, wouldn't think so either. I'd have to approach Justin first and hope he'd let me talk to his daughter. Nothing in the papers Karen gave me or anything I'd found on the net suggested Justin had been blamed for Karen's actions. No one had questioned his right or suitability to take over Sunny's custody either — not publicly, anyway. Given how closely the authorities must have investigated him, if Justin was using he must have been very good at hiding it. Or he had successfully stopped at the time of his son's death. It was possible, of course, that he'd never used — possible, but unlikely. I wondered if giving up drugs was what kicked the body building into action. Maybe they'd dealt with their guilt in parallel ways: Karen found sanctuary in the church and Justin had taken on the whole 'my body is a temple' number.

Wolf gave me what I swear was an ironic look as he dropped the Frisbee at my feet. He was bored with this game and knew my attention was elsewhere. With commitment this time, I hurled the Frisbee down the path again. Two things happened at once: a voice yelled in high-pitched outrage, and Wolf, barking and slavering with the kind of enthusiasm only a bored, one-eyed, overprotective ex-police dog can muster, launched himself at a besuited man, clutching his head with one hand and my Frisbee with the other.

Two cups of tea and a dripping packet of frozen peas later, Jason Baker had finally stopped shaking. But his mouth was still going strong. According to him, my reckless behaviour with the Frisbee had given him concussion and my dangerous dog should preferably be destroyed or, at the very least, be chained up at all times. Oh, please. I thought real-estate agents were made of tougher stuff. When he finally finished with the complaining I threw the peas back into the freezer, took Wolf into the office with me, closed the door and left Jason to click his well-polished heels through the house in what he called his 'appraisal process'. I'd offered to walk him through but he clearly thought Wolf and I were both dangerous. He was probably right — about me anyway. I'd pointed out that Wolf, as a well-trained ex-police dog, had merely pushed him to the ground and had not ripped his heart out as he was perfectly capable of doing. Jason remained unimpressed by my dog's restraint. Personally, the more Jason grizzled at me the more I admired Wolf's control. My dog's behaviour had been non-discriminatory; he'd have knocked over anyone who came onto the property uninvited, whereas I'd taken an instant personal dislike to the man. And that was after hitting him on the head with a Frisbee. He was just lucky I hadn't taken up the attitude before I let the Frisbee go.

Wolf sat bolt upright on his sofa, ears up in full alert. If I had ears like his I'd have done the same. I didn't like the sound of Jason clonking through my house with such proprietorial heels either. Our house, I mean. Sean's and my marital home. Wolf let out a low rumble of disapproval, which I suspect was just for my benefit. He's nice like that.

I picked up the phone. 'Karen? It's Diane Rowe.' I could hear her shallow breathing as she waited for me to continue. 'Justin and Sunny are living in Auckland.'

'That's wonderful,' she said. Nothing against Auckland, but I assumed she meant it was wonderful I'd found them.

'I'm not sure how I'll make the first contact, but I'd like to spend a couple of days up there sorting out how to go about things.'

'Yes, good. When?'

Jason was talking loudly on his mobile in the other room. I caught the phrase 'warm and welcoming'. I was pretty sure it wasn't me he was talking about.

'I can fly up first thing tomorrow,' I said. 'And all going well be back by Friday with a full report.'

'You can stay at my mother's place if you like,' she said. 'In Ponsonby. It's empty.' She was breathing fast. 'She's not there,' she added. 'I mean, Mum died a few months ago and I haven't got around to putting it on the market yet. I'm going to sell up and go live in a Christian commune in LA but I won't go until I know Sunny is alright. It's fully furnished and everything's still switched on.'

She fell silent as if embarrassed by her sudden chattiness. It was the most Karen had said in one burst. I realised she had no idea how close her mother's house was to where her daughter now lived.

'Okay,' I said. 'That sounds good.'

'The spare key is under the mat at the front door. Oh, and I'll put a cheque in the post to cover flight costs and all. I don't have internet banking, I'm sorry. There's a lot I haven't got my head around yet …'

I let the sentence peter out. No doubt there were a number of things other than internet banking she'd have to get her head around. High on the list would be how to live her life knowing she'd killed her five-year-old son and done her best to murder her seven-year-old daughter. Maybe living in that Christian commune would help.

Her offer of more money reminded me I needed to deposit her down payment cheque or risk getting an embarrassing call from the bank. 'We can sort out the money when I send you my report,' I said bravely. The silence stretched on. She wasn't an easy person to talk to by phone. Jason, on the other hand, was laughing loudly with someone as he opened and slammed wardrobe doors. Presumably, he was making sure they worked. Or looking for skeletons.

I forced myself back to my phone call. 'If Sunny doesn't want you to know anything about her, I won't tell you. That's the deal.' It felt cruel to remind her. The silence went on forever.

'Yes. I understand,' she said, finally. As I lowered the handset to the cradle I heard her add, 'God bless.' A little nervously, I thought. She must have heard what I did to the last person who tried to bless me. It was at Niki's funeral. Apparently, Father Fahey's index finger still bears the scar.

CHAPTER 4

I've never understood the 'fine dining followed by great sex' thing. Who wants great sex on a full stomach? Luckily Robbie agrees with me on this. So we had great — actually, we had excellent — sex and then we dug into our instant pasta meals with almost as much appetite as we'd had for each other. When the sex is excellent even microwave spaghetti bolognese forked straight out of the plastic container tastes mighty fine. As a bonus I got to watch Robbie eat naked. He rested his pasta on the pillow in his lap and scooped forkfuls into his mouth between grins. Robbie had the most spectacular grin of anyone I'd ever seen. It hitched up effortlessly on each side like the house curtain at an old-fashioned movie theatre, hijacking his entire face. And it doesn't take much to make that grin appear either. As a habitual frowner, I liked that about him. There was heaps I liked about this man and that grin was right up there in the top three.

Don't ask.

I filled him in on my meeting with Karen and my imminent trip to Auckland. He said he was happy to look after Wolf while I away. As an ex-police dog handler Robbie would have been an ideal dog-sitter anyway, but even without their shared occupational background my dog and my boyfriend had developed a relationship of some depth and complexity. A few months earlier I had been kidnapped by a nutcase who thought I should pay for what he perceived my sister had done to him. I was missing for days, during which time everyone thought I was dead. I know I did. By the time I was found, alive though not entirely undamaged, Robbie and Wolf had seriously bonded. I suspect they had spent several days comforting each other; which was fine with me.

That Robbie had also bonded with my ex-husband, Sean, during this time — not so fine. As far as I could tell, Sean and Robbie had just three things in common: they were both cops, they both loved Wolf and — well, me. They had me in common. Now I lived in fear of them becoming gym buddies, which just goes to show the level of my paranoia since neither of them belonged to a gym. Not as far as I knew, anyway.

'I've got a rostered day off tomorrow so I can take you to the airport and then I'll just keep him with me,' Robbie said. 'And he can come to the station with me on Thursday, Friday. He'll enjoy being back in a cop shop. The boys'll like it too,' he added, leaning sideways to put the empty spaghetti container on the floor. 'You know, once a police dog and all that.'

I watched the way the muscles in Robbie's stomach bunched as he stretched over and then relaxed as he settled back on the bed. He caught me eyeing him and grinned in response. Cocky. Wolf waited obediently for a sign that he could lick the spaghetti container clean. Robbie deliberately kept him waiting. It's part of the training. It occurred to me he might be using the same technique with me.

'Sean came round this morning—'

Robbie interrupted. 'How's he going with the Conway case? He's been working long hours on that with not much result.'

I didn't want to discuss Sean's latest case with Robbie. Anyway, Sean didn't share that stuff with me any more. Robbie finally made a small hand gesture to Wolf who launched himself at the container. I was determined to show more restraint.

'He wants me to sell the house,' I said.

Robbie dumped the pillow on the floor. 'I guess that's fair enough. He must need the money with the little kid and all.' Without waiting for a response, he padded through to the bathroom. Instead of admiring his naked butt, which I would normally do, I pulled a face at his back. Childish, I know, but I'd have preferred him to say Sean's request was unreasonable. I'd have liked him to commiserate with me, not understand Sean. I wanted him to take my side so that I could be the gracious and generous one to say that Sean wanting me to sell the house was fair enough. Grumpily, I finished off my spaghetti while Robbie peed. He came back into the room as naked as he had left it.

'So. You'll be buying a new place, eh? Any chance you'll be moving over the hill to the 'Mata?' It was a joke. Wainuiomata, where Robbie worked in the local cop station, didn't have a lot going for it apart from its proximity to a regional park and its low-priced housing. The high local crime rate was probably a plus for him, professionally.

'Yeah, well it might come to that, depending on how much we get for this.'

He climbed back onto the bed and placed my empty spaghetti container on the floor for me. 'We'd make such good neighbours,' he said, sliding his body alongside mine. 'I could drop by for a cup of sugar.' He grinned that ridiculously hitched grin at me.

While Wolf chased the plastic containers around the room, licking every corner of them, we did something similar. Robbie tasted of spaghetti bolognese. I guess I did too. Maybe there's something to be said for fine dining followed by great sex after all.

CHAPTER 5

We were nearly at the airport when Robbie slapped the steering wheel. 'Oh, shit. Sorry. I forgot to tell you. Sean rang.'

'When?' I asked. Which wasn't actually the question I was thinking.

'When you were in the shower,' he said. 'This morning.'

'You answered my phone?' I could hear the accusatory tone. I'm sure Robbie did, too, but he just casually threw that grin at me.

'No. I left it for the voicemail to kick in.' He pulled the police car into a temporary park outside the terminal. People stared, probably assuming I had been picked up for an offence. The murderous look on my face didn't help. If being really pissed off was an offence — fine. Hang me.

'When Sean didn't get a pick-up from you, he phoned me.' Robbie studied my face. 'On my mobile,' he added, going for the information overkill. 'He said to remind you that a friend of yours — Abi?' He waited for confirmation but I just kept staring out the window, controlling my sudden urge to hit him. 'Sean said she used to be a real-estate agent and he thought you might want to contact her and see if she could recommend someone to sell your place.'

I nodded and then busied myself organising carry-on and handbag, making a big fuss about looking for my ticket, saying goodbye to Wolf, keeping my head averted. The last thing I wanted was a fight but Sean and Robbie being mates was really doing my head in.

He put his hand on my arm. 'Hey, Di. Are you okay?'

'Yeah, fine,' I lied. 'Thanks for the lift. And Wolf. Thanks.' I opened the car door.

'Move in with me,' he said. I was gobsmacked but he repeated the offer as if I'd spoken. 'When you come back from Auckland. Move in with me.' He nodded in the direction of Wolf. 'You can bring your funny-looking kid too, if you like.' Wolf had his head out the window, tongue lolling, one ear up, one down. 'And then, when you've sold your house, we could buy a place together.' I suspect my mouth was hanging open. 'In the city,' he added, perhaps misinterpreting my look of dismay. I stuttered and stammered a non-reply, something stupid about needing a coffee before my flight. 'Just tell me you'll think about it,' he said.

'Okay. I'll think about it,' I said. I kissed that lovely mouth of his and walked towards the terminal. When I glanced back, he was whistling as he climbed back into the car. Wolf was leaning forward, trying to sneak a surreptitious neck lick. Neither of them was looking in my direction. They appeared blissfully happy. In the glass entrance doors I caught sight of my reflection. I looked pretty much like I always do. Then the doors slid open, splitting me in two.

CHAPTER 6

A long white plane moving silently across an expansive blue sky; strutting mynahs and jacaranda blooms; the sweet cloying smell of jasmine, the rotting stink of mangrove swamps; Rangitoto. All triggers. All invitations to the ghosts of my past to haunt me. I lived in Auckland when I was kid. We did, I mean. Mum, Dad, Niki and me. I remembered Mum here, shrugging the sundress straps off her shoulders. Bronzed legs. Shading her eyes from the late afternoon sun. Smiling. I don't know if they're real memories but I'll take them, they're all I've got of her. Memories of Niki surfaced, too. Us playing in the back yard, an Auckland back yard — there's still nothing to compare; Niki running ahead of me on the way to the corner dairy to buy ice creams, traversing tree roots that had erupted through the pavement; Niki looking back over her shoulder, laughing, squealing. Her smooth brown legs. She was a gorgeous two-year-old, all joy and madness. Fearless. Gone.

I realised with a jolt that my father's ghost was silent.

The Ponsonby house owned by Karen's mother was one of a big block of townhouses just behind Three Lamps, at the junction between Ponsonby and Herne Bay. The units were spread across three streets to form a triangle, with the interior of the triangle being the gated commons area and driveway access to the units' garages. I found the key under the front door welcome mat, as Karen said I would. A burglar would get a real hoot out of that little irony.

Later I'd ring Justin, introduce myself and ask if we could meet, but first I planned to walk by the house, get a feel for the neighbourhood. I wanted to try to sense how the family lived. In preparation, I'd dressed in trackies and gym shoes. Herne Bay is teeming with young trophy mums, keeping themselves in shape. Close inspection would give me away but with my hair pulled back in a ponytail and a pedometer clipped onto my waistband I'd pass a cursory look. If there was a car parked in the driveway or a sign of someone at home, like the song says, I'd just walk on by. That was the brilliant plan and, like all brilliant plans, it went totally to shit.

The house was a lavish icing-white Victorian villa set back from the street, with a high, wide visage. Two attic rooms had been added into the spacious roof, each with its own toy balcony. I guessed these rooms would have panoramic views of Cox's Bay on one side, the Disney-coloured Chelsea Sugar

Refinery across the water, and maybe even a glimpse of the Auckland Harbour Bridge. The property was what my father used to describe, accompanied by a clownish droop of the bottom lip, as salubrious. In other words, this place was serious money.

I crossed the road to gawk at the turquoise lap pool. Before I could wipe the envious drool from my chin and move on, a silver BMW M3 convertible drove up onto the footpath and stopped directly in front of me, cutting off my way forward. I immediately recognised both the man driving and the young girl in the passenger seat from my Google search. It was impossible to move past the car without getting in their way. Keeping my head down I feigned stretching as Sunny climbed out of the vehicle first and then her father.

Justin beeped the car lock over his shoulder, strode past me and went through the gate without so much as a glance. Sunny, too, stepped past and for a giddy moment it seemed possible I might not have registered on either of their radars. But as I edged around the metallic butt of the Beemer, Sunny spoke.

'Sorry about the parking,' she said. 'Dad always does that. He's going back out again in a minute.' She had paused to check the letter box but when I didn't answer she shifted her focus to me. Our eyes met and she smiled. She'd seen me, registered me and would remember me. It was too late to walk on.

'No problem. I'm a bit of a footpath parker myself,' I said. She smiled and pushed the gate open. 'Actually,' I added, and waited for her to turn back towards me. 'You're Sunny Bachelor, aren't you? Do you think I can have a word with your dad?'

Sunny stood very still, her long limbs twitching with a fight-

or-flight response. I tried to look as unstalker-like as possible. I didn't want to frighten her more than I already had.

'Who are you?' she asked. 'How do you know my name?'

Either I was doing an even lousier job than usual or this fourteen-year-old was more suspicious than most. I guess you learn to be wary of the unexpected if your mother has tried to kill you. Suddenly Justin was there behind her, car keys at the ready. He picked up the tension instantly.

'What?' he said to Sunny, then without waiting for a response, turned his attention to me. 'What do you want?' He advanced with hunched shoulders and straining pecs and didn't stop advancing until he was inches in front of me, fists clenched ready to plant me one. He had gone from easy, detached calm to fight-ready in point four of a second. The Beemer I was sweating against probably boasted a similar acceleration rate. I unstuck my body from his car and readied myself to fend a blow. Better a broken arm than a smashed face, I guess. Mind you, a comminuted diaphysial fracture of the radius and ulna is pretty painful. I should know.

'I didn't mean for us to meet like this. I just happened to be walking past.' Liar, liar, pants on fire. 'I'm Diane Rowe. Can I make a time to talk with you?'

'Talk about what?' he said, folding his arms across his chest. It looked more impressive like that. That was the point. But already his anger was dissipating. I'm five foot ten, athletic and can hold my own in more situations than most people, but he had it all over me in size and strength and knew it. The knowledge of it calmed him, just like that. I wasn't so sure he'd stay all that sanguine when I told him his ex-wife had employed me to check up on their daughter. Sunny stepped out from behind her father's bulk. She eyed me closely.

'You know Karen has been released from prison,' I said, as an opening gambit. They both tensed and glanced at each other but neither responded. 'I've been asked,' I said, skirting the point, 'to talk to Sunny. To see how she is. Check that she's okay.'

Justin swelled up like a baboon's arse as he closed the small gap between us.

'Who told you to check on Sunny? Tell me who told you to do that!'

He was right in my face, spit hailing my cheek. What Justin lacked in height he made up for in bulk. I was scared but knew I had to stay exactly where I was. I needed to keep my voice calm and, ideally, I needed to not shit my pants.

'Karen asked me to make contact,' I said, trying not to flinch in anticipation of a punch. 'I'm sorry it's happened like this. That's my fault, not hers. I should have phoned you first.'

'Who the hell are you?' He sounded more confused than angry.

'I'm a missing persons expert. I try to find people who are missing.'

He breathed heavily on me for a full ten seconds — I counted. Then, finally, he took a step back. My butt hole and half of my flight muscles relaxed.

'Well, you can fuck off then. Sunny isn't missing. She's here with me. I'm her father.' He wanted to say more but held it back because of Sunny. I saw him struggling and he knew it. 'Go inside,' he said, turning his back on me and attempting to usher Sunny inside the gate.

She shrugged his arm off her shoulder. 'No. I want to hear her.'

'I said go inside.' He knew she wouldn't.

'If she was sent by … M … by Mum.' She halted, embarrassed, I think, by her hesitation at the word, but then picked it up again. 'I want to hear what she has to say.'

He glanced up and down the street and then pushed the gate open aggressively. 'Let's take this inside.'

Presuming the 'this' to be taken inside was me, I dutifully followed Sunny down the path to the house. Justin walked close behind me. I could feel the warmth of his breath on my neck. It was meant to be intimidating. It was.

So far my judgment had been way off course, but I was determined not to make things worse by gabbling on about the impressive Carrara marble benchtop, although the kitchen was, without doubt, an impressive designer number, all grey on grey and white on white. Justin pulled a chair out from the billiard-sized dining table and leaned in to indicate I was to sit on it. I perched awkwardly with my bum on the hard wooden edge. The room smelt of burnt milk. Justin filled the space with his bluster, and it was a large space to fill. Eight metres by eight metres, would be my guess. Sunny tilted her shoulder against the wall, levelled a cool gaze at her father and then transferred it to me. Physically, she resembled her mother. The same almond-shaped eyes and long neck. She was painfully skinny but there was a steadiness about Sunny that her mother didn't have. This girl is brave, I thought.

'So why did Karen send a private detective to check up on me?' she asked. She'd been practising this question on the way into the house. Using 'Karen' instead of 'Mum' made it easier for her. We both knew it was bravado.

'I'm not a private investigator … I, I'm …'

She interrupted me with a forced laugh. 'Oh great, not even.'

I let the sarcasm sit there. She had every right to be smart-arsed. It had been unfair of me to catch her unprepared. Once I was out of here I would beat myself up for getting it so wrong, but right now my priority was to stop Justin doing that job for me. Hands on hips in a clichéd posture of an angry man, his eyes swung from Sunny to me and back again. He saw his daughter was close to tears and took control.

'Look, I don't want you here in our home,' he said. Unfairly, I thought, given that it was he who had ushered me in there. Sunny gave him a look. It wasn't one I could interpret, but Justin had. He scrabbled around in his wallet and threw a business card in my lap.

'Come to my office tomorrow, ten o'clock. We'll talk there.' I pocketed the card. 'Now you can fuck off,' he said, opening the back door for emphasis.

I placed a card of my own on the table. Gym shoes squeaking, I made the long trek across the floor. I made it all the way across the eight metres of polished recycled rimu without Justin thumping me in the ear. I'd count that as my best achievement of the day.

'I might be there or I might not,' Sunny called, with all the pluck of a poleaxed fourteen-year-old.

'We'll decide on that tonight,' Justin amended. 'As a family.'

He was addressing Sunny, not me, but I caught the response from her. It was a definite sneer. Was it the word 'family' she was reacting to? Hard to tell with teenagers. They do make a point of sneering at everything.

The decor of the townhouse was low-key designed living space, three floors, plus a garage, laundry and storage area underneath. There was no one hiding in the wardrobe or the showers. I checked. But there were women's clothes in the main bedroom's wardrobe and a few men's shirts and jackets in the smaller bedroom, facing the unit's common area.

A big antique clock ticked the minutes away as I studied the cluster of photos on the wall in the spare bedroom. It was a poignant soundtrack by which to study these captured moments in time. They were arranged in a semblance of chronology, starting with studio family portraits of Karen as a toddler with her mother and father. They were quite formal for the 1980s. There was no sign of other siblings. Parenting can be a big learning curve for someone who's grown up with no little brothers or sisters to look after. Still, 'learning curve' is a long way from murder. The most recent photos were of Karen's mother, Norma, in the company of a benign-looking bearded man. He looked a good decade older than her, but from the camera's point of view, they made a happy-looking couple.

In one of these photos a good-looking guy in his late twenties was squeezed proprietorially between the two of them. I pieced together the narrative of the family's life: Karen was an only child and after her dad died Norma had remarried. The looker in the photo was her new husband's son from a previous marriage.

One photo of Karen with Sunny and Falcon was set apart from the others, centred above a small oak side table on which a wooden cross and candle were placed. Judging from the age of the kids, the shot must have been taken shortly before Karen drove the car into the lake. Sunny leaned against the bonnet of an olive-green two-door Holden hatchback. Knock-kneed and ridiculously skinny, enormous sunglasses hid her expression. Falcon was unsmiling, his arm stretched towards the car as if reaching to anchor himself. Karen was in the driver's seat. She was looking at the camera with what seemed to me like a look of defeat. I chided myself for reading way too much into the image. This was me trying to understand how anyone could have driven their two children into a lake. Then it occurred to me that this was probably the car. If I was right, then it was a morbid choice of images for Norma to hang on the bedroom wall, even with the reverential cross and candle keeping it company. I went in search of a glass to fill to the brim with the wine I'd brought.

Feet up and alcoholic sustenance in hand I could now comfortably kick myself for stuffing up the first meeting with Sunny. It had been stupid to try a walk-by and risk getting caught. Now I needed to decide if I should tell Karen I'd met her daughter; cowardice won. Anyway, I reasoned, the deal with Karen was that I wouldn't tell her where Sunny was until her daughter had instructed me to. Sunny certainly hadn't done that. Not yet anyway.

Karen answered on the second ring.

'Have you seen her?' she asked, before I'd said a word.

'There's a chance I might get to talk to her tomorrow,' I said. Evasion isn't exactly lying.

Her breathing was loud in my ear. 'Good,' she managed.

'It's not confirmed yet,' I warned.

'Okay.'

She was grateful for anything I could offer. We chatted for a bit about her mum's townhouse; I thanked her for letting me stay there; she urged me to make myself at home and to use anything at all. Her phone manner hadn't got any easier. There were still long hesitations and she held the phone close to her mouth. The sound of her uneven breathing was unnervingly intimate.

'If I do see Sunny,' I said, 'and we can talk privately, is there anything specific you want me to check up on? Anything you're especially worried about?'

She didn't respond immediately. I waited. Her breathing had quickened. My normal response in the face of phone silence is to chatter, but I forced myself to wait. I took another sip of wine. Finally she answered. Her voice was so quiet I had to press the phone hard against my ear.

'It was Justin who introduced me to stuff. To drugs. I'm not saying it was his fault. It was my decision. Well, at first it was my decision, but then I got hooked and then I guess it was …'

I thought for one crazy moment she was going to blame the devil but, whoever or whatever it was, she left it unblamed. I poured myself another wine, taking care not to clink the bottle against the glass.

'And not the … the killing either. I take full responsibility.'

I wondered how long this had taken. Was it after Falcon's funeral? Had she taken full responsibility before the first anniversary of his death? Before he would have turned six?

'It's important to take responsibility. That's the only way you can ever forgive yourself.' So she'd forgiven herself for killing her five-year-old and trying to kill her seven-year-old daughter. Well, good for her. 'But unless you've faced things, admitted your sins to God, I don't think people change,' she continued. 'Not really.' I took another sip. 'Do you?' she asked, taking me by surprise. 'Do you think people change?'

'Well, you've changed, haven't you?' I said. 'You found God.' It was impossible for me to say this without sounding sarcastic. Admittedly, it might have helped if I'd uncrossed my eyes.

'That's different,' she said.

'Uh-huh.'

It's always a mistake to start a conversation about God, particularly with Christians. Ever since Niki was murdered I'd had trouble taking God seriously. When I was a kid I believed in Him, It, Them — whatever. Niki and I even got our school backpacks blessed by the local priest.

'Anyway,' I said, bringing my thoughts back to Karen, 'is there anything particular you want me to ask Sunny?'

I waited, going over in my mind all the things she might want me to ask her daughter. There was the obvious 'Can you forgive me?' question. I could imagine Sunny's response. The silence went on for so long I tried something else. 'Or any message from you that you'd like me to give her?' There were even scarier options here, like: 'Sorry I tried to kill you', or 'Sorry I murdered your little brother' or even 'Sorry about stuffing up your life forever'. Maybe she would even go for broke with the old 'I love you' chestnut. I hoped not.

'No,' she said and let out a long breath, like a sigh. 'There's nothing I can say to her, is there? Just check she's okay. Please.'

The phone went dead. She'd hung up.

I poured myself another glass. My second, I told myself, making that my number two lie for the day. No doubt about it, lying gets easier the more you practise it. There was a new sign going up on the building across the road, 'Shamrock. Love Business'. Was it an advertisement for a business recruitment firm or a brothel? Hard to tell.

The conversation with Karen supported my suspicion that she didn't want me to check Sunny was safe but to have me make the first approach on her behalf. Maybe she wanted to let Sunny know she cared enough to send someone to ask if she was okay. This didn't seem such a bad thing to me but I had seen how Justin reacted to the idea of Karen having anything to do with their daughter. It was predictable. Understandable even. I wondered how much of the drowning Sunny remembered.

A text alert interrupted my thoughts: *Caravan confirmed for 1 pm tomorrow. Cheers Jason.* I stared at the message for a full minute, trying to figure out what it meant. Then I got it. It was a message from the real-estate agent Jason Baker, confirming that a bunch of agents would be traipsing through my house — our house — tomorrow.

Just like that, a tsunami of sadness swamped me. Sean and I had been so happy when we bought it. We had walked through the empty house talking quietly, self-conscious of the echo. It felt to both of us as if we were trespassing. We couldn't believe we'd done something as grown up as buy a house together. We loved everything about it; even the flaking paint on the old window sashes. Later, when we had to scrape it back for repainting, we complained that it was a pain in the arse, but on this first day, possession day, we called it romantic.

When the movers rang to say the furniture truck would be late arriving we grabbed the opportunity. For some now-forgotten reason we ended up in the hallway, maybe because there were no windows or because the wall was warmed from the early morning sunshine, I don't remember, but I do remember we were interrupted by the neighbour arriving, armed with a plate of muffins, to welcome us to the neighbourhood. She cheerfully instructed us to carry on with it and not stop for her. She even insisted we'd enjoy the muffins more once we'd finished the job in hand.

Later we learned that eighty-six-year-old Madeleine's eyesight had failed some years earlier and she'd thought we were putting up a shelf. From then on Sean and I used the phrase 'putting up a shelf' as our private code. Over the years we put up a fair number of shelves. We even put up a real shelf against that sunny hall wall and let our books slowly fade there. Now I'd have to sort those faded books into his and hers.

It was never a good idea to ring Sean when I was feeling nostalgic but I needed to let him know I was on to selling the house. I didn't want him making any more buddy calls to Robbie with messages to pass on to me. Sean's mobile rang for a lifetime. I wondered which ring tone he had for me. Probably a song, 'We are Family'? No, probably not. He finally answered and without any preamble I told him I'd contracted an agent and there was going to be a caravan at the house tomorrow.

'So it's all go,' I said, repeating an upbeat phrase Jason had used on me. 'I don't need to ring Abi for advice.' I resisted the urge to point out I was unlikely to ask Abi's advice on anything. She'd had the hots for Sean for years. It had sparked at my party four years earlier when he'd done a joke striptease as a surprise birthday present for me.

'Thanks for arranging that,' Sean was saying, all business.

I could hear the cry of a baby and pots and pans banging in the background. My heart gave a lurch. Either the baby was taking out his frustration on the cooking utensils or Sean's partner was. Suddenly my anger and sadness lifted off somewhere.

'You're welcome,' I said cheerfully. I almost meant it.

'Well, if there's anything you need from me, just let me know,' he said.

I refused to let the formal phrase and its deeper meaning affect me. I felt no need to lecture him about talking to me through Robbie. Felt no necessity to remind him what our house had meant to us. And when I hung up I was smiling. It's impossible to explain why — probably those two glasses of wine.

I thought about ringing Robbie. I even hovered my thumb over his name in my contact list. Instead, I plugged the phone into the charger and fell asleep almost immediately.

CHAPTER 7

Justin's office was on the floor above his wife's gym in Jervois Road within easy walking distance of where they lived. At the back entrance were two car parks designated for the directors. Justin's silver BMW was parked in one of them. A sky-blue version of the same model kept it company in the other.

There were no surprises with the layout of the gym: a warehouse of equipment with low ceilings and mirrored walls. No surprises with the colour decor of Apricot either. The music was loud and vibrating. Sweating bodies pounded the treadmills. At nine-fifty on a Thursday morning the place was packed with penitents, feverishly working off their lifestyle sins. Who needs it? Give me a rosary or Stations of the Cross any day. Gym clothes, sweatbands, dietary supplements, health products, nut bars and probably the phone number of the cute guy working out beside you were all available from the reception area. No sign of Salena. A kitted-out twenty-something with a perfect body, hair and skin, smiled a perfect set of teeth at me. I grimaced my imperfect bag of tricks back at her. A boy of about five playing on an iPad gave me the briefest of glances. Presumably this was Neo, Sunny's half-brother. *The Matrix* had a lot to answer for. My phone beeped a text alert. It was from Jason, wanting assurance my dangerous dog wouldn't be at the house during the pre-open home inspection at one o'clock. I replied, *All good. No dog* and got a smiley face in return. Jesus.

I looked up from my texting as a middle-aged man approached.

'You Diane?'

I could handle the oiled chest on display above his low-necked singlet — just — but did my best to avoid looking at the eye-wateringly tight baby-blue Lycra shorts. 'Mr Bachelor said to take you up to his office when you got here.'

With that he turned and walked away. He had the classic gait of a body builder, arms forced outwards from his body to accommodate the bulk of water-wing biceps. I followed his muscular balloon butt up the narrow wooden stairway. We didn't say a word. What can you say when you're faced with a butt like that? Outside the office door he held his hand up like a traffic cop and peered at his watch, lips silently counting down the seconds until ten o'clock. Oh please, what drama. So Justin had a tame gorilla, big deal. He knocked once, opened the door and nodded in the direction he wanted me to take. I wasn't going to argue with him.

Sunny sat cross-legged in the middle of a blood-red sofa, a foot in one hand, the other holding her hair back from her forehead in a gesture of frustration. Justin hovered over her, his neck blotchy with emotion. They had been arguing. I pretended not to notice and spent a few minutes enthusing over the ultra-cool office space of brick walls and four-metre-high sash windows. The ceiling had been removed to expose kauri structural beams and a high arched roof cavity. Very nice. Signage and clothes samples lying around the place suggested this was where Justin ran the merchandise division of the gym business. One corner of the room was sectioned off by a bamboo-framed silk screen. Posters of disturbingly young girls in skimpy gym gear adorned the walls like hunters' trophies.

Sunny unfolded herself and padded barefoot to a coffee machine in the far corner. She was wearing a tiny pleated skirt that only just covered her bum. The sleeveless cut-away T-shirt was emblazoned with the word 'whore'. I hoped this was what she and her father had been arguing about.

'Coffee?' she asked, casually tilting her head over one bony shoulder. 'I do an okay cappuccino.'

I couldn't help but admire her bravado. 'Great. Thanks,' I said.

Justin glared at me. Meaningfully, I suspect. I followed Sunny, partly to get Justin out of my line of sight. He followed.

'Da-ad,' she protested. 'Leave us alone!' The habitual cry of the teenage girl.

'I checked you out,' Justin said, pumping his fists open and closed like he was preparing for a blood donation. I hoped it was *his* blood he was planning to donate.

'Good,' I said. 'It's what I expected you to do.'

After a brief respite his neck and chest had mottled up again. Just looking at him made me feel tired. How boring it would be to live with someone whose first and only response to everything was anger.

'Word is you're legit. If you weren't, I wouldn't have let you in the door.'

Sunny rolled her eyes theatrically. 'Da-ad, you promised!' She turned her impossibly fragile little neck to look at him. 'Please,' she added. This time without the attitude. It worked.

'Five minutes,' he said, splaying his hand in front of my face for emphasis. 'You get five minutes and that's it.' He turned to Sunny. 'Anton will be right outside the door.'

'I don't want him there.' Her eyes darted to the door. 'I don't want him ...'

'Okay, okay.' He held up his hand in the same stop gesture Anton had used on me. 'I'll tell him to go back downstairs. If you want me, you just yell, honey, and I'll be here in a heartbeat.'

Her back was to him, but she nodded.

The cappuccino was more than okay and so was Sunny. She'd built a little hard carapace about herself but it was surprisingly easy to get beneath it. We made a bit of small talk about why she didn't drink coffee or tea and about her dad's gym gear importing business, but we were both aware our time alone was short. I thought her first question would be, 'What's my mother like?' She surprised me.

'What's your mother like?' she asked.

I tried not to let the question throw me. Fair enough, I

thought. She has the right to find out about me before she gives anything of herself away.

'Well.' I let my breath out. 'My mother died when I was five so all my memories of her belong to a five-year-old.'

'Same,' she said, pulling her bare foot into her hand. 'Only the other way round.' I waited, not following her meaning but knowing more was coming. 'I wish my mother was dead and Falcon was alive.' She made it sound very matter of fact. 'He was five when she killed him.' She slid a little smile in my direction. 'I'd probably hate him. If he was alive, I mean. He'd be twelve. Twelve-year-old boys are so totally disgusting.' She hid her emotion in her oversized cup of hot water.

'I had a little sister,' I said, and took a sip of the coffee. 'I thought I'd hate her but I loved her right from the start. And even when she was an annoying twelve-year-old I still loved her.' The words were thick in my throat. The emotion surprised us both. I glanced at Sunny before adding, 'But maybe it's different with a brother.'

Sunny shook her head. 'Falcon was a really cute kid,' she said. Her eyes moved as she pictured him. She blinked slowly, shutting the image down. 'I try not to think about him too much.'

I could understand that. 'You get on okay with Neo?'

'Sure,' she said with a hitched shrug. There was a fierceness about her as she readied herself for the difficult stuff. 'What does she want with me?' Her eyes darted as she searched for another way to ask the question. She ended up just repeating it. 'What does she want?'

I took my time answering, aware every word I said was loaded. 'Karen says she wants to know you're alright,' I said.

'What do you mean alright?' she shot back. It was the first flash of anger.

'To be honest, I don't really know.' She'd drawn her legs up and was hugging them with skinny little arms. 'Are you alright?' I asked.

Sunny opened her mouth to speak. There was something there; some thought, some secret. Her eyes darted to the door again. I wondered if Justin was outside listening. Or Anton. Or if she thought one of them was. Whatever she'd intended to say was swallowed.

'Alright for someone whose mother tried to murder her, you mean?' She lifted her chin in a parody of pride. 'Oh yeah, I'm totally excellent.' Her voice hitched.

'I believe Karen cares about you, Sunny.'

This was pushing the limits of what I was prepared to say about Karen's feelings for her, but I had to give Sunny something. She feigned nonchalance and nearly convinced herself.

'Yeah, well, whatever.' A new thought took hold. 'You won't tell anyone at school, will you? Promise you won't talk to any of them. No one at school knows …' This was clearly her worst nightmare.

'I won't talk to anyone …' I began.

'And don't let Mum go anywhere near my friends! If she does, I'll … I'll …' She tensed. I reckoned there was a fifty-fifty chance of her making a run for the door.

'Listen to me, Sunny.' My chair squeaked as I leaned forward. 'I won't tell Karen anything you say to me. I won't tell her anything about you. Not unless you want me to. You are in charge of this. That's the deal. I give you my word.'

The seconds ticked away while she stayed frozen and stiff with indecision. Then the hand closed over the foot again with a comforting squeeze and the tension deflated.

'Okay.' She shrugged as if she didn't care. 'Whatever,' she added bleakly.

Suddenly the door clattered opened. Anton stepped back to allow Salena entry. 'So you're the person Karen sent.' She dismissed me in a single eye movement.

There was no reason to respond and she didn't seem to expect a reply. Neo slunk in behind her, iPad swinging casually in one hand. He perched on the sofa next to Sunny and continued his game. Anton remained in the open doorway, displaying his bulk. He was looking at Sunny in a way that made me uneasy. It was a relief when she put her feet on the floor.

'Justin didn't want Sunny to talk to you but I said she should. She has to come to terms with what her mother did.' Salena didn't even glance in Sunny's direction.

Sunny reacted. 'Hell-ooo,' she called, waving her arms above her head. 'I am actually here in the room, you know.'

Salena kept her eyes averted. 'I know you are, darling.'

An uncomfortable silence followed; well, uncomfortable for me anyway. Sunny glared at Salena with undisguised distaste. Salena shifted papers on the desk, ignoring her. No love lost or otherwise between these two. Neo edged closer to Sunny. His attention appeared to be focused entirely on his game, but I had my doubts.

'Are you alright, love?' Justin pushed past Anton, looking from me to Sunny.

'Why is everyone suddenly so interested if I'm alright. Of

course I'm alright. What did you think she'd do — kill me?'

An odd *boing* from Neo's iPad game was the only sound in the room. Salena threw Justin a 'this is what I have to deal with' gesture. He didn't respond. My knees clicked from sitting rigid for too long. In full view of Justin, I handed Sunny my business card.

'All my contact details are on there, Sunny. You can ring me any time you want.'

She studied the card intently, forcing the tears back. I resisted the urge to hug her goodbye. Salena called a sarcastic 'Bye now,' as I reached the door. Anton held it open for me. I was already anticipating the very deep breath I'd let out once my feet hit the pavement.

'I want to meet my mother,' Sunny said, addressing her father. I paused in the doorway, Anton's arm hovering above my head.

'No way, Sunny,' he said. 'I won't allow it.'

'You can't stop me, you know,' she said, without conviction. 'I have a right to see her.'

Justin looked to Salena for advice. She feigned interest in the wall. Anton stared at Sunny; he seemed fascinated by her. No one looked at me, frozen in the doorway, craving a cigarette for the first time in twenty months.

'I have to, you know, confront her,' Sunny said. 'Tell her how much I hate her,' she added, unconvincingly. Justin struggled to contain some emotion, his repertoire of emotions so limited I was guessing the emotion was anger. 'You have to let me do this, Dad. Please.'

Even the iPad had stopped boinging.

'Okay,' he said. We all breathed again. 'But I have to be there. I won't let you do this on your own.'

Sunny immediately got down to practicals. 'Not you, Dad. It would be impossible with you there. You'd just get totally angry and stuff.' There was no heat in it. She was stating a fact. Surprisingly, Justin nodded in agreement. I saw a thought take hold.

'You're right, honey,' he said, a barely repressed smile developing. 'It should be another female with you. Someone you trust.' Thrilled with the possibility, he looked the question at Salena. She offered a complex range of gestures in response, which I interpreted as meaning she would do it, but unwillingly.

'I want her to come with me,' Sunny said. Justin released the smile. He assumed she meant Salena. We all did. 'I want Diane to come with me,' she declared, studying the card in her hand, probably making sure she had my name right. Justin was speechless. So was I. 'I trust her,' she added. She might as well have said: Suck on that, Salena.

The iPad boinged.

Maybe Sunny chose me just to piss Salena off. Salena thought so, though she refused to give her stepdaughter the satisfaction of showing it. Whatever her intention, once Sunny had set the idea in motion she wouldn't back away from it and, having agreed to the deal, Justin knew he was stuck with it. Finally, he gave in and asked me to set up the meeting. Well, 'asked' would be a euphemistic way of describing his belligerent demands. He made it abundantly clear that I wouldn't have been his first or last choice as go-between. And from Salena's cool gaze levelled in my direction, she wasn't too big a fan of my involvement either. As for Karen, I was confident she would leap at the chance to meet her daughter.

Me? I wasn't so sure it was a good idea for either of them — or good for me either, for that matter. Taking charge, Justin instructed me to bring Karen to the Ja Coozy restaurant in the Wynyard Quarter at one o'clock on Saturday afternoon. No doubt he'd chosen a fishbowl-style setting where he could keep a close eye on us from a chosen spot close by. He confirmed my suspicion by assuring me he would be nearby at all times.

No amount of warning from me could dampen Karen's excitement. She was overjoyed at the prospect of meeting her daughter. Breathless with anticipation, she began planning an early flight up on Saturday morning in time to meet with me beforehand. The more she chattered eagerly about the meeting, the deeper my heart sank. Call me a pessimist but I couldn't help thinking it would go badly. When she asked for details about Sunny I reminded her of our agreement that everything about her daughter would remain private until Sunny chose to share it with her. Karen agreed immediately, apologised for her transgression and told me I was quite right. Such was her elation and gratitude she would have agreed to anything. Try as I did to remind myself that this woman had attempted to murder her daughter and had succeeding in killing her five-year-old son it wasn't enough to stop me feeling some compassion for her. I tried one last time to warn her that things might not go all that smoothly.

'She has a lot of anger towards you. You know that, don't you?'

'Of course she does. I understand.' But it wasn't enough to

extinguish the excitement in her voice. 'Do you think I could bring her a gift or something?' Before I could answer, she added, 'Or do you think that would be wrong?'

'I really don't know,' I said honestly. 'I've never been in this situation before.'

I didn't intend this as sarcastic but it must have sounded so. She was quiet for a full minute. I thought of apologising but decided not to. If she couldn't handle what sounded like a bit of sarcasm from me, she sure as hell wouldn't be match-fit for the meeting with Sunny.

'Neither have I,' she finally offered.

I'd punched the wind out of her. We wound down the conversation with me promising to get in touch if there was a change in plan. I thought there was a high probability either Sunny or her father would chicken out and call the whole thing off or Salena would decide she couldn't allow the meeting to go ahead. Before ending the call Karen thanked me for everything I'd done.

'Sunny must trust you to ask you to come with her.' I couldn't say anything without giving away more about Sunny's relationship with her stepmother than I was prepared to. 'Thank you,' she added. Despite all my dire warnings, she sounded happy. No doubt passengers on the *Titanic* were happy before they hit that iceberg, too.

Back at the townhouse, I called Robbie. I thought he'd ask why I hadn't phoned the day before, but that was just my own guilt talking. He said he was happy to keep Wolf until I returned on Saturday afternoon.

'He misses you,' he said. 'And I do too.'

I heard the grin, pictured it, too, and felt myself grinning back. 'Yeah, well, don't you go chewing up the furniture now.'

There was a pause before he spoke. 'Have you thought about my suggestion?' I swallowed. 'About us moving in together?' In case I was confusing it with some other suggestion he'd made.

'I've been really busy.'

Stupid and evasive. The truth was that I hadn't thought about it at all. Not because I was too busy or had other things on my mind. I hadn't thought about Robbie's suggestion we move in together because I was a big fat squawking chicken in big fat squawking chicken denial.

CHAPTER 8

I'm blessed with being able to fall asleep anywhere. Planes, trains and automobiles, friends' sofas, back seats of cars, motel rooms — it makes no difference to me. I put my head down and I'm out like the proverbial. No shallow sleep states for me. I've never experienced a stage one myoclonic jerk in my life; though I've had plenty of experience with the other kind. With only a brief pause at stage four, I plummet straight into stage five: REM deep dream mode. According to Sean I start sleep-talking in under thirty seconds.

Started, I mean. Sean is past tense. Present tense Robbie hasn't mentioned my odd sleep behaviour yet. Maybe that's the kind of conversation we'll have if we move in together, and whether the lawns need cutting and the fridge defrosting. Or maybe not. Most people, normal people, rotate from deep stage five sleep back up to stage two and then slowly back down again throughout the night. Not me. Once asleep, I pretty much stay there, way down the hole with only the occasional holiday up to stage four for a couple of minutes' light relief. When my brain decides it's time to wake up I rise to the surface like an abyssal diver in need of air, straight up and awake. Just like that. But try and wake me before my brain says it's ready — well, that's not easy.

The reason I know all this is because when I was a kid specialists studied the hell out of me. The end result of all their prodding and probing and sleep-wave monitoring was to be told my condition has no adverse effects — on me, anyway; in fact, it apparently gives me all sorts of health benefits I'm supposed to be thankful for. When I'm dreaming of flying or winning lotto it's an enviable little trick, alright.

But there is a downside: nightmares. When I'm in a night-mare I'm there for the long haul. I can be forced awake, jolted back to consciousness, but it takes a concerted effort. Mean-while, until my brain says it's time to wake up, I'm stuck in nightmare-ville. Believe me, that's no fun place to be.

The dream started off just fine. I'm swimming through clear, lucid water. Fingers stretching ahead in long easy breaststrokes. Forehead breaching like a ship's prow. My timing is perfect, rhythmical. I take a deep breath in, my forehead dips into the iciness. I lift my chin and breathe out as the stroke comes around again, weightless, like flying; blissful. I fill my lungs with air, flip and kick down into the deep cold. Hands clasped together, arms out in front, I dolphin kick down further and further, undulating my body through the liquid. The water parts in front of me and then folds back as I slice through. It's spectacularly easy. No drag. No effort. No struggle for breath. It's like I have gills.

Then I glimpse something below. Something in the murky depths. Something falling. Bubbles nibble my skin as they rise past me to the surface. One hard kick and I'm closer. It's a car. A car is falling below me in slow motion. Another kick down. Closer now, I make out a little white moon face, framed in the back window — Falcon. His eyes are wide; his hands are flattened against the glass. His mouth is a big 'O'.

And then in one of those time jumps that happen in dreams, it's me in the car. I'm not Falcon. I'm in the front passenger seat. The belt is tight across my chest. I'm wearing a pale blue cotton dress with lace trim on the hem. My knees are the knees of a young girl. Falcon is yelling something at me. He's yelling in another language, or he's yelling something I can't make any sense of. The car is still falling. Lake weed droops past the window. An old supermarket trolley lies on its side in the muddy bed. We're nearly at the bottom. We'll stop falling soon. There will be a bump. I wonder if it will hurt. Dying — I wonder if it will hurt. The water is as thick as mushroom soup. As if an un-mute button has been pushed, Falcon yells 'No!' as loud as a fire alarm. Over and over he's yelling it, 'Nonononono!' as if it's one word. His little arms are tight around my neck. I want to remind him to put his seatbelt on. Stupid. The car lands, *thud*! A soft landing, a parachute landing. Mud billows up with a *whoosh* and settles on the window. Pretty soon all the windows will be covered with it. The door won't open. I push harder but the weight of the water pushes back. Outside the car everything is soupy but the liquid that dribbles from the tops of the windows is clear. The river bubbles up through the floor. Already my ankles look wobbly and enormous.

Falcon's screams are right in my ear. He bashes my head with his fists. He's only little but it hurts. A distorted face appears at the windscreen. A hand brushes away the mud, left, right, left. I try to tell Falcon we're saved but no words come out. It's Karen. Her hand is a windscreen wiper. Or maybe she's waving goodbye. I point to the door and make pulling gestures, but she just looks at me. The car tilts as if hit by a big underwater tsunami. Falcon's hot face is on my neck. He's yelling at me.

'Stop.' He's yelling. 'Stop!'

'Stop!' I bolt awake. I'm on the bedroom floor, face down, cheek pressed into the carpet. 'Stop!'

A man is on top of me, pinning me down. I'm completely naked. His hand is pressed hard on the back of my head, forcing my face into the carpet. His other hand has pinned my wrist to the floor. He is straddled over my arse, knees pressed painfully into my ribcage. His hot face pressed against the back of my head.

'Stop! Just stop!'

Breathing hard, he gives my cheek a good shove into the carpet for emphasis. Memory and consciousness stutter back. I'm in Auckland. I'm not trapped in a car. I'm not underwater. I stop struggling. Immediately his weight lifts as he scoots backwards off me.

'What the fuck!' In the darkened room, he isn't much more

than a shadow crouched against the far wall, the king-size bed angled between us. The slatted streetlight illuminates his palms, held up in a placatory gesture. There's a raw patch on the back of my head. My cheek burns.

'Did you hit me?' My voice is slurred. I sound drugged. I'm still surfacing.

'I didn't hit you,' he said. 'I tried to wake you. You just flew at me like a madwoman. Are you nuts or what? You attacked me! Fuck!'

'Fook.' A faint Irish lilt. My world returned to normal. Normal, that is, apart from discovering myself naked on the floor with a complete stranger who has just attacked me, or me him — whatever. Given the circumstances, it seemed appropriate to go on the aggressive.

'Who the hell are you?'

'I'm turning the light on, alright?'

'Fine,' I said.

He waited, hands up in surrender, until I'd covered myself with the bed sheet. My cheek smarted. My neck was bruised. My pride wasn't in such good shape either.

Dark-haired, early thirties, ripped shirt — not in a designer way, more in a 'I've just been attacked' kind of way — one eyelid red and swelling. That would be the eye-gouging. Four distinct finger marks bloomed on his neck; they would go through the full autumn colour range over the next week. Eye-gouging and cheek-raking were techniques I learnt in women's self-defence classes years earlier. They served the dual purpose of effectively fighting off an intruder and leaving visible wounds to help with identification later. I'd send the self-defence girls an email in the morning. Tell them how well it worked out. But this was no normal intruder. If there is such a thing.

'I'm going downstairs to the kitchen now,' he said, loud and slow, like he was talking to a dangerous inmate. 'I'm going to put some ice on this so I won't have to explain to everyone that a madwoman tried to kill me.' The self-righteous type. All drama, he backed out of the doorway, his hands up in surrender mode. I needed ice, too, for the carpet burn. Grumpily, I pulled on sweat pants. He was muttering as he went down the stairs. 'Unless, of course, you'd rather go straight into round two. What'll it be this time? Knives? Nunchucks? Pistols at dawn?'

Ha ha. Funny guy. A bra seemed unnecessarily prudish given the naked tussle we'd just engaged in. I yanked a T-shirt over my head.

'Come on down,' he called. I heard the clatter of ice being dropped into glasses. 'Maybe we can try "Pleased to meet you" as an alternative introductory technique this time.'

I didn't need introductions. I'd already figured out who he was: the good-looker from the photo in the spare bedroom, Karen's stepbrother.

I probably hadn't made that great a first impression.

CHAPTER 9

According to Ned, he had used the spare room on a regular basis when Norma was alive and since her death he'd continued to stay there roughly one week out of every four or five. They were his clothes in the wardrobe. Karen, apparently, was happy with the arrangement. He had his own key, which was waggled in front of me as proof. In the excitement of learning she was going to meet her daughter, Karen had obviously forgotten to tell Ned and me about each other. He claimed to have been as surprised to discover me in the house as I clearly was to discover him. Though we had each, he repeated several times with increased emphasis, reacted rather differently to the situation. He had tried to wake me to introduce himself, whereas I had flown at him like a freakin' she-devil. Despite his words, it seemed to me he actually looked quite thrilled each time he said it and I noticed some new little detail was added with each repetition. Finally he settled on the story: I threw myself at him like a freakin' she-devil and set about ripping him apart with my bare hands. No doubt by the time the story had done the rounds I, the she-devil, would have ripped off each of his limbs and consumed them one by one. Even as a joke, I didn't want to encourage him by suggesting it. At least he'd had the decency not to refer to the she-devil being stark bloody naked when she attacked him. Not yet, anyway.

Eventually I apologised, begrudgingly. The explanation of my deep-sleep condition fascinated him. Well, he seemed fascinated. But he was an inveterate charmer from way back, this one, with his elaborate storytelling and the attention he paid. With every new story the accent grew stronger. I accused him of turning it on when it suited.

'Oh, well, everyone loves the Irish, you know.' He swirled his wine around the glass before knocking it back. 'Except the Irish,' he added, with a wink. Normally I hate being winked at, but I laughed.

'So where are you from then?' I asked.

'I was born here, if that's what you're asking.'

'And now?'

'And now I'm based in Perth, but I travel between here and Australia on a fairly regular basis.' He stopped as if he thought that was information enough. It was unusual to meet someone who didn't want to dominate the conversation with information about themselves.

'How come?' I'm a born questioner.

'Well, I'm one of the partners in a restaurant in Perth and another in Melbourne, though that's more of a bar than a restaurant, really. And I'm a silent partner in a little place here in Parnell.'

'What's the difference between a silent and a sleeping partner?' I asked. 'I've always wondered.'

'I thought you'd know all about that, being the expert on sleeping and all.' He tilted his head in my direction and I smiled and tilted mine back at him. He wasn't going to let the she-devil incident go easily.

'So why restaurants?'

He seemed to genuinely think about my question before delivering me an expressive shrug. 'I'm a useless cook.'

'You own restaurants because you can't cook? Seriously?'

'Well, no. The one thing you can say about me is I don't do anything seriously. I'm constitutionally unsuited for it. I'm told that's part of my charm.' They were right about that. 'But even though I'm a dreadful cook myself, I love food. Actually, I don't so much love food as the eating of it. With other people, I mean. There's just nothing that compares with sitting at a table with a bunch of people, eating and drinking and carousing. I love it, especially the carousing. What do you love, then?' Innocent though the question was, it made me blush. He smiled so readily in response, maybe the question hadn't been innocent at all.

We talked and drank wine and crunched the ice cube splinters from our makeshift ice packs, then at three o'clock he cooked up the only dish he claimed to be able to cook: a big plate of scrambled eggs and toast. We squatted on stools either side of the benchtop island, fork in one hand and ice-packed facecloths against our sore bits in the other, while he filled me in on the family history. His father, Arthur, had been in a relationship with Karen's mother, Norma, for ten years before he died unexpectedly of a massive heart attack. That was two years ago. Ned liked Norma. He was an adult when his father started up with her and he had no problems with their relationship at all.

'They made a great couple,' he said. Karen's father had been killed in a car accident more than a decade earlier and Arthur's first wife, Ned's mother, died when he was a teenager. After his father's death, Ned continued to stay at Norma's when he was in Auckland. He said he hoped Norma enjoyed his company. 'She and Dad used to have a good time together. He was good company and she missed that when he was gone. I could make her laugh,' he said, smiling appreciatively at the memory of her. 'She liked a good laugh.' Having spent a few easy hours with this man I could well imagine she did enjoy his company, particularly with her man-friend dead and her only child in prison.

'What about Sunny?' I asked. 'Did Norma see much of her after Karen went to prison?'

He shuddered dramatically and polished off a forkful of eggs before answering. 'It was a terrible, terrible thing Karen did. Norma never forgave her, you know. Well, who could? Even if you were her mother.'

'But she did keep up the contact with Sunny?'

'No. She decided it was best not to.'

I was shocked. 'How could that be best? She was the child's grandmother!'

'Norma didn't like to talk about it.' I waited while he forked some eggs onto a piece of toast. 'I do know that the day after —' He paused, toast forgotten. The Ponsonby clock chimed four times before he carried on. 'You know, I keep wanting to call it the accident but of course it was no accident.' I nodded. I'd done that too. 'Anyway, the day after the drowning, Dad and Norma went to the house to see Sunny. Karen was taken away that day, of course. The police came round and she just confessed. Anyway, Dad went off to the kitchen to talk to Justin, offer his condolences and all, and Norma went to find Sunny.' The accent was back in full force. He turned the ice pack over. I caught a glimpse of red and purple before he pressed it back into the eye socket. 'And the next minute Dad heard her screaming the house down.'

'Who was screaming the house down?'

'Sunny. She screamed and screamed. There was no stopping her. Justin told Norma she should go. Eventually, she turned around and left and Dad followed.'

'Why?' I was confused. 'Why would Sunny do that?'

He went back to the scrambled eggs. 'Dad thought maybe it was because Norma reminded the child of her mother.' He nodded in the direction of a framed photo of Norma and Karen on the shelf behind me. 'They do look alike, don't you think? Did look alike, I mean.'

A chip of melting ice was dribbling down his neck. I resisted the urge to wipe it away. Despite the intimacy of our earlier contact, I reminded myself we weren't that close. I craned to look at the photo. He was right. Mother and daughter did look very alike. Sunny continued the family resemblance. I wondered if she knew that.

'Dad said Norma was devastated. Far as I know, she never went back, never saw Sunny again. Personally,' he said, carelessly wiping that dribble from his neck with the back of his eating hand, 'I thought she should have gone back to see the child. She should have gone to the funeral. When all was said and done, it was a bloody selfish decision Norma made.'

'Selfishness seems to run in the family.' I clamped my mouth shut. It wasn't like me to make personal remarks about my clients, especially not to their family. I blamed the 4 a.m. supper and shared ice packs. Annoyed with myself, I carried the plate to the sink, sluiced it under the tap and stacked it on the bench. I leaned my head against the cold fridge door behind Ned. All this time he hadn't spoken or moved.

'It was selfish what Karen did, killing that little boy. And what she did to Sunny.' He swivelled on his stool to face me. 'But I blame Justin as much as I blame her. He was always so in control, you know?'

This was interesting but I kept my mouth shut. One indiscretion a night was enough, and if I included the freakin' she-devil attack my indiscretion count was already on the rise. Ned kept the ice pack on his eye with one hand and opened the cleverly disguised dishwasher door with the other. I stacked the dishes into it.

'And then Karen gets sent to prison, Justin cuts her out of his life, divorces her in a flash, turns his life around completely, marries a stupendous Polish blonde, sires a replacement son and makes himself a cool fortune.' He set the machine going. 'Plus he got Sunny. Karen can't have been happy that he got custody.' He looked at me expectantly.

'She's my client, Ned. Even if I knew how she felt about it, I wouldn't tell you. '

'Oh sure, sure,' he said, waving his hand in apology. His accent was back after a sustained absence. He dropped his ice pack in the sink with a loud clatter. His eye was the size of a purple golf ball. It was swollen shut so he probably didn't see me flinch at the sight of it. 'I was forgetting myself, us sitting here chatting and all.'

I didn't intend to go back to sleep and I thought my sore bits would make it impossible but my brain had other ideas. When I woke at nine Ned was already gone. The dishwasher had been unpacked, the bench wiped down. There was a note on it, held down by a wind-up monk wearing headphones: 'Prego. Tonight. 8 p.m. I'll be the guy wearing the eyepatch.'

It wouldn't hurt to have a meal with him. Okay, another meal with him. Call it research. But if the waiter gave me a funny look when I arrived I'd know the she-devil story had preceded me and I'd be out of there toot sweet.

I figured that since I was on the clock I should spend the extra time I had in Auckland finding out what I could about Justin. Apricot was a registered company, with both Justin and Salena nominated as shareholders and company directors. It was the same with the gym gear and health supplement importing business, which was registered under the company name of Orpheus. Both the websites for Apricot and Orpheus gave the impression of small-time businesses. Justin also had a specialty wine import business. From what I could make out it was so boutique as to be a company in name only, set up to provide tax-free expensive wines for Justin and Salena and their dinner guests. His own 'private cellar' I believe is the term used. I didn't get very far by tracking the line of imports and sales for Justin's gym gear and health products so I made a couple of phone calls complaining about missing deliveries and managed to glean much more information about the size of the import loads. On a roll, I followed this up by phoning the gym and posing as the personal assistant of a high-profile media celebrity who wished to remain anonymous. Eventually, after a lot of name-dropping on my part and a rather feeble struggle with confidentiality on hers, I convinced the receptionist to part with the gym's membership list. By the time I had hung up I was confident my first impressions had been pretty close. Both businesses were doing okay but were hardly mega money-earners, which didn't entirely gel with the house, the lifestyle and assets so ostentatiously on display. The Herne Bay multi-squillion-dollar villa with the barn-sized kitchen was owned by a trust, presumably for tax purposes — again — and presumably the trustees were Justin and Salena. I was about to check this when I realised it was five o'clock and I hadn't eaten anything since Ned's scrambled eggs in the early hours of the morning.

Over a coffee and muffin at Café Cézanne, a little place in Three Lamps, I thought over what I'd learned. It looked to me like Justin was spending more money than he earned from either the gym or the online store. This could mean the money was coming from somewhere other than from legitimate businesses. Possibly Justin had taken his alleged history of drug use to a new level and had switched from consumer to supplier. Possibly this was what Karen suspected, which would explain why she was concerned about Sunny — possibly. Justin's assistant Anton with his gold-spangled chest ornaments and bulging water-winged biceps would pass as a classic drug-dealer accoutrement. I made one more call.

Oliver was affectionately known by those in the media as 'accountant to the stars'. He had some luminary clients among the film and celebrity set, who paid him handsomely to look after their books. What made Oliver extremely hot property was that he was the most unlikely of accountants: convivial company, a popular spinner of unlikely yarns, an accomplished singer, lover of the high life and, most importantly, Oliver adored spending money. His own, that is. A generous big spender who was able to legally and legitimately protect his clients' money from the taxman — the only surprise Oliver offered was that he wasn't inundated with marriage proposals. I'd done some work for Oliver a couple of years earlier, tracking down his birth mother. It was an emotional time for him and by the end of it we weren't exactly friends, but we were definitely more than acquaintances. He'd said at the time he'd be happy to help if I ever needed anything. I wasn't counting on Oliver being Justin and Salena's accountant but I was confident he'd know who was.

'You want me to do what?' he responded archly.

'I'm just asking you to have a drink with their accountant

and if something should happen to come up in conversation that you think might be of interest to me, you could let me know.'

'And I would do this for you, why?'

'Okay, never mind. Forget it.' It hadn't occurred to me it was a lot to ask until he hit me with the tone. 'Sorry I asked,' I added belatedly.

His voice softened. 'What's this all about anyway?'

I thought over how much I could tell him. Not much. 'There's a kid involved, a young girl. I want to check that she's okay, that she's in a safe place.'

I waited out the silence. 'And you give me your word you're not working for the IRD?'

'What!' I was truly insulted by the suggestion. 'No. Of course not! What do you take me for?'

I heard him smiling at my outrage. 'I may or may not be in touch,' he said. Which was about as good as I was going to get.

Ned turned out to be one of the few men I'd met who could successfully pull off wearing an eye patch. Okay, he was the only man I'd met who had even tried it, but still … He admitted it was as much to avoid the double-takes from passers-by as it was for comfort. The Prego clientele and staff were way too cool to make anything of it. No doubt they thought it was a fashion statement. We were still studying the menu when Karen phoned. She apologised for failing to warn me that Ned might turn up but assured me he was harmless enough. Watching him flirt with the women at the table next to us, I wasn't so sure about that. Karen admitted she had forgotten about the arrangement Ned had with her mother. She and Norma had been estranged for some years and Karen knew very little about her mother's life.

'Luckily, we made up before she died. It would have been terrible if she'd passed away feeling all that anger towards me.'

Feeling a God lecture imminent I changed the subject. 'Will you move in to your mother's place now, or are you planning to sell it?'

'I can live with very little. That's the only worthwhile thing prison taught me. Actually,' she added coyly, 'it wasn't prison that taught me, it was God. God taught me that.' I bit my tongue. 'I'm selling up and leaving the country. But first I have to get things sorted with Sunny.' Sorted. As if. 'We're going to a Christian commune in LA. We'll live a very simple communal life, Manny and I. He has been so supportive.'

This was the first time I'd heard there was a boyfriend on the scene but it didn't surprise me. I wondered how supportive Manny was in helping Karen dispose of her inheritance. Call me a cynic, but I reckoned there was good chance Manny was supporting that inheritance right into his own pockets. Not my business, I reminded myself. Karen had hired me to find Sunny and I'd done that. She'd instructed me to find out if Sunny was safe and the meeting tomorrow would answer that question for her. My job would be completed and the final invoice would follow in the mail with indecent haste. My credit card balance would breathe a sigh of relief.

'It might not go too smoothly tomorrow, Karen. You should prepare yourself for that,' I warned her.

'Oh, I am.' Her voice lifted. 'Manny and I are having a prayer session tonight. We're asking God to grant me a successful meeting with Sunny. And if that's not His will, then we're asking Him to give me strength to know what to do next.'

'Well, good luck with that,' I said. Being Christian, she'd no doubt recognise the doubting Thomas tone in my voice.

'Thank you.'

Her genuine thanks shamed my sarcasm. I tried again to dampen her excitement about the meeting with Sunny but she was irrepressible. Finally, she told me she would write a cheque to cover my extra expenses. It was a gentle reminder of our employer-employee relationship. When I finished the call I was still struggling with an unease, bordering on terror. There was just no way tomorrow's meeting between Sunny and Karen was going to go well. I relayed this to Ned, who shrugged expansively. I asked if he could articulate what he meant.

'It means it's not your problem,' he explained. 'Choosing something for us from the menu that isn't going to break your bank account — now that's a problem.'

The menu took on a whole new meaning. 'I'm paying?'

'It's the very least you can do, given the state of my eye here, me hearty.'

There was a worrying red and blue streak leaking from below the eye patch, which appeared to be spreading down his jawline at speed. I ordered a salad and encouraged him to be equally extravagant in his choice but before I got to hear his order my phone rang again. Ned spun it around to face him. A photo of Sean I'd taken years ago lit up on the screen, his hand raised above his head in a gesture of farewell. I hadn't realised until now how prescient the image was. His contact name came up as a large 'X' on the screen. Not so subtle with the nomenclature. Ned raised an ironic eyebrow and spun the phone back in my direction.

'Hi,' I said.

'It's me,' Sean said.

'Yeah, I know,' I said.

This was another of those compact little exchanges that pretty much sums up my relationship with my ex-husband. I waited for Sean to pick up the conversation while I watched Ned engage in an animated discussion with the maître d' about his order. Ned did a lot of pointing at items on the menu. The maître d' did a lot of writing and nodding. I did a lot of frowning.

'Where are you?'

'What do you want, Sean?'

'How'd the caravan go today?'

'The what?' Then I remembered. 'Oh,' I said. 'I don't know. I haven't heard. I'll give him a ring in the morning.' There was silence at the other end. 'I'm kind of busy right now, Sean,' I explained. At that moment a woman at the table next to us shrieked with laughter.

'Yeah, I can hear that.'

Ned pointed and laughed at my grumpy face and ordered another bottle of what was no doubt an expensive wine.

'I gotta go,' I said.

'Obviously,' he said.

'Fuck you,' I said cheerfully, and hung up.

With the meagre salad and the two bottles of quality rosé, I didn't put up a fight when Ned took my phone into custody. 'Two phone calls during dinner is the limit,' he announced and made a big deal of switching both our phones to mute and placing them side by side on the far edge of the table. No sooner had he done this than mine lit up. Ned studied the photo of Robbie. I'd snapped him one morning as he was heading off to work. I had taken the photo from his bed, which I was still very nakedly in. His look reflected his response.

'Who's the good-looking policeman then?' Ned asked, waggling his un-eye-patched eyebrow at me.

'Robbie,' I said, holding my hand out for the phone.

'You're in no condition, girl,' he said, pocketing it. 'Best call him back in the morning.'

The image of Robbie disappeared into his breast pocket. There was definitely something proprietorial about the way Ned took possession of my phone. The way he spoke of the morning was as if it was going to be a shared morning, a morning after. My panic button was activated. Without making a big deal about it, I knocked back three glasses of expensive water, ordered goat's cheese and rock melon dessert, slipped the phone out of his pocket while he was engaged in a conversation with the table of women next to us and sauntered a little unsteadily to the ladies where I peed and texted (multi-tasking at its best). *Sorry I missed yr call. Goodnight xxx*, I wrote. I pulled up my knickers, washed my hands, slapped cold water on my bruised neck, checked for twenty-dollar lettuce in my teeth and finally Robbie texted back, *U2 x.*

I stared at the message for a long time, thinking of all the different interpretations I could read into that truncated little message. In the end I decided to accept it at face value. I owed Robbie that much. I signed the bill without looking at the total. We ambled the two hundred metres back to the townhouse. We slept in separate rooms. Eventually.

CHAPTER 10

Ned's bedroom door was shut, his jacket draped on the door handle. I'd booked a flight back to Wellington mid-afternoon, the plan being to catch a cab to the airport as soon as the meeting between Karen and Sunny was over. There was no reason to wake Ned to say goodbye.

At twelve thirty-five, I pushed open the big glass doors of Ja Coozy, the meeting place designated by Justin. Karen wasn't there, which surprised me. I was five minutes late and I'd been sure Karen would be there well ahead of time. A coffee later and still no sign of her, I was worried. I fired off a text, reminding her of the address and asking where she was. The second coffee arrived and still there was no sign of her and no response to the text. So much for the pre-meeting. Sunny was due in a matter of minutes. I rang Karen's number and it went to voicemail. I left a message.

'Please don't let Sunny down, Karen. If there's a problem, ring me.'

By now, the coffee was corroding my stomach lining. Surely Karen wasn't going to stand Sunny up. Surely. My only hope was that Sunny would be a no-show too. No sooner had I thought this than I spotted her swinging her way towards me. All show, she had adopted a striding catwalk lope. High heels, pendulum ponytail, layered skirt, tasselled shoulder bag; all movement, all real casual. As casual as any fourteen-year-old on her way to meet the mother who had tried to murder her could look. She spotted me through the window, saw I was alone and slowed her walk. By the time she pushed the big glass doors open, her shoulders had slumped. Her little mouth had clamped shut.

'She's not coming, is she?' Sunny dropped into the chair opposite but kept her bag in her lap. Her skinny little thighs were mottled with cold.

'She may be stuck in traffic or lost or something. I'll ring her, okay?'

She didn't answer but squinted out the window towards the sparkling harbour. The blackened volcanic crust of Rangitoto was stark against the expanse of blue sky. Even after Karen's phone had switched to voicemail again I kept mine pressed to my ear. This time I didn't leave a message. Sunny stared at her bony knees, most likely struggling to hold back the tears. Her square fingers, a girl's hand, splayed against her stomach as if pressing a bruise.

'Bitch,' she said, quietly. No argument from me there.

'She was really excited about meeting you, Sunny. I don't know what's happened. Something really ... urgent, must have stopped her'

Sunny pulled at the hem of her skirt. 'Yeah, right,' she said. Whorls of purple emerged like invisible writing beneath the translucent white of her skin. Bad circulation. I wanted to wrap her up tight in a soft woollen blanket, feed her good nourishing food, keep her warm and safe from harm — from further harm. I wanted to do all this, and yet I couldn't think of a single thing to say that would lessen the hurt she was feeling.

'Can I get you a coffee?' Then I remembered she didn't even drink coffee.

The chair screeched on the tiled floor, setting my teeth on edge. I followed her to the door and watched her stumble in her high heels across the courtyard. Justin appeared and walked slowly towards her. Stopping only long enough to throw her shoes away, Sunny pushed past him and ran. Following in her wake, I picked up the shoes, held them out to Justin. He ripped them out of my hands, spluttered an attempt to say something then gave up.

'I'm sorry,' I said to his departing back.

I didn't know if I was saying it for Karen or for me, but I was sorry. I was sorry to have raised Sunny's expectations and then dash them in this humiliating way; sorry to have had any part in it. Fingers looped through the straps of her shoes, Justin walked slowly away in the direction Sunny had run. He was giving her time, I think. No doubt he'd find her weeping in private somewhere further along the wharf. She wouldn't have gone far.

Only when they were both completely out of sight did I realise how angry I was. Furious, spitting, blood-pounding anger. I hoped the anger survived the flight to Wellington. I wanted to still be feeling this rage when I confronted Karen.

CHAPTER 11

Sunny

Dad makes me wear my blue summer dress with the daisies on it, even though the neck is scratchy. I ask him if Falcon is going to be lifted up to heaven by the angels and if heaven is like Rainbow's End only none of the rides are scary. And I ask if angels really are like fairies only fatter. I tell him I hope the angels make the coffin take off like a rocket ship with flames bursting out the bottom because I know Falcon would like that the best, but Dad looks out the car window as if I've said something bad, even though it wasn't bad and I whispered it so the man driving the car couldn't hear.

I've never been in a church before and I don't like it. Except

I do quite like the big windows with all the coloured glass pictures. The coffin is already there but I don't think the angels are coming to get Falcon. Kids from school walk up to it a bit scared and then the adults help them tie balloons to the handles on the side. Falcon's too heavy and the balloons aren't strong enough to lift it. Unless he's really light now that he's dead. If the angels don't come, they'll just have to put him in the ground with all the other coffins. Someone has put Robot Man and a football on top of the coffin. I've never seen the football before and I don't know why it's there. Robot Man is sitting there like he's waiting for Falcon to open the lid and pick him up. There's music playing and when I turn around to look for the person playing it the adults look at me but then their eyes slide away and they pretend they're looking somewhere else. I don't like it. And I don't like it when adults stand up the front next to the coffin and say all those things about Falcon and I don't like it when everyone sings really loud like they're yelling. I don't know any of the songs. Gran isn't here. I know that without looking because she told me she wasn't coming. She was mean to me and I hate her. Dad puts his hand on my knee and gives me his warning look to tell me to stop swinging my legs. I want to go home. Everything smells funny from the flowers. It makes my tummy feel sick and I wish I hadn't eaten my toast even though Dad said I had to. I think I might vomit and that wouldn't be good in the church. If the angels do come, they'll have to crash through the windows, right through the coloured glass. I hope they don't smash the one of the lady holding a baby. The lady and the baby both have big golden things like bike helmets on their heads but the lady's wearing a crown

94

with jewels under her helmet. She has a long blue dress like a princess and she looks really sad like a princess. And then the priest tells us to kneel and take a moment to think about Falcon, and everyone does but I don't think about Falcon because I don't know what to think about him. The wood smells nice and I put my teeth on it and bite it a little bit because Dad has his eyes shut. I like the feeling of it on my tongue. It tastes warm and brown and makes my tummy feel better. My teeth have left marks on it like when I bite my pencil. My teeth marks will stay there forever. Everyone stands up and Dad takes my hand so I know to stand up too. My knees are sore from when we had to kneel down but I don't rub them in case it makes Dad angry. Then Mrs Pritchard from kindy brings some of the little kids up and they have to reach up high to put flowers on the coffin. I can't see Robot Man any more because of all the flowers. He must be drowning in the flowers. I wonder what would happen if I saved Robot Man like the man saved me. The nurses were nice to me in the hospital and even let me keep the flappy slippers to take home, but they didn't tell me Falcon was dead. Dad told me. He said the man saved me first because I was in the front and when he went back down for Falcon he was already dead.

Everyone sings 'Somewhere Over the Rainbow' but I don't, even though I know all the words, and then some men I don't know lift up the coffin with Falcon in it and take it out of the church. Dad takes my hand and we walk behind it. Everyone stares at me, even though they pretend not to, and I can hear all the people sniffing and crying but I don't look at them. The light coming through the door hurts my eyes. Maybe all that light is from the angels and they're going to take us all up to heaven with Falcon. I tug at Dad's sleeve to tell him I want to go with Falcon and the angels but, instead of bending down to hear me, he picks me up in his arms like when I was little and carries me out into the bright light.

Outside the light isn't so bright any more but it's still weird. They're sliding the coffin into the back of the big black car like a tray going in the oven, but they leave the end sticking out and the back door open so people can put flowers on it. Dad puts me down and people come over and touch me and call me dear. I don't like it. But the man who saved me comes up and smiles at me and I like it, but then he goes away again without saying anything. Everyone looks strange like they're far away but their faces are really big, like balloons.

'Where's Mum?' I say to Dad, but he doesn't answer me. He's looking at the coffin with all the flowers on it. His face is wet and puffed up from all the crying. 'Where's Mum?' I say again and even though I know he's heard me he doesn't answer. The people beside Dad turn away, pretending they can't hear me either. 'I want Mum,' I say, but I don't really. I just want to see what Dad says. He turns his head and looks at me and I don't know what he's going to say. 'It's just you and me now, Sunny girl,' he says.

I think of Mum standing at the kitchen bench with the weird light coming in the window and the way her eyes slide at me and make my tummy feel sick, and how the policeman put his hand on the top of her head to stop her banging it when she got into the back of the police car. She didn't turn around to look at me when they drove away.

Dad hands me a flower. 'Go on,' he says. 'Say goodbye to your brother and then we'll go home.' He gives me a little shove so I know to put the flower on the coffin. Everyone stands back so I can go right up to the coffin. I reach in and put the flower in the middle of all the other flowers and I feel the shiny plastic of Robot Man underneath all the flowers, like he's drowned, like he can't get out. I catch him and pull him out and hold him tight in my hand where no one can see and then I put him way down deep inside my blue pocket with the daisies on it where he'll be safe.

CHAPTER 12

Karen's house on the rise of Mt Victoria was bigger and flashier than I'd expected. It's hard to break the old prejudice that criminals are all working class and poor. She had written her address on the back of the down-payment cheque I still hadn't got around to banking. First thing Monday I'd deposit it and send her an invoice for the extra days in Auckland, plus expenses. Given her no-show, I was tempted to add the cost of Ned's dinner to the invoice, plus extra remuneration for loss of pride over the naked she-devil incident. My anger had dissipated a little but the memory of Sunny running barefoot down the length of the wharf would haunt me for a long time to come. I resented being party to Sunny's humiliation and I was going to let Karen know it.

There was no response to my knock. Personally, I can't be confronted by a door handle without attempting to turn it. Turning being its only *raison d'être* and all, it seems impolite not to. That's my excuse, anyway. The front door opened into a T-shaped wide hallway with a warren of spacious rooms leading off on either side. All the doors stood open except the one directly on my right. I paused in the entranceway and called Karen's name, turning my head to one side to listen for a response. It had been a typically turbulent Wellington landing and one ear was still blocked from the flight. My stomach rumbled loudly in the silence. It wasn't just the cold breeze from the open door that made me shudder. There was an unnerving stillness in the air. The closed door on my right was paint-stripped rimu. Sanded and oiled. Closed. A big decorative brass doorknob confronted me, begging to be turned.

Karen was lying on the floor, her head propped up against the base of the bed. She was wearing a cross-over style silk dressing gown that was tied at the waist and decorated with large brightly coloured parrots. The slump of her body made the top gape open to expose a brown puckered nipple. Her legs were stretched out in front, crossed at the ankles, hands splayed open in her lap. My knees clicked as I knelt and held two fingertips to her throat. The skin was cool. I let my breath out but didn't seem able to take in a full lungful of air to replace it. Karen's head was tilted forward as if she was studying the upturned hands in her lap. Her hair smelt of Pantene conditioner. I knew already I'd never use it again. Squatting closer, I could make out a dark-bluish patch beneath the hair feathering her neck. A bruise or graze maybe. The silence in the room was complete. My toes cramped, forcing me to shift position. Now I was kneeling beside her, my head at the same height as hers. I twisted to look up into her face and caught the oily gleam of an eye. Mascara clumps weighted the lashes. How very still a dead body is. My fingers twitched with the desire to tug the gown up over the exposed nipple. What harm would it do? I could say I shifted it by accident when I was feeling for her pulse. My fingers edged towards the lapel … The shock of my phone ringing almost toppled me into Karen's lap. I recognised the ringtone: 'Hey, That's No Way to Say Goodbye.' The song was eerily fitting.

'Sean?' my voice sounded normal.

'Hey, listen, I banged into Joe Morton on the street this morning and he said he's interested in having a look at the house. You know he always loved our place.' He sounded so very alive. The body lying in front of me was so very dead. 'Shall I tell him to give you a ring, or get him to contact the agent?'

My stomach rumbled again. It seemed obscene to be hungry in the presence of death. 'Can you come here?'

'Where? I thought you were in Auckland.'

'No, I'm here.'

'What's up?'

'Someone's dead. My client, I mean. She's dead.' I turned my face towards the light from the bay window. It made talking about it easier.

'I only just got here and found her. It doesn't have to be you that comes, but can you send someone?' I gave him the address. He told me to go sit outside and instructed me not to touch anything.

'Touch absolutely nothing at all,' he repeated in the way that has always made me want to do the opposite.

I confirmed the address, told him I was fine and didn't need to keep talking to him until the car arrived. I managed to thank him for the offer, though. And I went outside like he told me to. And I didn't touch anything. But I did take photos with my iPhone. Since I did it without moving my feet more than absolutely necessary I reckoned it was fair. I turned my phone towards the overnight bag lying open on the window seat, some clothes folded neatly beside it, *click*. And then I turned it towards the clothes still on their hangers that lay across the unmade bed, waiting for Karen to inhabit them, *click*. From where I stood, pretty much in the middle of the room, I turned and took a whole panorama of photos and then from the doorway, I turned and took one more. Karen hadn't moved. Of course she hadn't moved, but I stared at her for a long time, willing her to prove me wrong. Her head remained tilted forward, her focus still on the upturned hands in her lap. From the doorway it looked as if she was reading an invisible book, or engaged in a silent remonstrative argument with herself. When I thought of all the cops and technicians who would soon be swarming over the place, I wished I had tugged the gown over her exposed nipple. But with Sean's lecture still echoing, it was too late now. My whispered apology to her hung in the silence. Then I went outside, sat on the veranda steps and waited for the cavalry to arrive. I knew the cavalry would be closely followed by the circus.

There's something about death that brings out the best in us. It's called life. Raging, adrenalin-fuelled, blood-surging life. It's obscene, I know, but that's just the way it is. Now, forty-five minutes after finding Karen's body, I could feel that adrenalin draining away. It left me feeling flat and a bit weepy.

Detective Inspector Aaron Fanshaw looked to be in his early thirties. That was young to have been made an inspector in a big city like Wellington. But I may have been wrong about his age. He was probably one of those perpetually youthful guys who don't age until they're in their sixties when they then suddenly let go of the reins. Right now he had a gym body and the height to carry it off. Maybe Aaron was the reason Sean had decided to get his own body into shape. He was already higher up the police hierarchy and pay scale than Sean. Or maybe it was having a baby that had made Sean aware of his own mortality and had initiated his bid for a longer life.

Sean had introduced Aaron and me and then walked away, leaving us to talk. We moved to a wrought-iron garden seat with a view of the gate and the entrance to the house. He slipped a little black notepad out of an inside pocket. The yellow Space Invaders icon on the bottom corner made me smile. I explained my relationship to Karen and the reason for turning up on her doorstep and he nodded but kept his eyes on the notes he made in a flowing longhand. I thought about skirting around how I had entered the house without being invited, but seeing the uniformed and plain clothes cops file down the path I knew this was too important to lie about or obfuscate. If someone had killed Karen, the cops needed to know the facts; the front door had been closed, but not locked. Aaron gave no response to my admission other than a nod, though he did underline the word 'unlocked'. He made the telling of it easy, letting me start at the beginning and talk my way through to the end without interruption. From the garden seat I could see Sean pacing up and down outside the dairy across the road, mobile phone pressed to his ear, free hand gesticulating as he talked. He may have been ordering fingerprint experts and photographers. Then again, he may have been telling the pixie that he'd bring home nappies for the baby and a bottle of wine for them when he finished work. I don't know what he says any more.

When I'd finished telling Aaron everything, he asked me to accompany him back into the house. In preparation, I clenched my hands and shoved them deep into my jacket pockets; it's the best way to ensure you don't touch anything at a crime scene. Aaron nodded in acknowledgement and indicated the plastic runner someone had placed on the floor to protect the carpet. Well, not to protect the carpet, but any evidence there might be on the carpet. If it was a homicide, at some point they would ask for my shoes, too. Hands on my shoulders, Aaron guided me carefully through the bedroom doorway, ensuring no part of me touched or brushed against anything. A squeeze of his fingers indicated I should stand still.

'Just point out exactly where you walked,' he instructed. His fingers were warm on my shoulder. 'And try to remember everything you touched.'

Maybe an hour had passed since I'd felt the coolness of her skin beneath my fingertips and in that time Karen had gone from being a person to being a dead body. Or, put more simply, Karen had gone, full stop. I marvelled again at the stillness. The beseeching upturned hands continued to beseech. The exposed brown nipple was a rebuke, but I was pleased now that I hadn't prudishly tugged the dressing gown over it. Maybe it was the presence of Aaron or the sound of hushed chatter as police and technicians gathered. Maybe it was that rigor mortis had begun to set in and the limbs were stiffening in the unmistakable rictus of death. Whatever it was, there was no mistaking this was a crime scene with a dead body at the centre of it. I thought I could smell death, but that was probably just the cloying smell of peppermints. Funeral directors, morgue staff, crime scene cops; they're always surrounded by the ubiquitous scent of peppermint. As I described to Aaron how I had approached the body, felt for a pulse, squatted and looked up into Karen's face, it was like watching a slow-mo film version of myself. I assured Aaron I hadn't touched any part of Karen's body except her neck where the carotid pulse should have been. And wasn't. When I finished speaking he ushered me back outside, ensuring I kept to the narrow plastic runner on the floor. His comfortingly warm hand remained on my shoulder the whole way. Oscar Fa'atua, a detective I knew from police barbecue days with Sean, was running crime scene tape across the doorway to the bedroom. He raised his eyebrows in a 'wassup?' gesture as I was ushered out. Oscar must have been put in as OC Scene then. Good for him. Aaron walked me down the path past a duck line of white disposable boiler-suited ESR technicians, each carrying their own little trade toolboxes. There was an unmistakable, barely suppressed air of excitement among them — homicide. In police bars and forensic scientists' and lab technicians' morning tea rooms, they would admit openly that homicides were the best crimes to land. Unless the victim was a child. I've never met anyone involved in a case who was blasé about the murder of a child; I hope I never do. As soon as we'd stepped outside the house, Aaron was besieged by cops, all needing answers to questions. I left him to it after promising to come into the station on Monday to give a full formal statement and fingerprints.

Sean was leaning against my car. He held out a paper cup.

'I'd rather it was a cigarette,' I said, but gulped the coffee anyway. Trim milk, two sugars. He remembered.

'You alright?' he asked, looking away from me.

'I'm fine,' I said and looked away from him too. I felt his gaze turn back in my direction. He was waiting for me to speak.

'Is there anything you want to tell me?'

I was feeling guilty about the photos I'd taken and had a paranoid notion Sean knew about them. My mobile seemed heavier than usual in my back pocket and I was excruciatingly aware of it. As if sensing the attention it was getting, it rang. It wasn't a number I recognised.

'I'd better take this,' I said, and waited for Sean to move away. He didn't. I gave him what he used to refer to as 'a look'. My phone kept on ringing. He took his time, looking from me to the phone and back to me again. I returned his look with a bug-eyed one of my own. It did the trick. He walked away with one hand raised. It was either a casual wave goodbye or him warding off the juju of my bug-eyes. I flicked the phone to answer.

'Is this Diane Rowe?' I knew immediately who it was. 'It's me. Sunny.' I walked quickly down the street, trying to put as much space between the phone and Sunny's dead mother as I could. It wasn't that I thought Sunny would overhear anything significant, and I knew Karen was past hearing anything at all, it was more a sense of decency.

'Have you seen her yet?' she asked. As I scrambled for an answer, I had a flash of Karen's exposed brown nipple; the beseeching hands in her lap; the oily gleam of her eye; the oppressive stillness. 'Well, anyway, when you do,' she continued, 'you can tell her from me she's a selfish bitch.' I listened to the break in her voice. 'I didn't think she could hurt me again but you can tell her from me that somehow she did. So, you know, well, tell her congratulations.' I saw again the overnight bag and the neatly folded pile beside it; the clothes carefully laid on the bed ready for Karen to give them shape. 'And you can tell her from me that today was the worst day of my whole life. Apart from the day she tried to kill me, that is.' She made awful little hiccupping sounds between words. It was heartbreaking to listen to. I had to say something.

'She was coming to see you, Sunny. I promise you.'

Sunny barked a laugh. 'Yeah? So what stopped her?' I bit my lip. It wasn't my job to tell Sunny her mother was dead. The sobbing got louder. 'What stopped her!' she repeated. 'It must have been something really important.' The sarcasm was flat.

Shit. I took a deep breath. 'Sunny, listen to me. I have something to tell you.'

'What? Unless you can tell me why she didn't meet me, there's nothing you can tell me.'

I waited until I knew she was listening. 'It's bad news, I'm afraid. I'm sorry, Sunny. Your mum—' I kicked myself for using the 'm' word.

Sunny was on full alert. She knew something was up. 'What? What about her?'

'She's dead, Sunny. Karen is dead. That's why she didn't come to see you today.' I listened to the uneven breathing. 'Is your dad there?' A long silence followed.

'No,' she said finally, her voice very quiet.

'Salena?'

Sunny coughed an ironic laugh. Fair enough, I thought. From what I'd seen of their relationship Salena wouldn't be of any use to her anyway.

'Are you totally sure she's dead?'

'Yes, I'm totally sure,' I said. She sniffed loudly. 'Is there someone you can go to now? Someone you can talk to? Someone you trust?' Again the silence. I held my breath, worried that I'd made a seriously bad decision in telling her.

'It's okay,' she said. Surprisingly, she did sound okay. I waited while she blew her nose. 'I'm alright. Dad will be back soon.'

I kept her talking until she heard Justin's car pull up outside. She broke down again when she knew he was there; when she knew she could break down. I sat in the car and knocked back the dregs of Sean's bitter coffee. Professionally, it had been wrong to tell Sunny her mother was dead but it felt ethically wrong not to tell her. Emotionally, it was fucked either way. The whole situation was what I think is called a lose-lose.

The last of the sun had dropped down behind the hills, leaving Oriental Bay in shadow. I flicked the car heater on. The warm air revived the homely odour of dog, but not just any dog. It was the distinctive, aromatic, comforting odour of my dog. I breathed it in deeply.

I was back in Wellington. Home.

CHAPTER 13

In my life, I've made love for a number of reasons. Love and desire, to name the two most obvious. But there are other reasons for making love that you only learn about when you've been together for a while. The list of reasons for having sex is even longer: lust, fun, tenderness, happiness, sadness and boredom … these are only a few. The great thing about being with someone you love is that you get to make love and you get to have sex. Robbie and I were at that awkward stage in our relationship when neither of us was quite sure if we could include making love in our repertoire of having sex yet. Though Robbie's suggestion that we move in together needed considered discussion, in the meantime we had plenty of less wordy stuff we could get on with. And though we couldn't yet decide on how deep our feelings were for each other, we were unabashedly confident of the depth of our feelings for my dog, which was definitely a plus. For Wolf anyway.

Sunday morning Robbie and I stayed in bed reading the paper, drinking coffee and dunking croissants. Wolf pretended to show no interest in the greasy croissant flakes but I was confident that as soon as we were in the shower he'd be on the bed sneakily hoovering them up, lips luffing. I hadn't talked work with Robbie except to tell him I'd found Karen's body and that, though the police were treating her death as suspicious, there was every chance it had been the result of an accident or natural causes. Robbie sensed, I think, that I didn't want to talk about it. I couldn't shake the image of Karen propped up against the end of the bed, her legs stuck out in front, ankles crossed, hands beseeching. Nor could I erase the image of Sunny throwing her shoes away and running barefoot down the wharf. Being the one to have told Sunny her mother was dead weighed heavily on me. It shouldn't have been me, I knew that, but at the time I felt I had no choice.

It might have been my distraction that drove Robbie from my bed. He claimed to have a game of social rugby to get to anyway. Cops have these friendly events all the time. The police are a closed society not entirely of their own making. People fall into two camps when it comes to socialising with cops. They either fawn, or feel compelled to complain about a parking ticket some arsehole cop gave them five years ago. Having lived with one for a number of years I understood why it was easier for cops to just hang out with other cops. Sunday morning rugby games were popular with the single cops. Single male cops, that is. There would be few women brave enough to insist on being included in that male bastion. I didn't ask Robbie if he was playing rugby with Sean and he didn't offer information one way or the other, which was a relief. Why do men think it's okay to buddy up with their girlfriend's ex-husband? We women know it is just so wrong.

We kissed goodbye. It was a good kiss. Then he said a loving farewell to Wolf who nudged him coquettishly, dipping his big skull between Robbie's knees to better facilitate the ear rub. His tail wagged out of control. I would have to have words with him about his unseemly display of affection — Wolf, that is.

I spent the next hour moping through the personal records Karen had given me the first time we met. In theory, Karen's death terminated our contract. In theory, I should parcel everything up and send it back to her, but that seemed rather pointless, her being dead and all. I decided I might as well hang on to it all until the investigation was complete. Presumably, Sunny would be the beneficiary of Karen's will and the parcel of childhood memorabilia would go to her. Karen's carefully kept record of her daughter's childhood milestones seemed even more poignant now. I was in no doubt Karen had been keenly looking forward to seeing her daughter. I wished for Sunny's sake she had been given the chance to meet Karen but whether she would ever have been able to forgive her mother was another matter entirely. It might have helped if she could understand her mother's attempt to kill her was an aberration, a terrible mistake brought on by her drug habit. I tipped an embossed card from a pocket-sized envelope into my palm. Inside was a lock of fine hair. *Sunny's first haircut* was written on the envelope in backward sloping script. A beep alerted me to a phone text. It was Jason Baker, reminding me that today was my first open home and requesting I vacate the premises before one o'clock. As I stared malevolently at the phone I remembered it held a set of photos that needed downloading. Crime scene photos no less.

There were a dozen in all. Six made up the panorama I'd taken standing in the middle of the room next to Karen's body. The photos looked as if they belonged in a game of Cluedo. Mrs Peacock in the drawing room with the knife. Maybe it was the light from the bay window heightening the colours that made the images seem lurid. More likely it was the dead body in the middle of the room. I downloaded them all to my laptop and used Photoshop to study each one in detail. I had no idea what I was looking for; maybe a clue to what happened? Who was I kidding? But there was one shot I stalled over. I couldn't figure out what it was that made me return to it again and again. Something about it bothered me. I gave up and stored the laptop in a file box labelled 'Tax'. That should put off any likely burglars among the open homers, unless of course they were employees of Inland Revenue.

Normal people spend hours preparing their house for an open home. I made the bed, did the dishes and vacated the premises before one o'clock, as requested, with a full 30 seconds to spare.

Gemma was waiting for me at the dog zone end of Lyall Bay, as arranged. She's my oldest and closest friend so I didn't take the scowl personally. She always looks like that. The place was crazy with canines of every shape, size and variety. In the five hundred metres of designated free dog area there must have been at least thirty freewheeling canines and their not so freewheeling owners. Wolf adopted an aloof and superior manner befitting an elderly ex-police dog until a youthful huntaway approached and sniffed his butt optimistically. That sorted, they cantered off together towards a yappy pack of short-legged terriers, tails and expectations high. We left Wolf to sort out his own social networking while Gemma and I sauntered along the waterline, enjoying the sunshine and sea air. Being a cop, Gemma already knew about the suspicious death in Mt Victoria, but she didn't know Karen was my client or that I had been the one who found the body.

'How did it look to you?' she asked.

'Dead.' I hid my shudder in a shrug. 'She looked dead.'

'I mean did it look like a homicide or an accident?'

I pictured Karen again. Still. Silent. 'I don't know. There was a big bruise on her neck but …'

'But what?'

'Well, the room showed no obvious signs of a struggle—'

Gemma interrupted 'It's pretty unusual to bang yourself on the neck.'

'Yeah, I thought that, too.'

'I'm talking about you. How did you get that bruise?'

Instinctively my hand went to my neck. I didn't realise the bruise from the she-devil incident with Ned was visible. Robbie hadn't mentioned it.

Gemma slid a sleazy smile in my direction. 'You and Robbie getting a bit boisterous?'

'It was just a misunderstanding with a guy in Auckland.'

Gemma raised an eyebrow but made no comment. We watched Wolf and the huntaway race side by side through the shallows, egging each other on. I was admiring the way Wolf's hair caught the sunlight. Gemma was thinking about something else entirely.

'So what is happening with you and Robbie?'

'Nothing,' I said way too quickly.

Gemma smiled cruelly. 'Uh-huh.' She always manages to get more information out of me than I intend to give. I guess that's what makes her such a good detective.

'He wants us to move in together.' Luckily for me, my phone rang, so I could ignore the surprised look Gemma turned on me. It was Oliver, accountant to the stars.

'Okay, I took your friend Justin's accountant out for a drink. I was forced to order from the top shelf.' No preambles with Oliver.

'Fine. Send me the bill. What did you find out?'

'Well, you were right about the gym not making a profit. It's losing money like the proverbial sieve.'

I watched Gemma wander off towards where Wolf and the huntaway were disputing the ownership of a stick. They were tugging at it from either end. Wolf's neck muscles were straining, his forelegs flat on the sand, butt high up in the air with effort. His blind eye as milky as an oyster.

'So they're in trouble financially?'

'I didn't say that,' he replied archly.

Wolf reluctantly gave up his stick to the huntaway who then dropped it dismissively. Wolf wouldn't like that.

'The vitamins or health supplements business or whatever

it is, seems to be doing okay. And according to Lou there's a lot of cash floating around. Your man claims he's lucky with the horses. If he is, he'll be the first.'

Gemma retrieved the stick and hurled it into the water for Wolf. The young huntaway got there first. Having won the race, he didn't even bother to claim the prize. He stepped over it and sauntered off. I thought I heard Gemma growl at the huntaway but it might just have been Oliver clearing his throat.

'Okay, thanks, Oliver. I owe you.'

'Yes, indeed you do. I'll round the invoice up to the nearest hundred, shall I?'

'Fine. Lovely to talk to you, too.'

I joined Gemma at the waterline. Wolf was walking backwards, his eyes fixed on the stick. Gemma would go to throw, but every gesture was a feint. At first Wolf lunged in the direction he thought the stick had been thrown, but already after half a dozen false throws he was smart to it. Gemma smirked at his cleverness. 'So are you going to move in with him?'

Instead of answering, I asked a question of my own. 'Are you going to be working on the case?'

Gemma feinted with the stick again. This time Wolf didn't move a muscle. 'Depends on what Smithy says. It might not even be a case. The body's still *in situ* but they're planning to move it later today. He's down to do the PM tomorrow.' Smithy doing the postmortem was good news. He and I went way back. Wolf crouched in the water, oblivious to the waves smashing on his butt, eyes riveted on the stick.

'So? Are you going to move in with Robbie?' Gemma never left a question unanswered. She was keeping half an eye on the huntaway who was circling behind her weighing up his chances of getting to the stick before Wolf.

'Maybe. Maybe not. I've got the house on the market.'

'Wow! That's big,' Gemma said, swivelling her head in my direction. Wolf thought her attention had shifted. She flung the stick in a high arc over his head. He was on to her though and trotted backwards under it, his one good eye locked on its trajectory. I was on to her, too.

'It was Sean's idea. But it's okay. It's time to move on.'

I ignored the cynical look Gemma turned on me. It was true. Even if I didn't really know what 'moving on' actually meant. Wolf leapt in the air and caught the stick long before it hit the water. The huntaway was impressed. So were the humans. Maybe it was the pleasure of it that made Gemma more forthcoming than usual.

'You know that if Smithy thinks there's anything suspicious, it'll be the full works. Seven years inside — she would have made a few enemies.'

I hadn't thought of that. If Karen's death was a homicide, the cops would be all over it. Some criminal networks are run entirely from inside prison and the death of a recently released prisoner would be thoroughly investigated. Karen may have been the link to the outside world for an activity run from inside. Or she may have thought she'd made the break from an inmate only to discover they had connections outside, too; connections prepared to deliver payback. The cops would be looking closely at all Karen's relationships, including her most recent cellmate, Vex. My sister's killer. I looked at Gemma. She nodded in confirmation. I'd finally got there.

I let Wolf keep the prize stick he'd proudly carried all the way back to the car. I heard him crunching away at it in the back seat. It sounded like small bones breaking.

Before unlocking the front door, I hosed and dried Wolf in the back yard and then checked the letter box. On top of my power and phone bills was an unstamped envelope. My name was handwritten on the front in backward sloping script. Inside was a cheque for two thousand dollars, tucked into a folded handwritten note.

This is to cover the cost of the flights and extra time in Auckland. And a small bonus. I know it's only money but I don't know how else to thank you. I'm so excited about meeting Sunny. It means everything to me. Even if she rejects me, you have no idea how much it means to me to be able to see her again. Just to know what she looks like now will be a blessing. Thank you, thank you. God bless. Karen.

And just like that I realised what had bothered me about that crime scene photo. Impatiently, I fired up my laptop and found the shot I'd stalled over. On the far side of Karen's bedroom, opposite the bay window, was a closed-off fireplace. In the middle of the mantelpiece was a group of photographs. One photo took pride of place in the centre. That was what had disturbed me. I rolled my finger down the mouse to enlarge the photo further and waited impatiently while it focused. It was a photo of Sunny — a recent photo; so recent in fact, she was wearing the same flouncy blouse I'd seen her in on Saturday. I slumped back in my chair. Karen had written that she was looking forward to seeing what her daughter looked like. When had she put that note in my letter box? It had to be after our phone conversation on Friday night when she had insisted on paying me for the extra time in Auckland. And obviously it was before I found her body on Saturday afternoon. Karen must have got hold of the photo sometime between those two events, which raised the most important question of all: who had given Karen the photo of Sunny in the hours leading up to her death?

CHAPTER 14

I faltered at marital status. Exactly how long are you divorced before you're single again? Or is being single like being a virgin — there ain't no going back, sister. Detective Sergeant Coleman waited patiently while I stared at the freckle on his lip and went through these mental gymnastics. He'd explained he was the OC Witnesses and that he'd be the one taking my formal statement. Detective Sergeant Coleman didn't offer me his first name but I noticed he was happy to chuck mine around freely enough. He led me into an interview room and asked if I minded if he taped our conversation. He said he hadn't quite mastered his Pitman's yet. I was fine with that, though the formality of a recorded interview made me a little uneasy about repeating the details of my illegal entry to Karen's house. What the hell,

I thought. It wasn't as if I broke in. The previous night, I'd tried to phone Aaron Fanshaw to tell him about Karen's letter but I hadn't been able to track him down and decided against babbling a message onto his voicemail. Better just to bring it up at the interview today, I thought. Coleman told me to make myself comfortable while he went to get us some water. It was a bit of a challenge to make myself comfortable on a hard-backed school chair in a barren grey police interview room. I was still squirming when he returned like a retriever with Detective Inspector Aaron Fanshaw in tow.

'G'day, Diane, good to see you again,' Aaron said, pulling up a chair across the desk from me.

His sudden appearance threw me. He and Coleman were now seated on the exit side of the desk while I was cramped against the wall. The wooden table was between me and the only way out. This positioning definitely put the interviewee — i.e. me — at a disadvantage. I reminded myself I was a witness, that was all. One of the good guys, here to help out the police with their enquiries. It occurred to me that there were probably a fair number of schmucks presently serving life sentences who'd thought the very same thing.

'Brett said you were trying to get hold of me,' he said.

Presumably Brett was Coleman's first name. I looked forward to using it the very first opportunity I got. Brett smiled wolfishly as he placed a single paper cup of water in front of me. For a big guy he looked remarkably comfortable on his baby bear-sized chair.

'I got a note from Karen,' I said, taking the envelope out of my shoulder bag and laying it on the desk between us. 'She must have delivered it before she was killed.' I realised the stupidness of my comment too late. 'Obviously.' I pulled a face and both cops smiled silently in response. I looked from one to the other. Okay, now I was really worried.

Aaron reached an arm towards the record button on the deck 'You sure you don't mind if we record this?'

I felt suddenly self-conscious. 'Sure. Yeah, sure.'

I reminded myself again that I had nothing to hide. Well, not much to hide. The little matter of the photographs I'd taken of the crime scene might be best left unmentioned. A red blinking light flashed above the deck's depressed record button. Only then did I notice the video camera clamped high on the wall above it. It was aimed in my direction. Both cops were looking at me expectantly. My mouth was dry but I wasn't going to pick up the paper cup. At least not until one of them had picked up the envelope.

'You were saying Karen sent this to you before she was killed,' Aaron prompted. Despite their casual demeanour I could feel the tension in the air, could see it in the way they sat with their shoulders hunched forward.

'Well, there's no stamp,' I said, sliding the envelope across the desk closer to them. 'So she must have put it in my letter box.' They looked at me. Waiting. 'Rather than sent it.' Still they looked at me.

'Before she was killed,' Aaron repeated.

'Well, yeah. I mean, obviously she put it there when she was alive.' What was this? Why was he giving me a hard time for a stupid slip of the tongue? I forged on.

'It's a cheque written out to me for two thousand dollars

and a note saying how much she's looking forward to seeing Sunny.' I pushed the envelope even closer to them but still neither of them picked it up. They were both working hard to appear relaxed as they nodded and smiled at me to continue. 'And what's interesting,' I said, nudging it a bit closer to them, 'is that she specifically says she's excited about being able to see what Sunny looks like now. And yet there's a recent photo of Sunny on her mantelpiece.' This was risky. I was pretty sure I could have seen the photo on the mantelpiece from where I stood next to the body, but the fact was, I'd only confirmed the girl in the photo was Sunny with the help of Photoshop. 'So,' I said, spelling it out for them, 'Karen must have got hold of that photo of Sunny after she dropped this note into my letter box.' Still they nodded and smiled benignly. They were really starting to piss me off now. 'Which must have been shortly before she died,' I added, just in case they hadn't got there yet.

'How do you know Karen was killed?' Aaron asked.

'What?'

'You said Karen delivered the note before she was killed. How do you know that?' Aaron's smile had gone but he kept the question sounding casual.

'Did I say killed? Killed … dead … I don't know why I said killed.' Why had I said killed? In the face of their suspicion I went with honesty. Sometimes it's worth a go. 'I guess it's because I think she was.' They looked at me. 'Killed, I mean.' Fuck, I thought. I sound as guilty as shit. Worse still, I felt guilty. 'Don't you?' My voice sounded squeaky. 'Think she was killed?' I managed to look Fanshaw in the eye but it wasn't easy. There was a creeping sensation on my scalp as the sweat cooled.

'Or are you telling me her death was an accident?'

Aaron looked at me for a long time before answering. 'We don't know yet,' he said, doing that neck-muscle-stretch thing I'd seen Olympic weightlifters do.

I saw his eyes drop to my neck and then back to my face. I resisted the urge to touch the bruise, but I was sure that's what he'd noted.

'Karen does have a history, of course,' Aaron said, stretching his legs out under the desk. 'She was a junkie when she killed her son and then she took up with a pretty heavy bunch in prison. She made a few enemies.' He paused long enough to rein in those legs under his chair. 'I believe you know Karen's cellmate?' He slid it in real casual and made a point of looking away as he dropped the bombshell. No need for him to study me now when he had the tape rolling for perusal later. There was no doubt about it, Case Officer Detective Inspector Aaron Fanshaw had me down as a possible suspect for Karen's murder. No wonder he'd made inspector at a young age. Though on this, our second meeting, I ramped him up to late- rather than mid-thirties. Then again, it was Monday morning and no doubt he'd had little sleep since landing the case on Saturday afternoon.

'If you mean Vex, yes, I do know her.' I could really have done with that water. 'And I'm sure you know exactly how and why I know her.'

Aaron smiled. 'I'm surprised you took on a job for Vex.'

'I didn't take on anything for Vex,' I said. 'Karen was Vex's ex-cellmate, that's all. According to Karen they were never friends.' It sounded like a weak argument, even to me.

'Where were you on Friday night?'

I laughed. It sounded like such a classic cop TV show question. Neither Aaron nor Coleman joined in the laughter. Shit! They were serious. My brain scrambled for an answer. I had a flash of Ned's eye patch.

'I was in Auckland. At a place called Prego. A restaurant. We left there about eleven, I think. Maybe midnight by the time I got back to where I was staying.' Neither cop responded. 'In Ponsonby,' I added, helpfully. Suddenly, I remembered. 'Karen phoned me while I was there!' This was vital information; it could help establish time of death. I'd forgotten it until now. I looked at them expectantly. Either this wasn't as interesting to them as I thought it would be, or they were playing it very cool.

Coleman doodled with his pen. 'What time was that?'

'Um …' I racked my brain. Was Karen's the first call that night? Before or after Sean's call? Or was it Robbie's? Both. Both had called. But Karen had called first. I had arrived at Prego not long after eight. 'Eight-thirty' I concluded. 'She called me about eight-thirty.'

Coleman made a note on his pad. His Pitman's looked fine to me.

'You were with someone?' Aaron's tone was flat. Unreadable.

'Yes.' He waited for me to elaborate. 'His name is Ned. I'm not sure he told me his last name.' I knew how bad that sounded but forced myself not to make it worse by blabbering on. I thought I detected a faint sarcastic twitch of Coleman's freckled lip.

'And Ned will be able to verify this?'

'Yes. I'm sure he will.' Shit! Can. I should have said he can verify it.

'You're going out with Robbie Lather, aren't you?'

I felt my face flush. 'What's that got to do with it?' It sounded defensive. I felt defensive.

Aaron shrugged. 'Robbie and I play footy together. That's all. He's a great guy.'

It felt like a slap, a rebuke, but that might have been my own guilt. I hadn't told Robbie about the dinner with Ned.

'Yeah, he is a great guy.' As a riposte, pathetic, but it was all I could manage.

Aaron picked up the paper cup of water and knocked it back in one motion. His Adam's apple bobbed up and down. Then he scrunched up the cup and dropped it into the wastepaper bin. I fantasised about un-scrunching the cup and licking the dribbles in the bottom. Now there was just the untouched letter on the desk between us. Coleman stared at a stick figure he'd drawn on his notepad, his pen poised. I was guessing that the stick figure was me. I expected him to draw a hangman's noose around its neck any minute.

'And you didn't return to Wellington until the following day. Saturday?' It was the first real question Coleman had asked.

'That's right. I waited for Karen to turn up for the meeting with her daughter at one o'clock. When she didn't show, I flew straight back to Wellington, picked up my car from the long term and drove directly to her house. That's when I found her.' We all stared at the untouched envelope. I was determined not to be the one to speak next.

'Karen had a visitor Friday night,' Aaron said. So that's why my phone call information hadn't impressed. They had already known she was still alive then.

'Well, it wasn't me,' I said, keeping it simple.

They waited, hoping for more, I think. I considered telling them about Karen's friend Manny who was due Friday night for a prayer session, but decided against it. Normally, I would have volunteered this information. Normally, I have a cordial relationship with the police; after all, it's from the police that I get most of my jobs. Used to, anyway. But right now, in this not-so-cordial environment, I wasn't going to risk saying anything more than I absolutely had to.

Aaron nodded. 'Mind if we keep this?' he said brightly, indicating the envelope.

'Sure.'

We all stared at the envelope. Still neither of them touched it.

Aaron shook hands with me and then Coleman led me out of the room, his palm poised centimetres over the small of my back. We waited in silence for the elevator. When it arrived he ushered me forward then leaned in and pushed the G button. He walked back along the corridor without saying a word. There is no elevator in the country that plummets at the rate of the Wellington Central Police Station's. As my stomach lurched I pictured them back in the interview room excitedly unzipping sterile glove and evidence bags. I knew there was no point asking if I could have the two thousand dollar cheque back. Not that it would be any more use to me than the unbanked down payment cheque still in the top drawer of my desk at home; Karen's bank account would be well and truly frozen solid.

Thinking the interview would take half an hour, I'd left Wolf in the back seat to gnaw on the prize stick he'd claimed at Lyall Bay. Instead I'd been trapped in a claustrophobic interview room for well over an hour. What I'd expected to be a friendly chat, with maybe a tolerant wrist slap for the uninvited house entry, had instead been an ambush with a double whammy interrogation. The bad cop-bad cop routine had totally unnerved me. Coleman's silence had been just as intimidating as the CO's pointed questions. The urge for alcohol was strong, but I fought it. No matter how rattled I felt, it was only ten-thirty in the morning.

As I approached the car, I spotted someone leaning towards the rear window. Sean. He was holding the baby in both hands so that he could see Wolf inside. Actually, it wasn't a baby so much as a little kid. I did the sum on my fingers. Sean and the pixie's son must be nearly eighteen months old. Patrick, they'd called him. That was Sean's dad's name. I'd loved Patrick. We probably would have named our first child after him. Though I'm not all that familiar with kids, I reckoned at eighteen months old, Patrick was a real person. As opposed to a baby, I mean. He waved a chubby little hand at Wolf. Luckily, I'm not the sort of person who would consider instructing Wolf to bite that little hand off. But I am the sort of person who doesn't want to play coochie-coo with my ex-husband's baby son. Fine. Shoot me.

I did a U-turn and sat on the bottom step of a nearby building, fighting off my urge for alcohol and cigarettes and turned my phone back on. First to appear was a three-page text from Jason, telling me the open home had gone really well and that there were two genuine buyers coming for another look at the house tomorrow. He finished with *I'm confident your house will be sold within days.* Well, yippee.

When I looked up, Sean had gone. He's really good at that.

In the time it took Wolf to stretch his legs and water the parched tree in the corner of the grassy knoll, I had arranged for Robbie to pick him up at the end of his shift and had booked myself a flight back to Auckland. Buying a ticket at such short notice meant paying through the nose, but, hey, what are credit cards for? I hadn't told the cops Karen had hired me to check on Sunny's safety; only that she'd hired me to find her. Foolishly, I'd dismissed Karen's concerns about Sunny, convincing myself she had only wanted me to smooth the way for them to meet. But it was obvious from the way the cops treated me that Karen's death was no accident. It was a homicide if ever I'd seen one. What if there was a connection between Karen's murder and her fears for Sunny? What if Sunny was still in danger? I would see the job through, remuneration or no remuneration. I owed it to Karen to finish what she had hired me to do. I owed it to Sunny to make sure she wasn't in danger. From who or what, I didn't know, but I was determined to find out.

Somewhere inside, hidden amongst all the other little denials I was an avid collector of, was the tight little nugget of knowledge that my commitment to finishing the job wasn't entirely altruistic. The surge of relief I felt when my flight was confirmed had as much to do with leaving Wellington as fulfilling my commitment to Karen. The real-estate agent's confidence that our house would soon be sold had made the acid in my stomach squirt. Every time I thought I'd moved on from Sean, I discovered I hadn't moved very far at all. Emotionally, I was still looking back over my shoulder at him. And then there was Robbie, asking me to move in with him — there was a lot going on that I needed to not think about for a few days. In short, making sure Sunny was safe was the perfect diversion from my personal life.

On my way to the airport, I decided to drop in and see my old mate Smithy. The fact that he happened to be the pathologist performing the postmortem on Karen was nothing more than a happy coincidence. Well, happy for me, that is; probably not so thrilling for Karen.

CHAPTER 15

When I'd last seen Smithy he'd dropped ten kilos and undergone a complete makeover; contact lenses, capped teeth, the works. An actual hairdresser had done the job, with scissors, instead of his usual efforts with a scalpel. Eye-wateringly, he'd even gone under the nasal tweezers. A new love interest when you're in your late sixties will do that to you. With relief I saw Smithy's little potbelly was back again and straining for attention between two perilously loose shirt buttons. The body's biological determination to return to its natural state is impressive. He'd ditched the contacts and gone back to glasses, which was a relief. The blinking mannerism that contact lenses had forced on him was one too many an addition to his already impressive repertoire of nervous ticks and gestures he used to punctuate his sentences. Smithy's previous glasses, those he'd stubbornly refused to replace for over twenty years, had been held together with an assortment of plasters, sticky tape and fuse wire, none of which really did the trick and had forced him to adopt strange nose-bridge prods and easily misinterpreted angled head movements to assist his focus. These new specs seemed to work fine but the habit of years of poking and shifting them around his face had clearly been hard to break. Despite all his eccentrics and oddities, Smithy was a brilliant pathologist. The best. I was very fond of him and I think he had a soft spot for me, too.

We sat in his small glass-walled office and simultaneously dunked ginger nuts into our mugs of insipid tea. After a decent passage of time dunking and slurping I asked after his love life. He sucked on his drooping ginger nut for some time before answering.

'May-Lyn is rather demanding,' he finally offered.

'In a good or a bad way?' I asked, dunking my last half crescent.

Smithy considered this as if I'd asked him about an intra-parenchymal haematoma. I was coming to that. 'I've reached the conclusion that I've become rather selfish in my older years, Diane. I must admit to having found it difficult to include another individual in my own personal domain.'

I performed a quick translation into normal speech. 'Oh, shit. I didn't know you'd moved in together. Bloody hell. That was a big step.'

'Rather bigger than I imagined,' he agreed morosely.

'How's Blinky?' I asked, hoping to cheer him up. Blinky was

Smithy's spoilt, overweight, grumpy black cat. He adored her.

'May-Lyn is allergic,' he said, and slumped into a depressed silence. I decided it was safer not to ask if that meant poor old Blinky had gone permanently.

'How's that lovely big dog of yours?' Smithy chirped up at the thought of Wolf. I did, too. Wolf had thrown me a pathetic, hard-done-by look when I dropped him at Gemma's. But then he'd spotted a block of sunshine by her glass patio doors and trotted off contentedly to spend the rest of the day lying in it.

'He's still gorgeous.' I conjured the sweetness of him. Grey muzzle. 'Getting old,' I added, realising with a gulp the awful truth of it. Wolf was getting old. It occurred to me I might not have him for much longer. 'I like old dogs,' I added, warding off the juju of Wolf's death. 'All dogs are smart, but old dogs are the smartest. They're busy when they need to be, but they're just as happy to sit in the sun all day and have their tummies scratched. He's definitely my kind of dog.'

Smithy removed his glasses to wipe the back of his hand across his eyes. For some reason he'd become all emotional. I hoped he didn't think my old dog reverie was an oblique reference to him. I avoided looking at his, no doubt scratchable, little protruding tummy just in case. 'And you?' he asked. 'Are you and the young policeman you were seeing planning to cohabit?'

'It's been suggested.' Now it was my turn to slump. He nodded sagely and we sat in companionable despondency until he held the ginger nut packet out to me. Third biscuit and refilled mugs cheered us both up.

'Hey, you did the post on Karen Mackie today, didn't you?'

He wasn't fooled for a moment by my casualness. 'You knew her?' His eyebrows puckered to form an unbroken hedge all the way from temple to temple.

'Uh-huh. Professionally.' That was true. 'She hired me to check up on her daughter.'

'Oh, I see,' Smithy said. 'How long ago was this?'

'Last week,' I admitted. I would never lie to Smithy.

'I see,' he repeated, more slowly this time. 'And you'd like me to give you a preliminary report on my postmortem findings?'

Sarcasm noted. Silence was my only defence. I paid close attention to my ginger nut-dunking. He downed the last of his tea, stood and stretched, hands in the small of his back like a pregnant woman; in fact, exactly like a pregnant woman. Stretched out like this, his little potbelly didn't look all that little any more.

'It will all be public information once I've sent my report to the coroner and he's ruled on it.'

I knew better than to push him. It looked like Smithy wasn't going to share on this one. Still, no harm trying.

'Okay, but hypothetically speaking ...'

Smithy raised those generous eyebrows. 'Oh, yes?' he said. Very droll.

'There wouldn't be many situations where someone died from hitting themselves on the neck, would there?' I said, recalling Gemma's astute reference to my own neck bruise.

That got a little flicker of amusement. 'Not in my experience, no.' He stared wistfully at his empty mug. 'But it's not my job as pathologist to decide on whether the deceased hit themselves, or was hit by someone else. Or for that matter, whether they sustained the injury — or injuries —' he added pointedly, 'in a hit or a fall.' Having segued into teaching mode he was on a roll. There would be no stopping him now. He turned his back on me and stared down the corridor at an invisible lecture theatre of students. 'The pathologist's job is to ascertain cause of death by meticulous examination of the body and, if required, to answer questions by authorities, such as the courts, as to whether a given scenario may or may not have been possible, or indeed plausible.'

I knew better than to interrupt. Smithy had, literally, written the manual on postmortem procedure and this sounded like a version of the preface to me. Smithy was a born teacher and would give away far more than he intended if I kept my mouth shut and my ears open. I focused my eyes on my last fragment of ginger nut but concentrated on listening hard.

'Some causes of death are more complicated to unravel than others. Take this latest case, for example.' I held my breath. 'The fact that the woman sustained a number of minor injuries — in all, I counted a total of twenty-three bruises down the left side of her body — may or may not be significant. Speaking as a pathologist, they are, I believe, irrelevant to cause of death. But to the police, those same bruises may be a clear indicator of events leading up to her death, and therefore are indeed significant to their investigation. Whereas the impact or blow to the back of the head was, in my opinion, the most likely to have caused the subdural haemorrhage that killed her. But—' he added, pointing his finger at an invisible crowd of medical students, 'there was also evidence of a number of small prior bleeds, which muddy the waters, so to speak. Unlike the bruises to her body, these may indeed be significant with regards to cause of death. Or they may not be significant at all but, without doubt, they deserve careful thinking about.'

He lapsed into silence, doing, presumably, just that.

'What could cause prior bleeds in her brain?' Smithy turned to face me, blinking rapidly. I'm pretty sure he'd forgotten I was there. 'Hypothetically,' I added belatedly. He turned back to stare out at the corridor.

'Well, cerebral amyloid angiopathy for one, but I don't think that's the cause here. Beatings. That would do it,' he said, thoughtfully. 'But I've also seen little haematomas like these in sportspeople, too, contact sports in particular. Or, in theory they could be caused by something as seemingly innocuous as a migraine.' He scratched at his comb-over before turning his attention back to me. 'Did your client have a history of high blood pressure or serious headaches?'

'I don't know,' I admitted. 'But she had spent the last seven years in prison, which would fit with the beatings theory.' He nodded, lost in thought again. It seemed a good time to take my leave. But I had one last thing to ask. 'Was it quick?' The question was no surprise to Smithy. It's what everyone asks.

'The subdural haematoma in her body had time to surface,' he admitted. 'But she wouldn't have suffered for long.' He threw a little smile in my direction, wanting to give me some good news, I think. 'She was most likely in a coma not too long after the blow to the head.'

I gathered up my coat and overnight bag. 'Well, thanks for the tea, Smithy.'

He took my coat and held it open for me.

'I'll be in touch when the report's made public.'

Smithy nodded. 'Sorry I wasn't able to tell you more.'

He didn't seem to realise how much he had told me. I was pleased about that. I didn't want him feeling bad. He ushered me out, a protective arm hovering tentatively over my shoulder. I couldn't resist giving him a peck on the cheek. He blushed at the touch.

When I turned back from the door to wave goodbye he was standing in the one little block of sunshine, deep in thought, patting his comb-over affectionately. I suspect poor old Blinky had been permanently dispatched to the big farm in the sky.

CHAPTER 16

For a full ten minutes I weighed the ethics of staying at Norma's place against my non-existent bank balance. Since I wasn't being paid for the work, free board seemed reasonable. No doubt the townhouse would eventually be sold as part of Karen's estate, but that wasn't going to happen in a hurry. Meanwhile it was just sitting there with the key under the welcome mat. There was no sign of Ned. If he did turn up, I didn't think he'd object to my company. As long as I didn't attack him again, that is.

On the flight up I'd thought about what I'd learned from Smithy. Karen had bruising down one side of her body and what had killed her was a blow to the back of the head; she hadn't died immediately and would have been in excruciating pain before slipping gratefully into a coma. And yet she hadn't called the police. All the scenarios I could think of for why she would have kept silent relied on the notion of her having known her attacker. According to Fanshaw, someone known to Karen came to see her on the Friday night. It could have been Karen's friend Manny, who was coming for a prayer session. Or it could have been someone else. Whoever it was, they were possibly the bearer of Sunny's photo. No doubt there were other possible scenarios but I needed more time than a one-hour flight to Auckland to come up with them. One thing was certain: Karen's killer was still out there and this meant there was a good likelihood Sunny was still in danger.

At nine o'clock I took a deep breath and used the landline to ring Sunny's house. If Justin answered, this was going to be one of the shortest phone calls in history. Luckily, it was Sunny who picked up. I hadn't spoken to her since I'd informed her of Karen's death, and then stayed on the phone with her until Justin came home. I had wanted to keep Sunny talking until she had someone with her who she knew and trusted; someone she could really talk to. We'd covered a lot of ground in that talk. She'd rabbited on about whatever came into her head and I'd just let her talk. Precipitated by the news of her mother's death our conversation had been unnaturally intimate. Two days had passed since that call.

'How are you handling things?' I asked.

'I'm okay,' she said. 'It wasn't like my mother and I were close or anything.'

'I know,' I said far too quickly.

The truth was I had no idea what it was like to have your

mother die hours before you're about to meet her for the first time since she tried to kill you. I kept my tone light. 'Hey, listen, I'm in Auckland for a couple of days and I thought maybe we could meet up.' I could almost hear the shrug.

'Sure. Whatever. I do reception at the gym after school. Salena thinks I should work for my miserable pocket money. Not that she ever works. Not unless you call pole dancing work. Did you know that's what she teaches at the gym? Pole dancing! And what makes it totally tragic is she's Polish! Which is a total joke only she doesn't get it. Anyway, you could come to the gym tomorrow, if you want. I look after my little brother Neo there too. Come at around six.' As if reading my thoughts she added, 'Tuesdays are Salena's hair days and Dad's not likely to turn up.'

The prospect of being confronted by Justin was daunting.

The remainder of last week's bottle of wine was still in the fridge. It was worrying how happy it made me. I thought back over the last few days. It was now Monday night. Yesterday was Sunday: open home day. Shit! That reminded me — I hunted down my phone and found this morning's text from Jason and forwarded it to Sean. Then I turned off my phone. I didn't want to talk with him about the likelihood of our house being sold within days. I didn't want to talk about it or even think about it. Real grown up.

In my little black notebook I drew a timeline. Working backwards I wrote Sunday and drew a line leading back to the day before, Saturday. The day Sunny and Karen were going to meet, the day I found Karen dead. I drew a line leading back to a box and labelled it Friday. I'd spent Friday investigating Justin and Salena's finances. That night, I'd dipped into my own meagre funds to pay for dinner with Ned. Too many wines at Prego that night but not so many that I didn't remember the phone call from Karen. She had been happy and excited about meeting her daughter for the first time since ... well, since she'd tried to murder her. I had a flash of the two-door Holden drifting down through the murky water. Falcon's pale little moon face pressed against the back window, Sunny screaming. I forced my thoughts back to the timeline. Sometime between Karen's call to me on Friday night and her death the following day, she had got hold of a recent photo of Sunny. Karen had dropped her letter and cheque to me at my house somewhere on this timeline, too. My pen wavered between the boxes. Friday night? Saturday morning? Karen had made a reference in the letter to not knowing what Sunny looked like. She had to have written this before she got hold of the photo. I wrote 'Dropped letter off at my place' and then drew a big question mark beside it. When? When did she drop it off? Was it Friday night or early Saturday morning before she was due for her flight?

I left a note on the stairs warning Ned that I was asleep in the main bedroom and put my phone under my pillow for safekeeping. Until I'd deleted the photos of the crime scene, I'd keep it with me at all times. The likely interrogation I'd have to endure with Detective Inspector Aaron Fanshaw and Detective Sergeant Brett Coleman if my phone was turned in to police with a bunch of illegally obtained crime scene photos on it, didn't bear thinking about.

I thought I'd have nightmares about death and dying, stiffened rigor-mortised zombies coming for me with outstretched arms. Marital homes collapsing around me, cops dragging me off to prison. I don't know what I dreamed. All memory of it had gone when I surfaced the next morning.

CHAPTER 17

Neo was playing on the computer in the gym's reception area. In the fishbowl workout room opposite, three gym bunnies feverishly cycled nowhere. There was no sign of Justin or Salena. No sign of Sunny either. Neo glanced up as I approached the desk but showed no further interest in me.

'Hi, Neo. Is your sister here?'

He yelled, 'Sunny!', without looking away from the computer screen.

Photos of Salena adorned the walls. In most of them her body was wrapped around a pole — not in a 'car accident' way and not exactly in a 'strip club' way either, more in an 'old-fashioned circus performer' way; glittery body suit, arched spine and arm thrown in the air in a theatrical 'ta-da!' gesture.

Sunny hadn't been joking when she'd said Salena taught pole dancing. Neo continued tapping, his fingers tripping expertly over the keyboard. Still no sign of Sunny.

'What are you playing?'

He hit me with a look. 'I'm not playing anything,' he said.

I stopped myself from responding 'whatever'. He yelled again, this time he stopped tapping the keyboard long enough to turn his head in the direction of the closed door leading to the upstairs offices.

'Sunny! That lady's here!' His job done, he went back to the tapping, his attention riveted. I wandered over to the glass divider and watched the gym bunnies huff and puff for a while. Their desperation was so dispiriting that I decided even a five-year-old uncommunicative brat was preferable.

I leaned on the counter. 'So what are you doing?'

'Trade Me,' he said without lifting his eyes.

I craned around to see the screen. He was on Trade Me. 'No way!'

A proud little smile tempted his lips. 'I make way more money than Sunny does.'

'Seriously?'

Now he was openly smiling, enjoying my surprise. 'I made two hundred dollars last week.'

'Wow.' Actually, I was impressed. 'What do you sell?'

'Games and stuff mostly.' His plump little shoulders lifted and relaxed again. 'When I get sick of my own things I sell them. I sell stuff for Sunny, too. For a commission.'

I was warming to this kid. With his attention focused on the screen I could study him at leisure. He would become a beautiful man one day, with those expressive blue eyes and ridiculously long lashes. 'I have to use Dad's account because of my age, but he doesn't mind.' It was the first time he'd spoken to me unprompted. Having launched himself into conversation, he became downright chatty. 'I could get into all his online accounts if I wanted. He uses the same password for everything. All dads do that.'

Before I could respond, the inner door opened and Sunny swung into the room. I balked. She was wearing an oversized singlet and shorts. The transparent material adhered to her little breasts, revealing pink juvenile nipples. The singlet ended at her crotch where the words 'eat me' were emblazoned.

'You like?' she said, pirouetting to show me the back view. The cutaway shorts revealed three-quarters of her little buttocks.

'Not so much.' It was all I could manage.

She laughed and pulled a sweater over her head. 'Salena will totally loathe it!' Her face emerged, smiling brilliantly. 'It's Dad's latest import.' Thankfully, the sweater dropped over her buttocks. 'I think it's awesome.'

I hoped she was only wearing the gear to get a reaction from her stepmother. If she wore that outfit on the street I was pretty sure she'd get a whole different kind of reaction.

'You okay, little bro?' she called, leading me to the two sofas by the entrance windows.

'Yup,' Neo replied, clicking away at the keyboard.

'Don't worry about Dad turning up,' she leaned forward to whisper conspiratorially. 'He won't be here until after eight now.'

I was still recovering from the sight of her pubescent flesh but managed to produce a response. 'Does he use the gym much?'

'He's mostly just into importing this stuff now,' she said, adjusting what there was of the shorts.

We each claimed a sofa, our knees facing. Sunny looked at me, waiting. I launched right in. 'When Karen hired me to find you, she gave me a pile of stuff. Her treasures, I think. Things she'd kept. I thought you might like to see some of them.' I'd put together a selection of photos of Sunny and Karen, the record her mother had kept of her childhood milestones and the lock of hair. The photos of Falcon I'd left in my faux 'Tax' file box back at the office. Sunny looked from the envelope to my face and back again, but made no move to open it. My heart gave a lurch. I hoped this wasn't a mistake.

'Have they figured out what she died of yet?' Sunny obviously didn't know or suspect her mother had been murdered.

'They're still working on it, I think.'

'She probably OD'd or she was high and did something stupid.' She threw me an unconvincing sneer. 'She was always doing stuff like that when I was a kid. It was bad when she had taken something. She'd be all hyper and that. But when she couldn't get anything, that was far worse. Falcon and me used to try and keep out of her way when she was like that. She used to call it the yips. "I've got the yips," she'd say, and I'd try and clear us both out of her way.'

It was safer not to respond. Feigning a casualness I knew to be false, Sunny slid the contents of the envelope into her lap. Head bent, she studied each item. Her long fine lashes fluttered. I had the creepy feeling I was looking at Karen again, the day I found her dead; head bent and long lashes pencilled against her cheek, the beseeching hands in her lap.

'I wish Karen had been able to tell you how sorry she was.'

Sunny's head snapped up. 'Yeah?' Her eyes were dry. 'Go tell Falcon that. He's buried in the same cemetery as Gran.'

I didn't respond. I had no right to. Sunny slid the photos back into the envelope. I noted how carefully she did that.

'Shall I take them back with me or would you like to keep them.'

'They're mine, aren't they?' she snapped.

'Sure.'

The booming of the gym music still vibrated but something had changed. The keyboard clicking had stopped. Neo was staring at Sunny wide-eyed.

'I'm okay, Neo,' she called across to him, her voice softened. He said nothing but continued to stare at her. 'Seriously. I'm okay.' She poked her tongue out at him and laughed at his surprised response. 'I'll raise your commission to sixty per cent on that top if you sell it.' Neo held her look for a long time and then reluctantly went back to his trading.

It was time to come clean. 'Look, Sunny. I'm not here to defend Karen or put her case to you or anything like that. I hardly knew her.' She was about to say something but stopped herself. 'I think Karen did a dreadful thing and maybe you can never forgive her for that.' Her eyes flashed up at me. 'That's none of my business,' I added quickly, 'and not why I'm here. The truth is, Karen hired me to check that you were okay. She thought you weren't safe.' Sunny had gone very still, very quiet. The keyboard clicking had stopped again. These two were uncannily tuned to each other.

'What else did she say? About me, I mean.' She turned her

head away. 'Did she tell you she hated me?'

'What? No, of course not. She didn't hate you, Sunny.' I stopped myself from reaching a hand out to her. Her head was turned away but her profile was calm. I reminded myself Sunny had lived with these demons for seven years. Almost her entire life. 'She didn't think you'd want to see her again but she was really happy when you decided to.' It was all I could think to say.

She turned back to face me, her eyes still dry. 'What did she mean I wasn't safe? What did she think was going to happen to me?'

'She never said,' I admitted. 'It's possible she just told me that so I'd go all out to find you. Maybe there was no reason at all for her to think something was wrong.' I waited, giving her the opening. Nothing. Nothing at all. 'But if she was right and there is something — if you feel you're not safe — you can tell me. I promise I'll help.' Still nothing. That was as far as I was prepared to go. Suspicious as Karen might have been, I wasn't going to ask Sunny directly if Justin was sexually abusing her. 'If you don't need my help, I promise I won't bother you again.' She stared across the room for a long time without moving or saying anything. Just when I was about to stand she spoke.

'Friday night I wanted to hang out with my friends so I wouldn't have to, you know, think about meeting ... think about seeing Mum the next day.' Apart from the falter over what to call her mother, Sunny's voice was calm and steady. 'But Salena said I wasn't allowed to go out and I wasn't even allowed to have anyone to stay because I had to look after Neo. She always does that when Dad's away. When he's here, she's all kissy to me like she actually cares. She's such a selfish moron.'

I waited for more, but that was it. Was this code for something? Or was the concern for her safety, coming as it did from the woman who had tried to kill her, so ludicrous Sunny refused to even acknowledge it? Sunny was looking at me now, her face still and thoughtful. I looked back, willing her to explain. She didn't.

'Okay,' I said, even though it wasn't. 'I'll go away.'

I gave it a moment, but she didn't try to stop me. Didn't say anything to make me stay. Enough. What the hell was I doing with this girl, chasing her around, insisting something was wrong. Sunny was as okay as any fourteen-year-old girl; in fact, she was more than okay, given her history. I was behaving like a stalker and worse still I'd been using her as an excuse to avoid facing my own life. Shame rose in me and I blushed. It pushed me up from the sofa.

'Can I use your computer? I want to book a flight back to Wellington.'

Sunny retreated to the upstairs room and Neo slumped on the sofa with his iPad. Using the computer at reception I checked both airlines. Same-day flights back to Wellington were too expensive but I found a cheapish Air New Zealand flight leaving at one o'clock the next day. It would have to do. I clicked on it and scrabbled in my bag for a credit card. What was Sunny's rant about? Was there some deeper meaning to it? Was there something I was missing? I copied the credit card details into the box and clicked confirm, then I clicked through to obtain a boarding pass. So she was home Friday night by herself — big deal. Sure, I could see why she was pissed off about that, but I didn't understand why she would bring it up in response to my question about her safety. What was that all about? Was I carrying any dangerous goods? Only my smart-arse mouth. I clicked no and waited while the website uploaded the information. Suddenly, a thought hit me. It was so clear I hoped one of those lightbulbs wasn't beaming above my head. Neo's attention was on his iPad. The door to the room Sunny had retreated into was shut. I flicked across to the main computer screen. It listed two hard drives and a back-up. I clicked onto the main A: Drive. Folders scrolled onto the screen. This was obviously the company drive. I clicked on the Finder icon, narrowed the search parameter to folder name and typed in 'travel'. Nothing. I stared at the blinking icon some more and then typed 'flights'. I blinked as a folder labelled 'Flights' appeared. Too easy. Before I could question if what I was doing was ethical, let alone legal, I clicked it open and typed November 2012 into the search box. And there it was: a flight to Wellington on Friday 23 November 2012 for Justin Alexander Bachelor.

'What the hell are you doing?'

'Shit!' I nearly jumped out of my skin. It was Anton, all two hundred-odd pounds of him. Instinctively, I flicked out of the A: Drive before he got too close to the desk.

'Does Justin know you're here?'

'I left my jacket here the other day,' I lied, indicating the one I was wearing. Neo stared at me, his jaw slack. His obvious fear of Anton helped improve my usually useless lying skills. 'There was no one behind the desk so I was just calling myself a cab.'

Anton was still looking at me suspiciously as Sunny swung back into the foyer. She froze at the sight of him. I couldn't tell if this was her usual response or if it was because his arrival was unexpected.

'Thanks for the jacket, Sunny. I'm always leaving it.'

'No problem,' she said, circling around behind Anton. His body swivelled in my direction and his eyes never left my face as I made my way out from behind reception. Sunny held the entrance door open for me but avoided my eyes.

Once outside I thought over the significance of what I'd learned. As much as I loathed to have a conversation with Detective Inspector Aaron Fanshaw and loathed even more to tell him how I had unearthed the information, this was too important not to pass on. Justin had flown to Wellington on Friday night. This put him right in the middle of the frame as Karen's killer.

Back at the townhouse, I left a long rambling message on Aaron Fanshaw's voicemail. There was no sign of Ned; I could have done with company to take my mind off what I'd discovered. I opened the fridge. I closed the fridge. Anton would no doubt tell Justin I had been at the gym. I hoped it wouldn't get Sunny into trouble. Neo's fear and Sunny freezing in her tracks at the sight of Anton worried me. Failing to contain my nervous energy I put on my sweat pants and sneakers and headed out for a run.

CHAPTER 18

There is a perfect loop along Jervois Road, down the steps past the scout hall into Cox's Bay, through the park and then up Richmond Road into Ponsonby Road and back along the home straight to Three Lamps. I reckoned I could run it in forty minutes. Not that, strictly speaking — or any other way of speaking, in fact — I could call what I do running. With my technique and fitness level it would better be described as an out of sync slow lurch. When I was a kid living in Herne Bay I dawdled this loop on my way home from school, greeting all the resident animals on the way. Those long walks home were the forever of my childhood. Niki was with me, of course. Niki was always with me — she still is. What I had told Sunny was true; I had loved my little sister right from the start. Even though her birth heralded the death of my mother — our mother —I'd loved Niki right to the end. Dad had never been a major figure in my life before her death and he became even less of one after Mum died. It seemed to me he set about replacing her with a series of good-time women, none of who were interested in taking the time to win over a couple of needy motherless girls. No doubt I'm being unfair. No doubt I made it difficult for them. I let the memory of those walks home with Niki drift away. I'm careful with memories of Niki. I don't want to wear them out with overuse. I take them out like treasures, touch them gently with the tips of my consciousness, then wrap them in tissue and put them away again.

I don't run often enough to learn the tricks seasoned runners have been taught that enable them to keep going, but even with my stop and start method, it still works for dissipating nerves. After twenty minutes or so, red-faced and panting, it'll even quieten, if not completely mute my chattering inner voice. Personality disorders that include voices must be the pits. I have trouble enough with my so-called normal mental narration. Plugging into music helps to both quieten that chattering brain talk and to help keep me moving.

By the time I'd tried to get hold of Fanshaw, failed, left a message, lost my key, found my key, lost my phone, found my phone, opened the fridge door several times to eye up that bottle of wine, admonished myself and closed the fridge door an equal number of times and then finally changed into my running gear, it was coming up to eight-thirty when I left Norma's place and started on my run. The traffic had thinned out again after rush hour on the Jervois Road stretch, leading to the harbour bridge on-ramp. I plugged in my headphones and started at little more than a walk while I warmed up, and k.d. lang singing 'A Case of You' was well under way by the time I passed the street Justin and Sunny lived on. About an hour had passed since I'd left the message for Fanshaw. I glanced along the street, half expecting to see police cars parked outside the house, but all was quiet. No cops; in fact, no people at all. All those big empty mansions; in the wealthy suburbs no one is ever home.

The steps leading down to Cox's Bay were slimy and I had to watch my footing. A spring dusk was looming and the temperature would drop dramatically as soon as the sun dipped behind the hills. The tide was well out in Cox's Bay, leaving nothing more than a shimmering snake of water to reflect the last of the blue sky. The beached yachts tipped sideways in the mud exposed their rudders like sea lions displaying rotund underbellies to their harem. A heron high-stepped through the mud, pausing occasionally to prod the glutinous swamp, but it was just going through the motions, unconvinced. It would have to wait for the tide to turn to deliver up a quivering morsel. By the time I crossed the road into Cox's Bay Reserve a heavy purple cloud hovered directly above me. Like a cartoon depression cloud, it followed me through the park. I'd got my second wind slowing for the traffic on West End Road and ran easily now past kids playing soccer, a young boy checking the paw of his muddied terrier. The Dusty Springfield song 'The Look of Love' started up at the exact moment the terrier held up its paw and turned a beseeching look on its young owner. The appropriateness of the song and the pathetic look from the canine made me laugh out loud. The emptied culvert waited patiently for the tide to return, mangroves on tiptoes, roots exposed. The soft warm breeze accompanied by the scatter of leaves above was a reminder that summer was close by. Such a time of promise is spring. It was all beautiful in the way a previously ordinary place and time can suddenly seem to have meaning; can seem to be packed full of fragile life. Maybe it was the endorphins kicking in from the run. As I hit the boardwalk leading through the mangrove swamp I caught sight of a small plane banking into the curdled rain clouds, its tilted wing catching the last of the day's slanting sunlight. The voice in my head was drowned by the music and the harsh sound of my laboured breathing. I'd reached that stage of exhaustion when I was thinking about nothing; aware of the pain and exhilaration, conscious of the way the light hit the wing of the titling plane as it circled above, my thoughts freewheeling with it as I left the last of the light and dropped into the dense shadows of the manuka scrub, canopied over the mangroves. The walkway had been built on stilts to accommodate the stinky swamp below and the breathing tide. It vibrated and shuddered with each pounding footstep. A white-faced heron prodded optimistically around the mangrove roots. Coldplay's melancholic 'Fix You' was filling my head as I neared the bridge at the Richmond Road park end of the walkway. A red jacket hung on the bridge pole. Someone must have come across it and hung it there for the owner to find. Under the bridge, the deserting tide had exposed a rusting supermarket trolley, drowning in the mud.

Someone grabbed at my shoulder. I hadn't heard or sensed anyone. I tried to pull away but the shock of it made me twist awkwardly. I tripped and fell heavily onto the bridge pole. It knocked the air completely out of me and I went straight down onto my knees, dragging the red jacket with me. The thin sound of vocals reached me from the headphones, dangling in the blood, blooming warm and sticky around my kneecap. A menacing form loomed over me but all that mattered was getting air into my lungs. It was like they'd been squeezed tightly closed and held there, unable to re-inflate. Bright sparks drifted in front of my eyes. The pain in my solar plexus was excruciating. Anatomy was never my best subject but it felt like I'd ruptured one of those soft, red bloody organs I'd never quite got my head around the purpose of — spleen? Liver? Gall bladder? Whichever it was, I was about to find out if it was possible to survive a ruptured one. One little gasp in … and out. Better. Another one in … out. The sparkly stars were disappearing. My assailant was leaning over me, yelling. Justin. It was Justin. I made a desperate grab for my phone but he kicked it out of reach and it skidded along the planks of the bridge. Only now did I realise he'd been yelling at me the whole time, spit flying.

'Fucking bitch! You had no fucking right to see her without my permission!' The pain was receding enough for me to know I was in big trouble. Justin's eyes were red, his skin mottled, his breathing almost as ragged as mine. 'You think you can just do what you like? She's my daughter, you hear me? *My* daughter. And you will stay the fuck away from her! You hear me?'

There wasn't enough air in my lungs to say anything. The boardwalk was empty. The park at the far side of the bridge was in darkness. No park lights. Night had suddenly fallen. Where the hell was everyone?

'Fucking bitch!' he repeated, unnecessarily, I thought.

He'd run out of things to yell at me and I could see the heat in him was cooling. That made him all the more dangerous. Slowly, carefully, I repositioned my body against the railing. Blood dribbled down my shin, pooled in my sneaker.

'Take it easy, Justin,' I said and raised my hand in a peace-making gesture. It was a mistake.

'Don't fucking tell me what to do! I tell you what to do. And I tell you to stay the fuck away from my kids.'

'Okay, okay, I get it.' His teeth were bared in a strange animal expression. 'I heard you,' I said, using the bridge railing to pull myself to my feet. My knee stung like a bugger as the leg straightened. My sweat pants were ripped, my hands and jaw slimy with mud.

'You don't tell me anything, you hear me? You stay away from Sunny or else.' He walked a couple of steps away from me, hands pumping.

Unexpectedly, anger flooded through me like a much-needed shot of whisky. 'Is this what happened with Karen? Is this what you did to her? I know you killed her, Justin.'

He stopped and turned to face me, his fists clenched. It should have been enough to shut me up.

'You flew to Wellington Friday night. You went to Karen's house and you killed her.' He took a step towards me. 'It's too late to shut me up, Justin. The cops already know. I told them.' He opened his mouth and closed it again. I couldn't read his expression. ' You knew Karen wouldn't show on Saturday. You knew she was dead. But you let Sunny think she was going to meet her mother. You put Sunny through that.'

He looked at me for a long time and then slowly shook his head. 'You stay away from her.' And with that he turned and walked off into the park. I watched his back until he disappeared into the darkness of the trees, then I knelt and scrabbled around for my phone. The screen was shattered and there was no light behind it but I held down the on button and waited, hoping it would come back to life. To calm myself I listed all the rubbish below the bridge: red ballpoint pen, lime-green ice cream wrapper, bottle without its label, plastic milk cartoon, blue bottle cap, inner sole of a sneaker, dog collar. Right now, bloody, ripped and broken, I felt I was just one more object among all this discarded human waste. Life's like that. One minute it's all beautiful — the dog with the beseeching look being attended to by its young owner, the sunlight reflecting on the tilting wing of the plane, the poignant spring breeze — then the next minute some bastard attacks you and suddenly all you can see is the rubbish.

Fuck him.

I did my best to swipe the mud off my grazed palms and peeled back the ripped trackies to check out the cut in my knee. I'd live. The unnamed internal organ still reminded me it was there and hurting, and there was a loud ringing in my ears that I was pretty sure, though wouldn't swear, wasn't a police siren, announcing the arrival of the cavalry. I dragged myself off the bridge into the park and kept up a speedy limp until I was out of the gloom of the trees and onto the safety of Richmond Road. Once more in the comfort of traffic and people, I perched my arse on the fence and did my best to wipe the shattered phone clean. Blood poured from my knee and though the enigmatic organ probably wasn't ruptured after all, it was definitely bruised. Or whatever the equivalent of bruised is for an internal organ. I'd have to ask Smithy one day. The screen of my phone was cobwebbed with shattered glass, a pathetic visual reminder that there was no one in Auckland I could think of to call for help. I was still staring at it and feeling mighty sorry for myself when it rang. I didn't recognise the number. Tentatively, I held the shattered glass to my ear.

'Hello?'

'Diane? It's Inspector Aaron Fanshaw.' I immediately teared up with a ridiculous surge of relief. It was short-lived.

'Do you know what police officers do, Diane?' I took a breath but he continued before I had a chance to answer. 'They investigate and, sometimes when they're left to do their work un-interfered with, they solve crimes. That's their job. Some even call it their profession. In short, it's what we do.' If tears could harden, mine would have. 'I know you have done some work for the police department and I know you're involved with police on a personal basis, but you are a civilian.' Right now I was feeling more like a wounded pit bull, but I bit my tongue, rolled my eyes and heard him out. 'Listen to me, Diane. I don't want you interfering in this case any more than you already have. You can take this as a formal warning.'

'Jesus,' I said, 'I left a message for you with some information about Justin that is obviously relevant to the case. I didn't go to bloody *Campbell Live* with it. That's what civilians are meant to do, isn't it? They pass on information to the police?' There was no way now I was going to tell him what Justin had just done to me.

'You told Sunny her mother had been killed.' It was a statement, not a question. Shit. I knew this was going to come back to bite me in the arse.

'I told Sunny that Karen was dead. I didn't say she'd been killed.' He wasn't going to catch me out on it a second time. 'Sunny rang me because she knew I had gone back to Wellington and would see Karen and I … I felt I had to tell her.' I listened to his breathing.

'You had no right to do that and you know it. Given your special relationship with police, I assumed you knew not to speak to anyone about Karen's death or I would have formally warned you not to at the time.'

I was suitably chastened but with it went a feeling of righteousness. Special relationship indeed — prick. I don't like being told off no matter how justified it is. He probably thought it was time for me to say I'm sorry. I didn't say it.

'You didn't mention your phone call with Sunny during our talk at the station on Monday.'

'Our talk, as you describe it, wasn't quite what I was expecting it to be,' I responded, feeling ridiculously close to tears. The delayed shock and the cold were taking effect; I wasn't sure if I was shaking or shivering, or both. I wanted to finish the call, go home and clean myself up, get some antiseptic onto my knee and spend some time feeling sorry for myself. I hadn't done quite enough of that yet. 'Okay, fine. I'm …' I tried to say the sorry word but my mouth just wouldn't do it. 'I'm admonished.' There was the distinct sound of a guffaw on the other end of the phone, which I ignored. 'But I hope you'll follow up on the information despite it having come from me.'

I heard the long sigh. No doubt I was meant to hear it.

'We already know Justin saw Karen on Friday night.' I stopped breathing. I think I even stopped shaking. 'He went down to talk her out of meeting Sunny. He thought it would be bad for his daughter, that she was too young. He wanted Karen to wait a couple of years.' The photo on the mantelpiece, it must have come from Justin. 'He brought a photo of Sunny to give her.' I wondered if I'd spoken aloud. 'Bit of a peace offering, I think. He hoped it would hold her off for a while.' Fanshaw's tone had become downright chatty.

I risked a question. 'How did you find this out?'

'Like I said, it's our job to investigate and solve crimes.'

I breathed through my teeth and tried counting to ten. By the time I got to six he relented, realising, I think, how prissy he sounded. 'In this case it was easy. He told us.'

'Justin told you this? When?'

'He rang us as soon as he heard Karen was dead.' Fanshaw jumped at the opportunity to remind me of my transgression. 'Thanks to you, he heard that from his daughter on Saturday night. Ideally, we should have given him that information and been there to witness his response first hand.'

Of course he was right and I knew it. He definitely knew it, too. 'Okay,' I said defensively. 'So he's a suspect?'

'Everyone connected to Karen is of interest to the enquiry.' Meaning, he was including me in that everyone. 'But we don't believe Justin was responsible for his ex-wife's death.'

'What? Why not?'

'Because Justin returned home to Auckland on Friday night.' I opened my mouth to speak but he answered my question before I had a chance to ask it. 'We checked.' I opened my mouth again. 'Thoroughly,' he answered. This guy was uncanny. I decided to keep my mouth shut. 'As far as we're concerned,' he said, spelling it out for the thick but thankfully now silent person on the other end of the phone, 'we have eliminated Justin from our enquiries.'

'So it is a homicide?' It wasn't much but it was the only point I could score.

'We are treating the death as suspicious, yes,' he admitted. 'But I have already informed the family of this so there's no need for you to tell them.'

Touché.

Bastard.

CHAPTER 19

TUESDAY 27 NOVEMBER 2012

A blindingly hot shower is a truly wonderful thing. I prescribed a glass of wine and a couple of paracetamol for my damaged internal organ and it accepted its medicine gratefully. It probably wasn't my liver then. A cold wet cloth on my knee eased the sting, but my pride still smarted from the confrontation with Justin, followed by the smackdown Fanshaw had given me, topped off by an ignominious limp home along Ponsonby Road. Still, I couldn't help feeling I'd got off lightly from my encounter with Justin.

My smashed phone had turned itself off again but responded to a gentle but persistent hold-down press of the on button. I'd have to get it fixed before the shattered screen fell out and I lost everything on it, including, I reminded myself, the crime scene photos. My phone seemed to have taken on a perverse life of its own since being bashed, turning itself on and off whenever it felt like it. A message from Jason had been sent directly to voice-mail, not that I minded too much having missed that call. He had left an excited message asking me to ring him ASAP. He actually used the acronym ASAP instead of the words. Jesus. Okay, sure. I'd ring him. But first I wanted to check those crime scene photos. Discovering that Justin had flown to Wellington on the Friday night had seemed like a breakthrough. Learning that the police already knew he'd gone to see Karen that night was a surprise and hearing from Fanshaw that he'd discounted Justin as a suspect was a whole new curve ball I needed to get my head around.

I went through the crime scene photos one by one, careful not to dislodge the shattered glass each time I swiped my finger across the screen. My knowledge of pathology is about as good as my knowledge of anatomy, and my understanding of the process of rigor mortis is rudimentary, to say the least, but I did know that in normal circumstances, it begins to set in a couple of hours after death. The muscles on the face are the first to stiffen. I used two fingers to enlarge the image of Karen's face on the screen. Close-up there was a definite rigidity to the set of her jaw. I remembered being aware of it when I bent down and looked up into her face. I remembered the oily gleam of her eye, the lashes weighted with mascara. Normally it takes twelve to twenty-four hours after the heart stops beating for full rigor mortis to set in. It is an unmistakable and quite shocking phenomenon. I also knew it was a chemical reaction affected by temperature and atmospheric conditions and I was pretty sure some medical conditions could alter the time of onset as well but, as a basic rule of thumb, if Karen had died on Friday night, by the time I found her late-afternoon the next day, not to put too fine a point on it, she would have been as stiff as a proverbial plank of wood.

The exposed nipple beneath the dressing gown, the strong smell of Pantene conditioner, the clothes laid out on the bed ready to wear; it was obvious Karen had showered, put on some make-up and was preparing to dress for her flight to Auckland when she was killed.

According to Karen's note to me, she didn't know what her daughter looked like, which means she must have written the note and dropped the cheque into my letter box sometime on Friday evening, after she'd talked to me but before Justin gave her the photo of Sunny. And in that phone conversation, she had said her friend Manny was coming over for a prayer session. I'd had the chance to mention this to Fanshaw and Coleman during my interrogation, aka interview, with me on Monday, but I had decided against it. There was no way I was going to mention Manny or anyone else to Fanshaw now. Not after my formal warning and all. Allowing an hour for the flight from Wellington to Auckland, another hour from Auckland airport to the city, plus a bit of extra time in case of flight or traffic delays, I figured Karen would have had to book a flight no later than nine a.m. on Saturday to get to our arranged meeting at Wynyard Quarter at twelve-thirty. This would mean leaving home by eight at the latest.

Putting all this together, the time of her attack could be pinpointed pretty accurately to sometime between seven and eight on Saturday morning. Smithy said she would have fallen into a coma and most likely died a couple of hours after that. This scenario was backed up by the onset of the early stages of rigor mortis when I found her late Saturday afternoon. If Justin had returned to Auckland on Friday night, which Fanshaw said he had thoroughly checked out, Justin was in the clear. One by one, I deleted the photos of Karen while I still could.

Staring into space, I thought about the bruising on Karen's neck and remembered Smithy's description of the previous small bleeds in the brain. Had she been caught up in something in prison? Something she was unable to escape from even after she was released? Prisons are pressure cookers for the worst of human nature, but they can also bring out the best sometimes, I reminded myself. One of the most moving and powerful shows I'd ever seen had been performed by inmates of Arohata Women's Prison: a series of little one-act plays written and acted out by the prisoners based on the crimes they had committed. The vast majority were tragic domestic stories. Perhaps Karen knew something about an inmate; something that wasn't safe for her to know once she was released. Or maybe she had failed to fulfil some promise, failed to follow through on something she was supposed to do once she was on the outside. Is this where the threat to Sunny came from? I could theorise forever, but what I needed was information. And painkillers. My glass was empty and my knee stiffening. Who could give me information? Karen's ex-cellmate could, but I wasn't keen to see Vex again. The last time I saw her was shortly after she was imprisoned. As part of a deal for a reduced sentence, Vex had agreed to provide details of how she had procured my sister's murder. And she had agreed to talk to me — restorative justice, it's called. It didn't give me closure or allow me to move on. And it certainly didn't restore Niki. Niki stayed all the way dead. I realised with a kind of guilt that I thought about her less often now. Her ghost had tired of haunting me.

The sound of a key in the lock interrupted my gloomy thoughts. Ned. I was grinning before the door fully opened. Interesting.

He admitted to being useless in an emergency but excellent help once the patient was in recovery mode. He eyed me up from head to foot and declared that, in his learned opinion, recovery was 'without doubt the very mode I was in'. When he removed the bloody cloth from my knee we both flinched. The gash was raw and oozing.

'Do you think it might be needing stitches?' he asked. 'Not that I'm offering. But I will go with you to the hospital. It won't take long. We could get you stitched up and be back here in no time.' The stress of seeing my injury had turned up the heat on his accent.

'It'll be fine,' I insisted. The last thing I wanted to do was sit in A and E for a couple of hours while nurses assessed me, prodded me, then moved on to more serious complaints.

'Alright then. But let me get you something nice and cold.' He made a dismissive wave towards my knee. 'And I'll get something for the knee as well.'

He was, in fact, a surprisingly gentle and confident nurse, placing a towel-covered cushion under my knee and a wrapped packet of peas gently on top of the wound. 'If I'm not mistaken,' he said, casually wiping away an escaped dribble of ice from my thigh, 'this is the same packet of peas I used for the injury to my eye.' He flattened the peas between his hands before gently placing the packet back on my knee. 'Shared intimacy with frozen peas takes our relationship to a whole new level, don't you think?' I didn't think it was the legumes so much as the touch that threatened to do that.

'I'm sorry about Karen,' I said, only partly to call the physical intimacy to a halt. 'No doubt you heard …'

He lowered himself onto the sofa, casually lifting my feet onto his lap to make room for himself. 'I did, yes,' he said, sobering. 'The police came here actually, looking to inform next of kin. I gave them Justin's address.' I considered telling him it was me who had found Karen's body but it seemed crass to mention it; besides, it would raise questions I didn't want to answer. Ned absent-mindedly stroked my foot. 'What a tragedy for little Sunny. It would have been a good thing for her to have met her mother,' he said. 'Don't you think?'

'Mmm,' I agreed. 'It would have been better if they'd had a chance to meet.' There was more I could say but I stopped myself. It all sounded trite, too easy.

Ned looked over at the photo of Norma and Karen on the far wall, his eyes soft. 'It was quite a sum of money Norma left to Karen, you know. When she died, I mean.'

'Really?' I said, straightening. 'I didn't know that.' This was new. I wondered if the other prison inmates knew about Karen's wealth. 'She told me she was giving away all her worldly goods and was going to live in a commune in LA.'

Ned shrugged it away. 'Well, I guess it will go to Sunny now. And that's got to be a good thing.' My mind wandered, thinking of all the implications of Karen's wealth, until Ned waggled my ankle for attention. 'We'd better be looking for a new place to stay when we're in Auckland, hadn't we?' He had deftly used the pronoun 'we' to suggest an intimacy that right now was also being expressed in the way his fingers made easy with my foot. An innocent enough act, you'd think, given the knee and all. Perhaps even an unconscious one. That's what I told myself, anyway. Then Ned threw me a look and suddenly that touch didn't seem innocent at all. None of it did. He smiled at me. And I smiled right back at him. It was a deciding moment …

… shattered by the loud insistent ring of an old-fashioned phone.

'You should get that,' I said.

He cupped his warm fingers around my heel. I didn't pull away. 'It won't be for me,' he said. 'I've never given the number to anyone.'

The phone rang insistently.

'Neither have I,' I said.

'Well then, it won't be for you either.'

The phone stopped ringing. We looked at each other. The answerphone message started up in one of those robotic American voices.

'I need to pee,' I said.

He laughed and released my foot. I could feel his eyes on me as I hobbled unattractively across the room towards the bathroom. I didn't need to pee. What I needed to do was remove myself from his body heat before I did something I was very likely to regret. I ran the tap and splashed cold water on my flushed neck and gave my reflection a silent talking-to. Robbie and I had never said we were exclusive but, given the recent developments, such as the suggestion to move in together, sleeping with Ned, though technically not wrong, would not be technically all that right either. As I bent to splash more water on my face, I startled. There was a woman in the living room, talking to Ned. I knew that voice well. The woman was undeniably, unmistakably, Karen.

Ned was wide-eyed. His face white, his hand pressed theatrically against his breast. I suspect the hand still hovered there from when he'd crossed himself. Karen's voice boomed loud and clear from the answerphone.

'... just so excited. I know, I know you've told me not to expect too much, but I can't help myself. Anyway, I'll ring you on your cell. I just thought you might pick up if you were there.' A faint sound in the background and Karen's voice yelled, 'Hang on!' It was so loud, both Ned and I jumped. Karen laughed as if she'd seen our response. 'Sorry,' she said. 'There's someone at the door. I'll ring you back in a minute.'

A click followed by a long beep ended the call. Ned and I stared at each other as the automated voice announced, 'Call ended. Saturday 24 November, seven thirty-two a.m.' We waited out the entire next message from a telemarketing firm in silence. Neither of us moved. I don't think we breathed. Only when the long beep finished and the answerphone clicked to a halt did we breathe out. We knew what we had heard. The call was from Karen to me on Saturday morning. And it was her killer she had gone to open the door for. Ned crossed himself again without any attempt to hide it. Normally it's the sort of thing I would have a person on about, but I didn't. I was pretty close to making the talismanic gesture myself. Hearing Karen's voice was creepy enough. Hearing her killer knock at the door was even creepier.

Ned was the first to speak. 'I'll take it into the police station first thing in the morning.' He stared wide-eyed at the phone but made no move towards it.

A fraction less superstitious, I picked it up. 'I've never seen one like this before,' I said, turning it over. It was all in one piece with no obvious place for recording. 'Where does the tape go?'

Ned lifted his shoulders but didn't offer to check it out himself. He hadn't seen a ghost but he had heard one and it had clearly given him the heebie-jeebies. The thought of ringing Fanshaw to tell him about Karen's message made my head pound. It was doubtful he'd even take my call. Better to drop the phone into the station and let the message speak for itself. Ned hovered nervously as I pulled the wire out of the socket and unplugged the whole phone-answerphone contraption from the wall.

'I'll take it,' he repeated, but still made no move to reach for the phone.

'It's fine,' I said, hiding my amusement. 'I'm flying back to Wellington tomorrow. I'll give it directly to the CO.' Ned looked puzzled. 'The case officer. A guy called Aaron Fanshaw. I've met him,' I added, hoping Ned wouldn't ask how or when. He didn't. Now that the phone was out of sight, he regained some of his composure, though he clearly needed the wine he was pouring with a trembling hand. I needed it, too. Hearing Karen's voice had undoubtedly been a very spooky experience. First the posthumous letter and now the call. Karen seemed determined, even insistent, on talking to me from the grave. I gave myself a mental rap over the knuckles; Karen wasn't trying to tell me anything, wasn't trying to urge me to stay on the case. I was reading way more into these things than they deserved. I'd spent too much time of late in the company of a superstitious Irishman and it was rubbing off on me. That's what I told myself anyway, but I wasn't entirely convinced. I've heard of people leaving messages on the phones of the dead. Declarations of love or messages, asking them to come back. It made sense to me. I can understand why they'd ring the familiar number, listen with exquisite pain to the voice on the answerphone and then be unable to hang up without saying anything, without leaving some message of love or yearning.

Ned held out a glass of wine to me, but it wasn't the wine I had to decide if I wanted. I've always been a one-guy girl. One at a time, that is. But ever since Robbie had buddied up with Sean something had shifted in my feelings for him. Ned smiled as if sensing my internal dialogue. There was no denying I wanted this man. I looked at him for an indecently long time and then leaned forward and kissed him on the cheek.

'Goodnight,' I said.

'Are you sure now?'

'I'm sure,' I lied. As I limped ignominiously up the stairs, I half expected Ned to call out to me with an offer I couldn't refuse.

CHAPTER 20

You'd have to be crazy not to be scared landing at Wellington airport on a windy day, and my way of dealing with fear is to be pissed off. Psychiatrists would have a field day with stuff like that but, honestly, there's something manifestly wrong when passengers applaud the captain just for landing the plane. Surely landing the plane isn't an optional extra that deserves praise.

My foul mood hung around like a bad smell. Even the taxi driver didn't try to engage me in conversation. This was a first. Chats with taxi drivers were often a highlight of my day. In my perversely honest heart I knew the roller-coaster plane landing wasn't the cause of my bad mood, though it hadn't helped. What was bothering me was the close escape

I'd had with Ned. The dilemma now was whether I needed to tell Robbie about it. I took a break from my angst to carefully turn my munted phone back on. Two voice messages had been left during the flight. The first was from the real-estate agent, Jason. He started right in, pointing out that this was the second message he had left asking me to contact him ASAP. He used the acronym again. He was the only person I had ever heard do that. My mouth was still working on a response when the second message started up.

'It's me. Sunny,' she said, barely controlling the panic in her voice. 'Dad's been arrested. I don't know who else to call. Please ring me. Please!'

I immediately pressed the dial icon, careful not to dislodge the shattered glass. The call went straight to voicemail. Justin arrested? Fanshaw had convinced me Justin wasn't responsible for Karen's death; assured me his alibi had checked out — thoroughly. What the hell had happened to change the cops' minds? An awful thought occurred to me: maybe Fanshaw told me Justin had checked out just to keep me out of their way. I blushed at the idea of it. If this was so, it was a pretty clear indication the police had lost confidence in me and I had little hope of getting any future work with them. I would have to hang up my missing persons operator boots and do some-thing else for a living. Justin was arrested for Karen's murder — well, it was what I had suspected. He hadn't wanted Karen back in his daughter's life and there was no doubt he was very protective of Sunny. I'd experienced that first hand. How he had got himself to Wellington, killed Karen and made his way back to Auckland in time to take Sunny to the wharf for the meeting puzzled me. No doubt all would become clear.

Sunny's call had taken my mind off my own personal dilemma: was I obliged to tell Robbie about my near miss with Ned? As the taxi pulled into the curb and my house came into view, I made a decision. I was being way too serious about the whole thing. Sure, I'd tell Robbie about Ned. Why not? I'd turn it into a story, make a joke of it, cast myself as foolishly swooning for the rakish charms of a flirtatious Irishman. I'd assure Robbie nothing had happened. Because nothing had happened. Ned had held my foot, that's all. Cupped my sorry ankle, to be precise. There was no reason at all why I should feel guilty about that. I'd done nothing wrong; in fact, I decided, as I lugged my overnight bag up the path, I'd tell Robbie about Ned straight away. Get it over with. He'd wind me up a bit, we'd have a laugh and that would be the end of it.

Robbie was drinking coffee at the kitchen table. Wolf lay across his feet. A bunch of yellow tulips wrapped in white paper lay on the bench. I stalled in the doorway, my mouth ready to deliver the silly story about me and Ned. Robbie stood, his smile already hitched. Wolf dragged himself off Robbie's feet and arthritically clicked his way towards me. It wasn't anything like his usual excited greeting. My mouth opened and closed. Robbie's beautiful smile slowly unhitched. I didn't have to tell him anything. One look at me and he knew. And just like that I realised why I had been in such a foul mood. Ned may have been the cause or the effect but, either way, my relationship with Robbie was in deep shit. It had taken me all this time to acknowledge it. Robbie knew it instantly. Into the awkward silence that lengthened between us, I garbled something about having to go straight back to Auckland, deciding on the spot it was what I needed to do.

'There's a problem there,' I said, excruciatingly aware there was a problem right here, too.

'You do what you have to do, Di,' he said quietly, and took his cup and saucer to the bench. He placed them carefully in the sink and stayed like that, his head bowed, breathing slowly.

I felt the tears threatening. 'I can ask Gemma to look after Wolf … if you'd rather.'

My voice seemed to waken him from his thoughts. He shrugged himself into his jacket.

'No, it's fine,' he said, laying an index finger on Wolf's nose. 'We're fine, eh boy?' I watched the hairs on the top of Wolf's head rise in response. I think mine did too. I envied the intimacy of that touch. He moved into the doorway where I was still stalled. 'I'll pick him up after work.' He paused long enough to run cool fingertips gently down my face. 'You'll be gone,' he said.

Wolf followed Robbie outside and stayed there watching him drive away. Okay, it's official: I'm a shit girlfriend; a shit dog owner; a shit missing persons so-called expert; a shit everything. Shit! Wolf didn't disagree with me one bit. Once Robbie was out of sight, he walked back inside without so much as an affectionate lean on his way past. I followed meekly, determined not to plead or make a craven idiot of myself in any other way. Wolf slumped back down on the floor where Robbie's feet had been and let out a deep sigh. Fine. Be like that. There was a sheet of paper on the table I hadn't noticed until now. It bore the letterhead of Jason's real-estate agency and was headed 'Offer on Sale of House'. I skimmed down the page until I got to a number: $860,000. I held the paper up close to my face and counted those zeros again. An eight hundred and sixty thousand dollar offer. It was fifty thousand more than Jason thought we'd get at auction. It should have made me feel good.

My newly independent-minded phone had turned itself off again. When I rebooted it, there was another panicked message from Sunny asking me to *please*, *please*, *please* ring her. When I tried, all I got was her voicemail again. Making true what I had told Robbie, I booked a flight back to Auckland, closing my eyes while the website confirmed my credit card payment. I knew I was perilously close to my limit but I couldn't work up the courage to check exactly how close. Departing at six o'clock meant I had only a couple of hours to do everything I needed to before heading to the airport. I put my recalcitrant phone on the charger and used the landline to ring Jason. He confirmed the offer on the house was genuine and still live, whatever that meant. If he was expecting a squeal of delight he must have been disappointed. I said I'd give him an answer by the same time tomorrow. He started to remonstrate with me but I hung up. Then I rang Sean and matter-of-factly told him what the offer was.

'Wow. That's more than I expected,' he said, his voice pleased.

'Yeah. It's definitely a good offer.'

'So, what do you think?' he said, failing to suppress the excitement in his voice.

I squeezed my eyes shut tight. 'I think we should take it.'

'Okay,' he said, a little too quickly. 'As long as you're ...' he hesitated, 'if you think so.' I knew he was trying to let it be my decision and I appreciated that. 'Do you want to grab a coffee or something?' he said. 'It would be good to talk.'

'I can't, sorry. I'm flying back to Auckland this afternoon. But listen, Sean. It's okay. I'm okay about it. You were right. It's time to sell up.'

'Actually, Di, it wasn't the house I wanted to talk to you about.'

I waited, feeling oddly detached while he struggled to find his opening line. Wolf still lay on the phantom of Robbie's feet. He had turned his back to me, maintaining an unmistakable posture. Who needs teenagers when you've got a dog with attitude?

'Are you and Robbie going to move in together?'

I wasn't expecting this. 'What?' Wolf's ears pricked with interest at my raised voice.

'Robbie's a great guy, you know.'

I tried for a second 'What?' but nothing came out.

'I'd hate for you to stuff it up, that's all.'

Finally my outraged voice made it all the way past my throat. 'What the fuck's it got to do with you?'

'Don't be like that, Diane. I just wanted to say, Robbie's a great guy and you're a great, um ... woman.' He ignored my snort and pressed on. 'You two are good together.'

I sucked in some air and kept my voice steady and quiet. 'Go fuck yourself, Sean,' I said, keeping it friendly. We breathed intimately into the silence some more, our breaths mingling in a way they hadn't for a very long time.

'Bye,' I said, and hung up.

It took only a twenty-minute hobbling walk along the lower track of Mt Victoria and the occasional lower back scratch and I had Wolf eating out of my hand again. Literally. Smackos will win over the most standoffish of dogs. Tragic, really. I picked up a pine cone, a young one, firm and closed with a shiny golden sheen the colour of its needles, and lobbed it up the slope. Wolf and I watched it roll back towards us. He glanced at me then continued to breathe deeply at the bottom of a rotted tree trunk. Chasing pine cones has never interested Wolf much. Neither had running round in circles chasing his own tail. That was my specialty.

By the time I was back home re-packing my bag, Wolf and I were best buddies again. He even awarded me his most loving of gestures, a surreptitious lick to the inside back of my knee. I bet he wouldn't mention that little intimacy to Robbie. The knee laceration worried him and he spent some minutes sniffing a diagnosis, while I tried ringing Sunny's number again. But what with my useless phone continuing to turn itself off and Sunny's always flicking to voicemail we didn't make any voice-to-voice contact. Justin's arrest would have come as a complete shock to her. As far as I knew, she had no inkling that her father was a suspect for Karen's murder; in fact, she didn't even know Karen had been murdered. It was a relief when my phone finally rang. I thumbed the answer icon and tentatively held the phone six inches from my head. When the shattered screen did eventually drop out, I didn't want it falling into my ear.

'I'm Manny Spears,' the voice said. 'Karen Mackie's friend.' He made it sound like he was her only friend. 'I want to talk to you.' This was a bonus. Tracking down the friend Karen had been planning to go to the commune with had been top of my to-do list. 'Can we meet?' he said. 'I want to talk face to face. I don't like phones.'

I had two hours before I needed to be at the airport. A gust of wind buffeting the house reminded me of what to expect at takeoff.

'Sure,' I said. 'What are you doing now?'

Manny arrived less than fifteen minutes later. Giving a stranger my home address is not something I would normally do, but already it felt more like a house than my home. No doubt in preparation for it being sold, I was separating myself from it ASAP, as Jason would say.

Wolf went through his usual theatrical routine with strangers while Manny stood in the doorway: head bent, eyes averted, weighing him up like an old enemy. The prison tattoo on his hands and cheekbone reinforced my suspicion he'd had run-ins with Wolf's compatriots in the past. Normally I'd tell Wolf to rein in his performance, but this time I let him go the full three acts. After a few days separation from me, he needed to reassert his role in our relationship, and it didn't hurt for this stranger to know I had an ex-police dog in the room on full alert. Wolf turned on a top-notch performance, baring his teeth and raising his neck hair. I almost forgot myself and applauded. When he had finished announcing his full credentials, I instructed him to stay by the door and offered Manny a coffee.

'I'll take a seat but I won't take up your offer of a drink, thank you,' he said, and lowered himself tentatively into the chair furthest from the door. He stole furtive glances at Wolf but kept his eyes out of reach of mine. Once seated, he slid a hand into a pocket and extracted a soft-leather black book. It looked suspiciously like a Bible. I didn't notice any change in Wolf, but it sure made my hackles rise. Manny made no reference to it, but kept the book squeezed tightly in his palm. The cut in my knee oozed blood as I lowered myself into a chair opposite him. 'What can I do for you, Manny?' If he started to preach at me, I'd set Wolf on him.

'Karen liked you. She thought she could trust you. Thought you were straight up.' He shifted in his seat, uncomfortable. 'I want to meet Sunny. Karen's daughter. I want you to arrange it.'

Tiny blisters of sweat formed on his upper lip. It was hard to tell if it was me or Wolf causing them. Maybe neither. The simple act of conversing seemed to be a real strain. He had a past, this man. An unpleasant one.

'I don't think I can do that, Manny.'

For the first time he lifted his eyes to mine. I saw the sweat bead on his forehead with the effort. 'I know how I look with the prison tattoos and all and some folk can't see past them. I don't blame them for that.' He'd reached his limit of comfortable eye contact and turned to look out the window. A fine drizzle slurred the glass. 'I marked myself as a criminal so the world would know it and I have to live with the consequences of that.' His hand squeezed the Bible, tightly clutched beneath four white knuckles riddled with tattoos. 'But this has left more of a mark on me than any ink could.'

I remained unmoved by the Bible, but Manny's use of it as

an emotional anchor was real enough. 'Why do you want to see Sunny?'

He struggled with some inner argument before deciding, 'I can't tell you that.'

His eyes darted around the room and returned to touch down on Wolf. Possibly he was looking for an escape route that didn't involve passing my dog. Wolf kept his unblinking stare fixed on Manny. His milky blind eye appeared all-seeing.

I relented. 'If there's something you want me to give Sunny, something of Karen's, I can do that for you.' This was a big offer on my part. The Bible he was clutching was most likely what he intended to offer and I wasn't keen on being the gift-bearer of it.

'It's nothing like that,' he said, frowning at the floorboards. His whole body was stiff with tension. 'Karen already organised all that. With us preparing to go away and everything.'

He stalled. 'Karen had come into quite a bit of money recently,' I prompted. 'When her mother died.' I posed it as a statement, unsure how much he knew.

Manny threw me a quick glance. 'She kept that pretty quiet, especially while she was still inside. It can be dangerous if word gets out that you've got money stashed away.'

'Is it possible word did get out? And that's what got her killed?'

He thought about the question for a long time, turning the Bible over and over in his hands like worry beads. 'We were giving up everything we had anyway. It's one of the rules of the commune. If it was her money they were after, well, that would be a ...' he struggled to rein in his emotion. 'Well, that would be a crying shame now, wouldn't it.' He stopped, his voice thick. Out of respect, I looked away. Untethered from my gaze, he continued. 'Karen didn't need anything. Except God, of course,' he added matter-of-factly. 'Prison teaches you that. As for me, well, I've never had much anyway. Giving it up is not as big a deal as you'd think.'

'You're still going to the commune?'

'Aye. As soon as I've sorted things for Sunny.' His jaw clenched in determination. Whatever Karen had feared for Sunny, she'd passed on that concern to Manny. I leaned forward, trying to catch his eye again. 'Do you think Sunny's in danger, Manny?'

He looked at me directly. 'Aye.'

'Then tell me what it is. I'll help. I won't drag you into it.'

He closed his eyes and shook his head. 'I gave my word.'

He had retreated from me. Lips moving in silent prayer, he stroked the leather with his thumb, smoothing out the corners. There was a fine filigree of gold tracing the edges. His unconscious stroking gesture was an old learned one. At sometime in his life Manny had calmed animals. I let my frustration with him go.

'Well, I'm sorry, Manny. I can't help you.'

There was no way I was going to let him Bible-bash Sunny, particularly now with her father arrested for her mother's murder. She was vulnerable, a prime candidate to get sucked into anything on offer. 'I keep my clients' information confidential. That's the deal. Karen knew that when she hired me.'

We had reached an impasse. I stood, an indication there was nothing more we could say.

Neck bent, Manny frowned at the floor for a long time, breathing heavily through his teeth. He ran his hand repeatedly over the pliable leather as if he was kneading shiny pasta dough.

'I'm the only one who can give it to her,' he repeated.

If I had been wavering, his sudden intensity convinced me. Wolf felt the tension build and rose to his full height, letting out a high-pitched whine of displeasure. Manny's chair screeched painfully as he pushed it back. Wolf moved rapidly. Pushing in front of me, he pressed protectively against my legs, a low rumble of discontent vibrating against my damaged knee. Manny wasn't the eye-popping, muscle-bulging gym type but he had an intensity that hummed with strength. I looped my finger lightly through Wolf's collar. I would release him if Manny made even the slightest move towards me.

As quickly as he'd coiled, Manny relaxed. 'Fair enough,' he said. 'I wouldn't have expected less. You shouldn't be putting someone you don't know in touch with that little girl.' He reached his hand across the table to me and when I eventually took it, he squeezed mine with convincing force. 'Could you ask your dog to let me leave unmolested, please?' he asked politely.

'He won't attack unless I tell him to,' I said confidently, and put my hand flat on Wolf's head to remind him of it.

Manny walked slowly to the door, his shoulders hunched, the Bible clutched in front of his body. The holy book might have effectively warded off any number of dangers but not Wolf. He was most definitely an atheist. The only god Wolf paid homage to was the heaven of late-afternoon sun on his pelt, the sacred smell of a bitch in season and the state of ecstasy reached after long hours gnawing on a bone.

Manny lifted his collar against the drizzling rain and bobbed his head in farewell, all the time keeping his eyes lowered. I was sure his aversion to eye contact was nothing more sinister than a symptom of his shyness.

For Karen's sake I tried one last time. 'I'm sorry I couldn't help you, Manny. Are you sure you won't let me give something to Sunny for you?'

For the first time he smiled at me. A transforming smile, all sloped around one side of his face. 'No, girl. It's not something you can give her.'

He was halfway down the path when I called out. 'Manny.' He turned. 'What time did you leave Karen's place on Friday?'

'The police have already asked me that.' I bet they had. Many times, no doubt. He paused, hoping it would be enough for me. It wasn't. 'I left around nine-thirty. We were going to have a prayer session, but she was too excited about meeting her little girl the next day so we called it an early night.'

He lifted his hand in a silent farewell, turned his back and continued down the path. Only when he was completely out of sight did I breathe properly again. His tension had been infectious.

Arohata Women's Prison is laid out a bit like an army barracks with one long single-storey wooden building serving both as dining room and visiting area. My visitor's permit was already on file from the last time I was here; to hear Vex describe the details of my sister's murder. I remembered it word for word.

I could still hear the thrumming of a desperate bumblebee against the window, the background noise to her confession; could still picture it, image by image. An unexpected tsunami of grief threatened to engulf me. I held it back but the effort made my eyes sting.

Having previously been vetted, this time I only had to turn up, show my ID, endure a pat-down and relinquish my phone. The warder on entrance security studied my shattered mobile suspiciously but made no comment other than a derisive snort. She had the same response to my driver's licence photo so maybe the snort was an habitual response. Visiting hours were coming to an end and fractious kids, bored with being cooped up all afternoon, were being packed up to go. The room smelt of soiled nappies. But it wasn't all doom and gloom; in fact, there was a surprising family picnic atmosphere I hadn't been expecting.

Vex spotted me before I saw her and had a chance to hide any reaction my unexpected appearance might have caused. She stayed seated and waited for me to approach. It's one of the few defiant exertions of power available to inmates forced to deal with people from the outside. Inside the razor wire-topped nine-metre-high fences, the everyday power struggles between inmates are very real; whether you survive or not depends on your ability to understand and negotiate them. Vex was smaller than I remembered. The level grey eyes were the same, though, the whites, once startling in their healthiness, were now the colour of two-day-old hard-boiled eggs. I recognised the smattering of freckles across her nose. Her innocent look had been a staple of her prostitution work before she was incarcerated. I doubted she would be able to pass herself off as the girl-next-door type any more.

It is oddly deflating sitting opposite the person responsible for your loved one's death. This prison visit was starting to feel like a mistake, but it was too late to pull out now. I cut straight to the chase. The sooner I was out of here, the better.

'Why did you send Karen to me?'

Vex raised her eyebrows at my bluntness, but her tone was flat. 'It's what you do, isn't it? Find people? She wanted to find her daughter.' My eyes were fixed on the filigree of fine lines extending from her eyes to her hairline. How dare she grow old when Niki would be stalled at twenty-one forever. She was aware of me studying her and didn't seem to mind it one bit.

I forced my attention back to why I had come here. 'Do you know who killed Karen?'

'No. Do you?' she shot back.

It would be public knowledge soon enough but I wasn't going to be the one to break the news of Justin's arrest. I forced myself to breathe slowly. If I was going to get anything out of this woman, I had to play it way more softly than this. Before I could come up with my next question she spoke.

'How's Sean?' she asked, going back to first moves, making it clear whose terms this conversation was on. Vex had had dealings with Sean.

I answered honestly. 'I don't know.'

She smiled at that. We were both quiet for some time, while she decided what, if anything, she would tell me.

'You know that Karen turned Christian,' she said, and glanced around the room. 'A lot of them do that in here. There's all sort of benefits.' She studied one of the guards for a long time before continuing. 'But with Karen it was the real deal. She went straight; got off the drugs, stayed out of trouble …' she said, counting off Karen's achievements on her fingers. Her nails were nibbled to the quick. 'Believe me, it's not so easy in here.'

'When was this?'

'As soon as she got here. Years ago now. Before my time,' she said, batting my question away with a swipe of the hand. 'She was totally infected with the God bug by the time we roomed together.'

If this was true, it was unlikely Karen's conversion had been a cynical pretence to win back her mother's approval. Vex read my thoughts.

'It was real alright. I should know. I had to put up with the endless bloody praying.'

'Is that how she and Manny met?'

'Yeah. He visits Christian prisoners. He's been doing that for years. Well,' she added slyly, 'since he got out himself.'

'What did he serve time for?'

Vex leaned back, arms folded over her breasts. 'Maybe I should be charging you for this.'

I was about to get up and walk out but she started up again before I had the chance to.

'Not long after we roomed together she wrote to her mother, asking for her forgiveness. Christians are big on the whole forgiveness thing.' She couldn't resist a coy look at look. 'Me, not so much.' She was baiting me, but I ignored it. It was just as well Vex wasn't big on forgiveness. I would never forgive her for killing Niki. Not in this life, or any other. 'So,' she continued, relishing the power the role of storyteller gave her, 'her mum came in to see her and they made up. All was forgiven. Mother and daughter reunited. Alleluia. Then the mum up and died and Karen suddenly has all this money. It was news to her that the mother even had any money. They'd had nothing to do with each other for years. Since before Karen killed the kid, I think. But Karen wasn't into the money, anyway. She was going to give it up. Her and Manny were going off to live in a Christian commune. What a waste.'

'You didn't try for some of that unwanted money yourself?'

'Sure I did.' She smiled at me, one corner of her mouth sliding up. 'I came straight out and asked her for it. Who wouldn't? She didn't want it! All I ended up with was a fee for giving her your contact details.' She laughed out loud at that. 'There's a word for that, isn't there? Irony? Something like that?'

I ignored the gibe. 'Did Karen get into fights? While she was in here, I mean.'

She gave me a deep look before answering. 'I didn't tell anyone about her coming into money. It would have put real heat on me and I didn't need that kind of shit. All sorts of people would be working me to get my hands on it for—' again she looked across the room and studied the guard for a long time but the guard appeared to be paying her no attention, '—for other people,' she concluded. 'But there were rumours about the money. And Karen got the occasional rough-up to see what would shake down, but no more than anyone else really.' She studied my face. She was on full alert. 'Why?'

I wasn't going to tell her about the little bleeds Smithy had found.

'No reason. I just wondered if she'd made any enemies who might have wanted to have her killed.'

Vex shrugged. If she knew or suspected anyone, she wasn't going to tell me. 'Did you find the daughter?'

I hesitated. Was this a trap? Was it possible Vex was the danger to Sunny? I kept my response on safe ground. 'Karen never got to meet her.' Vex waggled her head. If I didn't know better, I'd think it was a gesture of sympathy. 'Did Karen ever talk to you about her husband? Justin.'

'What about him?'

'Karen was worried about Sunny. She seemed to think there was some threat to her, but I never got to the bottom of it.' I waited, thinking she might give me something. Just when I'd given up, she spoke.

'I used to wonder if it was him who drove the car into the river. Not her. The husband, I mean. She just didn't seem to have it in her.' My mouth was suddenly dry. 'But, you know, when drugs are involved, people can do anything. Only idiots take drugs.' It was a not so subtle reference to Niki. My sister had been an addict and Vex had been her supplier. She gave me another of those long looks. 'I asked Karen once.'

'What did she say?'

Vex shrugged. 'She said it was her. That she did it.' She looked around the room. Some of the women returned her gaze. 'You know, in the men's prison, they all claim they're innocent. But not here. No one here says that. We all know what we did.'

No one smiled in response to Vex's gaze, but the looks they returned to her weren't threatening either. There was something that passed along the lines of sight between these women; some shared emotion that I couldn't quite decipher. Vex turned that look directly on me. And that's when I got it. It was pride. That's what these women felt; what they communicated with each other. They were proud of what they'd done. 'Most of us would do it again if we had to,' Vex said, confirming what I'd sensed. Niki's silent ghost rose up between us. I swallowed bile. I refused to be baited.

'Did you believe Karen? When she said she did it?'

Vex looked away from me towards the guard who was now watching her closely. 'I don't believe what anyone here tells me.' It seemed to be aimed at the guard as much as a reference to Karen.

The air outside felt fresh and cold and clean. Since the prison is right on the shoulder of the motorway, that's saying something. I sucked it in anyway; petrol fumes, sheep truck effluent and all, relishing the freedom of it. Was it possible, as Vex claimed to believe, that it was Justin who had killed Falcon and attempted to kill Sunny and not Karen? Was that why Karen believed Sunny was in danger? Is that what Karen confronted Justin with in Wellington? Is that why Justin killed her?

I was already swinging the car around the last roundabout to the airport, picturing Wolf as I'd left him: gnawing contentedly on the bones I'd picked up for him on the way back from the prison while he waited for Robbie to collect him, when I remembered Norma's phone was still in the bottom of my overnight bag. In fear of wiping Karen's message, rather than attempt to dismantle the phone I'd ended up throwing the whole thing in with my luggage. It would be cutting it fine, but I figured there was just enough time, if I got lucky with the lights, to drop the phone off to Inspector Fanshaw at the Wellington police station and still be back at the airport in time to catch my flight.

The uniformed cop behind the desk eyed me suspiciously. It might have been because of my urgency. More likely he was wary of the phone I was handing over, wires and battery pack dangling suspiciously. When I viewed it with the sceptical eye he was trained to look at things with, I had to admit it appeared not dissimilar to a home-made explosive device. He kept his eyes riveted on it as I repeated several times that I wanted him to give the phone to Detective Inspector Aaron Fanshaw and tell him to listen to the message from Karen Mackie that she had left for me on the morning she was killed. He kept asking me to wait right there and refused to even touch the proffered phone. We argued back and forth for a while and things were looking downright ropey until I offered to write my name and address down for him. He visibly relaxed, and handing me a police issue notepad, waited patiently while I wrote on it. It was endearingly naive of him. If this was a bomb I was delivering, it was unlikely to be my real name and number I'd written down.

With the phone delivered, I broke a couple of speed limits getting to the airport and was soon back in the air, struggling with an Anzac biscuit encased in cellophane that was impossible to open. It all felt a bit déjà vu really. But despite the sensation of my stomach falling out of my anus during the roller-coaster takeoff, and despite the migraine-inducing buffeting as the pilot attempted to level out, it was a relief to be back in the air high above Wellington and winging my way back to Auckland.

Though I'd managed quite successfully not to consciously think about what had happened between Robbie and me earlier in the day, in truth the memory of his grin slowly unhitching haunted me.

CHAPTER 21

WEDNESDAY 28 NOVEMBER 2012

One hour later I was charging my way along the air bridge, juggling overnight bag, sunglasses and mobile. There were no new messages from Sunny. I carefully pressed her number but her phone clicked straight to voicemail again. Salena might give me shit for turning up unannounced, but Sunny had asked for my help and I'd flown back to Auckland to give it to her. I had no idea what that help might involve but I owed it to Karen to go find out. I still couldn't figure out how Justin could have killed Karen, but presumably the cops had a tight enough case for them to have made the crucial move of arresting him. It's not something they ever do prematurely.

Sunny sat cross-legged on the sofa. Pale and dishevelled, she

193

was eyeing the woman opposite her with a look of repugnance. As soon as she caught sight of me, she unravelled her long legs and ran to me, throwing her skinny arms around my neck like a distraught two-year-old. Salena put a comforting hand on her back but Sunny shrugged it off and kept her face turned into my collarbone. The woman moved towards me, her hands twitching with the desire to pull Sunny away from me. I gave her a look not dissimilar to the one I'd seen on Sunny's face.

'And you are?' she asked, her irritation with my sudden appearance barely suppressed.

Ignoring her, I pushed the hair from Sunny's face. 'Okay?' I asked. Sunny sniffed loudly and nodded her hair back into the tears and snot.

'She's a friend of Sunny's mother,' Salena explained, not unkindly.

'My name's Maggie. I'm the assigned social worker,' she said, and held out her hand for me to take.

Sunny pulled herself out of my embrace but stayed close. 'I don't need a social worker. I don't even know why you're here,' she said over her shoulder.

'As I explained to you,' the woman said in the slow irritating way some professionals adopt. 'I've been appointed by the courts to check on your wellbeing.'

She looked directly at me, willing me to leave. I wasn't going anywhere. I put my hand lightly on Sunny's back. Her whole bony little frame was trembling.

'In cases like this we need to be confident the children are safe.' Maggie was addressing me. She was enjoying her role up there at the front of class, telling the poor students how it was going down from now on. 'Sometimes removing the perpetrator isn't enough.'

Salena advanced towards her. 'Are you crazy? What are you saying? That I was involved?' Salena's face was flushed. 'I knew nothing about it! How could you think I would allow such a disgusting thing!'

I had no idea what they were talking about. Sunny dropped herself to the sofa. Hands over her ears, she rocked back and forwards. I lowered myself down beside her and placed a gentle hand on her. I felt the fragile shoulder bones beneath my fingers, the warm vibration of her movement. Maggie continued in her irritatingly calm voice.

'It's my job to assess the home environment and to ensure the children are safe here. I'm just doing my job, Mrs Bachelor.'

'Don't call me that. I don't want that name any more.' Salena wrapped her arms around her stomach as if in pain. 'I don't want anything to do with him ever again.'

Something was most definitely wrong here. A husband murdering his ex-wife is not usually met with such a harsh response from the incumbent. The room had lapsed into silence except for the regular squeak of the leather couch as Sunny continued to rock back and forwards, feet on the sofa, forehead tucked into her knees. Salena and the social worker had stopped yelling at each other and were watching her, but neither seemed able to decide on their next moves. I was pretty sure Sunny was ready to spring if anyone else came near her.

I risked a question. 'What was Justin charged with?'

The women glanced at each other but neither offered a response. It was Salena who finally answered. 'He's been charged with obtaining objectionable material.' Sunny wrapped her arms around her legs but kept her face hidden against her raised knees. 'But that was just to get him away from …' she glanced at Sunny but couldn't say her name. 'They said there are more serious charges pending.'

The pained face Sunny turned towards her was devastating. I was struggling to keep up. Porn charges? Justin had been charged with obtaining porn, not for killing Karen?

Sunny was shaking her head, hair swinging from side to side. 'I can't stand to be in this house one minute longer. I'll just … I'll just go totally crazy!'

Maggie moved towards her. 'That's the right decision, I think, Sunny. I can take you to stay with some caring people—'

'No!' Salena glared at the social worker. 'I won't have her staying with strangers.' She turned to Sunny. 'We can go up to the bach, Sunny. We don't have to stay here.'

A ghastly animal moan started from somewhere deep inside Sunny's birdlike little frame. The sound built and built, louder and louder until she was screaming; a wild high-pitched ululation. She threw back her thin body, arching her spine to an impossible curvature. Feet pounding the floor, she smacked mercilessly at her head. Niki used to do this. I always thought it was something similar to a petit mal, a kind of epileptic seizure. Just as uncontrollable anyway. From experience, I knew it would only make things worse if anyone tried to restrain her. The social worker obviously didn't know this and strode purposefully towards Sunny, her hands ready. I blocked her. In that frozen moment in which Maggie and I were eyeballing each other, Salena running her hands through her hair, Sunny screaming and pelting herself on the head, Neo entered.

'Sunny?'

And just like that, Sunny stopped. She ran to her little brother framed in the doorway, the sunlight creating an angel's halo of his hair. His plump face was pale and frightened. Sunny put her arms around him as if it was he who needed the comfort.

'Sorry, Neo. I'm so sorry.'

'Are you okay?' he asked, his voice breaking.

Sunny hurriedly pushed her hair back behind her ears, used her sleeve to wipe the saliva and tears from her face. 'I'm totally okay. I lost it for a minute, that's all. I'm okay. I promise.' This transformation must have taken a huge effort on her part. It was impressive.

Neo's chubby little arms folded around her, too, and they stayed like that, a tableau, until the social worker broke the spell.

'I don't think the children should be together. Not while Sunny is so reactive.'

Sunny straightened and gave the social worker the cool direct look she had once turned on me. 'I'm going to stay with Diane,' she declared. I nodded my agreement, but she didn't even look my way. Salena hurried to take ownership of Neo. Her hands rested proprietorially on his shoulders.

'I'm happy for Sunny to stay with Diane until things settle.' She put one hand gently on Sunny's arm. 'But only if it's what you want. Of course you're going to get upset. That's completely understandable. If you want to stay here with us, I won't let this woman stop us. We're a family — even without Justin — we're still a family.'

Sunny was clearly moved, and surprised. So was I.

'I'll be okay,' Sunny said. In that moment anyway, everyone believed her.

Salena offered me her car, saying she'd use Justin's. I waited in it, heater turned all the way up while Sunny packed a bag. I was struggling to get my head around Justin being arrested for downloading porn, and not for Karen's murder as I had assumed. Salena said the cops had told her more serious charges were pending. Presumably, that would be the murder charge, but the whole thing seemed odd and I couldn't figure out what was going on. I still hadn't got it sorted when Sunny slammed the car door shut and threw her bag over her shoulder onto the back seat.

'Let's get out of here,' she said bleakly, staring straight ahead.

I started the engine. 'Are you okay staying at your grand-mother's?'

'Why wouldn't I be? I had nothing against her,' she said, making no attempt to disguise her bitterness.

We were halfway along Jervois Road before she spoke again. 'My friend Jasmine was there when the cops arrested him. It's all over Facebook. All my friends know.' She stared out the window at the rain-soaked streets. 'I'm never going back to school. They can't make me. I'd rather kill myself.'

I was trying to find a way to phrase the question. In the end I just asked it straight out.

'What exactly did the police find, Sunny?'

She turned her bleak face to me. 'Me. Disgusting photos of me. Naked and … and everything.' She turned away again. 'He took photos of me.' The lights from the street strobed.

'Shit,' I said.

'Totally,' she agreed.

CHAPTER 22

Sunny curled up on the sofa with a soft blanket wrapped around her. Like a malingering seven-year-old she picked fastidiously through a container of steamed rice and vegetables. It had been a challenge to find anything of the fast food variety that she was prepared to eat and from the way she expertly weeded out any of the coloured items, it looked like this attempt had failed too. She responded to my critical look with a shrug.

'I only like food that's white,' she explained.

She seemed to want to talk about what had happened, replaying events over again and again with little variation. Details were being etched into her memory and with each retelling they would sink deeper. Trauma does that.

'Jasmine and me were in the kitchen. Neo was eating Coco

Pops and Salena was lecturing him about having fruit as well, then Jasmine said there's a cop down by the swings so Salena went to look out the patio doors. Then there was like, this knock on the front door.' She mimed a fist knocking, visualising it, even though she couldn't possibly have seen it. 'And I went down the hall, and I could see them, see the police uniform, through the stained glass on the sides of the door. The glass made them look, like, all wavery. And I opened the door and there were these two cops asking for Dad. And then Dad came down the stairs ...' She turned her head, seeing the invisible stairs, seeing Justin, 'and when Dad saw the cops, he froze. His hand was on the stair whatsit — the railing — and he kept saying "What's happened, what's happened?" And then he kind of just sunk down on the stairs, with his hand still holding on, like his legs wouldn't hold him up any more.' She choked a loud hiccup, her face flushed with the effort to hold back the tears. 'I think that was because of Falcon. The cops coming to the door like that reminded him of when they came to tell him Falcon was dead.' She looked down at her hands before adding, 'And to tell him I was okay, I guess.'

Sunny was silent as I poured a glass of water and handed it to her. She took the glass but studied the liquid suspiciously.

'It's just water,' I reassured her.

'From the tap?' she said, screwing up her face with disgust.

I nearly responded 'It won't kill you,' but stopped myself in time. There were so many things that were inappropriate to say to this girl.

She put the glass on the floor and picked up the story exactly where she had left off.

'And this cop, he was quite old, he walked right into the house and said he had a warrant for Justin Bachelor's arrest and a warrant to search the house, and Dad went, like, nuts! And poor Neo was there holding his bowl of Coco Pops with his eyes all big and scared, and Dad was, like, yelling at Salena, "Call my lawyer! Call my lawyer!" And she was standing there holding this warrant, just staring at it and staring at it and then she looked at Dad like … like he was evil or something and then she spat! Right on his bare feet. Salena just spat this big glob at him.' She lapsed into silence, eyes bright with the memory of it. 'That was so not Salena. We're not even allowed to wear shoes in the house.' A little smile flickered at the corners of her mouth. I suspect she was impressed by Salena's visceral reaction. 'I made Jasmine leave but she was all "Oh no, let me stay with yooou", pretending she wanted to be there for, like, me, but it was just because she thought this was the most exciting thing that had ever happened to her, which it probably was. She was probably filming the whole thing on her phone …' She stopped abruptly. The other filming, Justin's filming of her, smashed into her consciousness. Her eyes were huge with the horror of it.

'You shouldn't have been there when the police arrested Justin,' I said. 'They handled it really badly.'

'One of the cops said they hadn't meant for me to be there. They were supposed to wait until Neo and me had left for school, but they stuffed up.'

They sure had. I didn't think Fanshaw would have been thrilled by the way the Auckland cops had handled it.

'Did they take anything from the house?'

'They took Dad away, to the police station, and Salena and Neo and me had to sit on the sofa with the policewoman watching us while they went through the house. That was when Salena told me what he'd been arrested for and I went to the bathroom and vomited with the policewoman standing beside me checking her make-up in the mirror.' She leaned forward to place the rice tray on the floor, then tented the blanket over her knees. 'Salena said they took all our computers, but I don't know what else they took.'

'So where did the police get the photos from? The ones he was arrested for?'

'They were on the computer at the gym. Salena said they told her they were like soft porn. But, well, they would have to be, wouldn't they? I mean, I've never done anything gross. Except undressing and being naked and … and posing, and maybe dancing and all that. But not in front of anyone! Just by myself.' Her eyes moved, figuring it out. 'He must have been hiding behind the racks of clothes, where he keeps the new imports. He was always saying I could go in there and try on whatever I liked but not to wear them on the street.' She buried her face in her hands. 'It's so gross to think he was watching me when I was, you know, playing around, thinking I was on my own, and all the time he was taking photos of me.' She glanced shyly at me, a blush spreading across her face and neck. 'You know the sort of thing you do on your own … posing and stuff?' I nodded. I remembered trying out sexy poses in front of the mirror when I was her age. Sunny had lapsed into thought, her eyes darting. It seemed she hadn't yet considered the possibility Justin had taken the photos not only for his own use but for trading on the internet. It was impossible to know if Sunny would think this was better or worse.

'What sort of father would take photos of his daughter like that? I've had, like, five showers today already. Salena said that's understandable.'

'How's she been?'

'Who?' she asked petulantly, not yet ready to relinquish being the centre of attention.

'Salena.'

'Oh. She's grossed out too. Neither of us ever wants to see him again. She is actually being quite nice to me,' she added, 'which is a first. I hope he stays in prison for the rest of his life. I hope he dies there.'

'Has Justin done anything before? Anything that creeped you out?'

'No way! Dad's totally old school. He always knocks when I'm in the bathroom and stuff like that. I thought maybe it was Anton who took them. He's such a creep. I told the social worker. I mean, Anton has keys to the gym. Maybe it was him who took the photos.'

It had occurred to me, too. 'What did she say?'

'Just that she was sure the police had got the right person.'

Oh, well, if she thinks that, it *must* be right then.

Sunny followed me into the spare bedroom and stood, arms crossed, leaning against the wall while I stripped the sheets and pillowcases off the bed.

'Whose is that?' she asked, nodding towards a jacket draped over the back of a chair.

'It's Ned's. He stays here sometimes.'

'With you?' she asked, looking me up and down as if she thought it unlikely.

'No. He's a friend of your gran's.' I found him in the photo and pressed my index finger under him. 'That's him there.'

She studied the photo closely. 'Cute,' she finally pronounced. She lifted the photo off the wall to study it more closely. 'His dad was called Arthur, eh? The old man who lived with my gran?'

'That's right.' She didn't turn but instead held the photo closer to her face to examine it better. 'Do you remember him? He would have been around when you were a kid.'

'I don't remember the cute guy, but I remember his dad. He had this totally Irish accent that made everything he said sound funny.'

'Yeah, well Ned's a bit like that, too.'

With the bed stripped I went in search of clean sheets. Sunny was studying a photo of her mother and grandmother when I returned. The sheet cracked like lightening as I flung it over the bed.

'That smell reminds me of Gran. Her things always smelt like that.' It was lavender. I'd noticed the sachet in the linen cupboard.

'Did you like your gran?'

Her skeletal shoulders went up and down. 'Falcon was her favourite. She liked boys more than girls, I think. Or maybe she just didn't like me.' She lapsed into silence but remained staring at the photos. 'Mum said Gran wasn't a very good mother.' A harsh laugh. 'Not that Mum was that hot either.' She tried to make a joke of it but it fell flat. 'I guess there's not much hope for me.'

'Great sisters make great mums,' I said confidently. I'd made that up on the spot but thought it was probably true. Sunny wiped away a tear. I hadn't realised she was crying. 'Are you okay?' I asked. She nodded. 'You're a fabulous sister to Neo, Sunny.'

She didn't respond, but her fingers reached out to touch the image of Falcon.

'Gran came to see me. After I got out of the hospital. I think it might have been the day Mum was arrested. It was before the funeral anyway.' She lapsed into silence again.

This must have been the time Ned told me about, the day Sunny had screamed and wouldn't stop. When Sunny spoke again she addressed one of the photos of her gran. 'That's when she told me Falcon was her favourite. She said he had always been her favourite. She told me she never wanted to see me again and she said she wished it had been me who drowned, not Falcon. I was only seven years old when she said that to me.' There wasn't a lot I could say. She turned to face me. Her eyes were dry now. 'Pretty harsh, eh?'

Now there's an understatement.

I left her studying the photos and went to bring in her bag from the car. When I returned she was sitting in the middle of the bed, the photos arranged around her like a magical circle. She had a framed high school photo of her mother clasped in both hands.

'I look like her, don't I?'

'A bit,' I agreed, keeping my tone neutral.

'I wish I had met her now. Just to check out stuff like that. I'd changed my mind about meeting her, you know, at the last minute. I said no way, I'm not going, but Dad made me.'

'Really? That surprises me. He was so dead against it.'

'I know. He was in such a weird mood that morning. Not that I blame him. I mean, he totally hated her for what she did to Falcon. He probably just lost the plot, knowing he was going to see her again.'

So she still didn't know Justin had seen Karen the night before they were supposed to meet; she didn't know he'd flown to Wellington on Friday night to plead with her to leave Sunny alone. The only reason I could think of for why he would then insist that Sunny go to meet Karen was to maintain his cover. It would look suspicious if they didn't turn up to an arranged meeting. Some might even make the leap that he didn't go because he knew Karen was dead.

'He was never, ever going to forgive her for killing Falcon,' Sunny continued. 'You know, after the funeral he never mentioned Mum again. He never went to visit her in prison or wrote to her or anything like that. And I just knew never to talk about her. We never talked about Falcon either. It was like, to him, both of them were dead.' She put the photo of Karen back down on the bed. 'I thought I had a good dad ...' she said, and shook her head. 'Now there's nothing about him I believe any more.' She picked up another of the photos and studied it for a long time. It was the photo of her leaning on the bonnet of the car her mother had attempted to drown them in. Karen was in the driver's seat, looking towards the camera with what seemed like a look of defeat. And Falcon, unsmiling, was reaching towards the car as if to anchor himself. She studied the image so closely her face was hidden from me. Her fingers slid down the glass like a blessing. She kissed the glass and then, embarrassed, sniffed back her tears and rubbed the kiss away with the sleeve of her jumper.

She was struggling enough knowing her father had taken pornographic photos of her. I had no idea how she was going to handle it when he was charged with her mother's murder. I tried to steer Sunny back there to see if she had any suspicion at all.

'Justin was so against you and Karen meeting. Do you have any idea what changed his mind? Why he insisted you go?'

'It was probably Salena,' she said, her old nemesis rearing her snaky head again. 'Dad does whatever she says. He probably just got sick of her nagging at him and wanted it over and done with. He came home late and she was yelling at him half the night. Neo came into my bed, he was so freaked out.' She looked at me intently. 'Someone killed Mum, didn't they? She didn't, like, OD or anything like that?'

Luckily, before I had to answer, Sunny's phone rang. Her skin turned waxy as she listened to the caller. I could hear Salena's tinny voice still talking as Sunny threw the phone on the floor.

'They've let him out,' she said, her voice barely a whisper. 'He got out on bail. Anton has already picked him up from the police station.' She grabbed a pillow and buried her face in it. I retrieved her phone. Salena was still talking, unaware Sunny was no longer listening.

'He's not allowed to come anywhere near you, Sunny. And he won't. I'm sure of that. But if you want us to get out of town, we can do that. We can just—'

'It's me, Salena. Diane.'

'How's Sunny? Is she alright?'

'She's okay. Give us a minute. I'll get her to ring you back.'

Sunny was biting into the pillow, her arms wrapped around it as if it was a giant teddy bear. 'Justin's not going to come here, Sunny. He knows better than to do that. You're completely safe here with me.'

'How can they just let him out after what he's done? That's so sick!'

'Listen,' I said, hunkering down beside her. 'How about we get out a movie and just forget about Justin. Forget about everything for a while. We can buy some popcorn—'

'Are you totally crazy?' She looked at me in horror.

I thought I'd made a dreadful mistake but her horror had nothing to do with my insensitivity. 'Do you know what kind of crap they put in popcorn these days?'

She chose *Bridesmaids*. I'd managed to steer her clear of anything that looked like it might resonate with today's events. We were at the hilarious scene where the bridesmaids are all vomiting on the white carpet of an expensive bridal outfitters when we both startled at a noise outside. Sunny leapt from her couch to mine and leaned into me, one hand on my shoulder.

'Dad!' she whispered, her fingers trembling.

I made steady eye contact with her, motioned her to get behind the sofa and made a quick dash to the utensils drawer where I'd seen a heavy marble rolling pin. I knew better than to draw a knife. Knives can too easily be turned against you with devastating results. There was a scrabbling sound at the door handle. I mimed 'phone' to Sunny, thumb and little finger extended. She responded with an expansive gesture indicating that she had no idea where her phone was. Mine was plugged into the charger upstairs. The landline would by now be sitting on Aaron Fanshaw's desk at the Wellington police station, waiting for him to listen to Karen's phone message. Excellent. I motioned for Sunny to duck down behind the sofa and readied myself to hit the intruder with the rolling pin. The door opened.

Half an hour later and we'd forgiven Ned for the fright he'd given us. He was good at eliciting forgiveness, probably because he'd had plenty of practice at it. But when I came back into the room to find Sunny making pancakes with him and doubled up laughing, I decided he had more than paid for scaring the hell out of us. Sunny adored him and we spent a happy couple of hours laughing, playing charades and eating. She didn't even mention the pancakes not fitting her picky white food-only criterion. He most definitely had a way about him, this Irishman. At midnight Ned said he had to be off, but not before gallantly offering to sleep on the sofa so as to ward off any late-night bakers who might decide to break into the house, looking to steal the impressive marble rolling pin I'd brandished at him. When I assured him we were fine, he packed a bag of overnight necessities and then stood staring at the side table with a look of bewilderment.

'That's very strange, now where's the telephone gone?'

'I couldn't figure out where the tape went so I took it to Wellington, remember?'

'Oh, that's right. So you did. Well, I'll just go up the road and grab a taxi off the rank then.'

'What tape?' Sunny asked, her back to us as she searched for her own phone between the sofa cushions. Ned and I exchanged a look. Neither of us wanted to say the tape with the message from your mother, recorded moments before she opened the door to her killer.

'The tape on the phone needed replacing so I took it to the manufacturers in Wellington,' I lied.

'Found it!' Sunny declared, holding her phone in the air triumphantly. 'Okay, I'm going to bed now. Goodnight, you two.' She pecked me on the cheek but hesitated in front of Ned, as awkward as the fourteen-year-old she was. Without any hesitation, he kissed her on both cheeks in the French manner and, though she flushed, her eyes were bright as she bounded up the stairs; a different girl to the one she had been a couple of hours before. I felt ridiculously grateful to Ned and when he repeated the cheek kisses with me I returned them with one in the Diane Rowe manner — the lips on lips version. It was a long sweet kiss that made us look at each other when it was finished. His smile mirrored mine. We had crossed a line into something else and we knew it.

CHAPTER 23

I have the dream again. The one of the car drifting down through the murky water thick with weed. Again it's me inside the car. I'm in the front seat. My knobbly knees jut out from beneath the lace edge of my dress. The seat belt is tight across my chest as the car plummets down. Water bubbles up through the floor. Already it's above my ankles, making my feet swollen and wobbly. The water is desperate to get into the car, cascading down from the tops of the windows, squirting out of the dashboard. The metal creaks and yaws with the pressure of the water trying to force its way in. The supermarket trolley, draped in long fingers of river weed, is buried in the silent grey mud beneath me. Falcon's hands are around my neck. He's crying. I take his hand in mine. Sticky, chubby little fingers. I look into his face, all gluey with tears and snot. It's not Falcon. It's Neo. 'I don't want to die,' he says. 'Don't let me die.'

I startled awake to the sound of mynahs arguing in the tree outside the bedroom window. A distinctively Auckland sound; one of the sounds of my childhood. Sunny was curled up in bed beside me, her knees pulled up tight to her chest, her chin tucked into her neck. She looked heartbreakingly vulnerable. I hoped my dream hadn't leached across and infiltrated hers. She must have plenty of nightmares of her own without mine adding to them. Slowly I extricated myself, careful not to wake her, and crept downstairs to make coffee.

I'd bought white bread for toast from the corner bakery and found some butter and marmalade in the fridge. I was pouring the coffee when Sunny rushed in, clutching her phone. 'Neo's totally freaked out. Dad's at home and he and Salena are having this, like, huge fight. I'm going to get him. You can't stop me.'

I flicked off the coffee and grabbed my jacket. 'Neo rang you?'

'I don't care if it means I have to see Dad. I'm getting him out of there. He's totally terrified.' She held out her hand. 'Give me the car keys.'

I pocketed them and made for the door. 'Stay here. I'll get him.'

She paused, unsure whether to argue with me, but I was already at the door. 'I'll bring him back, Sunny. It'll be okay. Stay here.' I closed the door before she insisted on coming with me.

It took less than ten minutes to get to the house. Justin's BMW was parked across the pavement. Anton lounged in the driver's seat, window down, elbow triangled across the frame. He watched me through the side mirror until I reached the gate, then his eyes lifted to stare directly at me. From the pavement the sound of Salena yelling could be heard all the way from the back of the house. Anton's eyes were on me as I pushed the gate open and made my way towards the sound.

They were locked in a scuffle. Salena, red-faced, was trying to wrench her arms free, but Justin pinned her forearms against her hips and advanced on her, pushing her back towards the fridge. He kept his body close to hers so she couldn't get any leverage. Over his shoulder Salena spotted me as I came through the open patio door. She increased her efforts.

'You won't get anywhere near her ever again and if you try I will kill you!' Salena yelled at him and then set about trying to do just that.

I spotted Neo curled in a wicker chair in the corner of the room, his eyes squeezed shut, his hands over his ears. His eyes sprung open in fright from my touch.

'It's okay, Neo,' I said. 'I'll sort this. Are you alright?'

He nodded. His sticky, tear-stained face brought my dream back to me in a rush.

'I didn't do anything,' Justin said, struggling to keep Salena's arms pinned. Her back was against the fridge, Justin's body pressed against hers, so Salena did what any self-respecting street fighter would do. She kicked his shins.

'I don't ever want to see you again. You disgust me,' she yelled and spat directly in his eyes. Instinctively, Justin let her go to wipe away the spit. With her arms freed she slapped him, a real roundhouse wallop across the side of his face. It made an impressive whip-crack sound that seemed to surprise them both. It must have hurt.

I closed in on them. 'Stop! Stop now, you two, before things get really ugly.'

Justin turned at the sound of my voice. Salena took that as an invitation to punch him on the jaw. His head swung round from the impact. Instinctively, he grabbed her shoulders and pushed her hard against the fridge.

'Don't do that again, Salena.' It sounded like a last-chance warning growl an animal makes before it attacks. Calm and very threatening. Most people would have backed off but it seemed to have the reverse effect on Salena.

She pushed her heated face up to his. 'Or what? You're going to hit me? Go on then! Do it!'

Justin's fist pumped. I took a breath and possibly my life in my hands and squeezed in between them. The acrid smell of Justin's sweat enveloped me. Facing Salena I held my arms up, hands open in the classic gesture of surrender. It effectively put my body as a block between them. I felt Justin pull away, leaving me pressed up against Salena's body. Her breasts seemed incredibly hard and, well, there. I wasn't used to grappling with breasts. I did my best to ignore them.

'Don't do this, Salena. Come on, don't be stupid.' I was definitely stronger than her and she didn't fight me but her body was rigid with anger.

Justin headed purposefully towards the hall, then paused, his voice shaky. 'I just came to get my things, that's all. I'll be out of here in ten minutes.'

Salena pushed against me, wanting to have another go at

him. I blocked her.

'Go cool off somewhere, Salena. Come on. Let him get his things.'

Justin was paused awkwardly in the doorway. 'I don't want him touching anything of mine,' she yelled across the room at him. 'And don't you go anywhere near Sunny's bedroom! You hear me?' I was pretty sure the whole neighbourhood had heard her.

'Listen, you two. I'll stay here, okay?' I looked to Justin for agreement. 'Until he's got his overnight stuff.'

Though his mouth worked, he nodded an agreement. I looked pointedly at Salena.

'Okay. Okay,' she said and grabbed her clutch purse from the table. 'I'll go to Courtney's. Down the road,' she added for my benefit. A long manicured nail was directed at Justin. 'I will be back in fifteen minutes and you'd better be completely gone.'

Justin shrugged an agreement, his jaw clenched. Both of them seemed to have forgotten Neo, tightly curled in the wicker chair, his eyes darting from one parent to the other.

'I'll take Neo with me,' I said, hoping to jog their memories. Neither responded, though I knew they'd heard me.

'Just make sure this prick doesn't take anything of mine,' she said and left through the patio doors without so much as a glance towards Neo.

Justin watched her go, muttered 'Crazy bitch' and made for the interior of the house.

I knelt down in front of Neo and put my hands gently on his, which were capped over his ears. 'It's okay, Neo. They've stopped. It's okay now.' Slowly he lowered his hands. The dark rings under his eyes contrasted with the pallor of his skin. A strand of fine hair was stuck to his cheek by a smear of jam. He clutched his mobile phone in his chubby little hand like it was his only hope of rescue. 'Why don't you go and wait in your mum's car.' I handed him the car keys. 'It's parked right outside. I'll be with you in a minute and we'll go to my place. Sunny's there. She's waiting for you.' He nodded and used his sleeve to wipe his nose. 'You sure you're okay?'

'Yep,' he said, his voice croaky. 'Is my mum okay?'

'She's fine. She's gone to have a coffee with a friend. She'll be back soon.' He nodded again and unfolded himself from the chair.

'Text Sunny that you're okay. Tell her we'll be there in fifteen minutes.'

'Okay,' he said. He was already texting with one hand as he opened the back door with the other.

Justin was in the bedroom, throwing clothes in a travel bag haphazardly. 'It's just my stuff, alright? I'm not touching anything of hers.'

I perched on a stool in front of the dresser. He looked a wreck. His bottom lip was swollen and his jaw bloomed from Salena's punch.

'I didn't come here to police you, Justin. I came to get Neo. Sunny was worried about him.'

He glanced nervously at me. 'Is she okay?'

'Not really. No.'

He stared at the contents of the bag as if it didn't make sense. It didn't. Half a dozen shirts and no pants or undies. But he wasn't really looking at his packing.

'I didn't do anything. This whole thing is bullshit. She needs to know that.'

I gave him my most cynical look. He glared back at me.

'I would never take photos of Sunny undressed! Jesus. I'd never go anywhere near her like that. The whole idea disgusts me! It wasn't me who took the photos.' He wrestled another half a dozen shirts out of the wardrobe. 'But I'll tell you this: when I find out who did, I'll kill the bastard!'

'Stay away from her, Justin.'

'I'm not going anywhere near her. Actually,' he said, and paused to yank the bag's zip closed, 'it's probably better if I don't see her again.'

I tried to study his face, but he kept his head averted from me. There was something odd about his behaviour. Something I couldn't quite get a handle on.

'If you are innocent, how can that be right for Sunny?' He didn't answer, just hefted the bag onto the floor.

'What happened in Wellington, Justin?'

He turned to me, hands on hips. 'What?'

'Friday night when you went to Wellington to see Karen. What happened?'

'Nothing happened.' He walked into the en suite, talking sullenly over his shoulder. 'I went to ask her not to meet Sunny. I thought it was too soon. I wanted Karen to wait until she was a bit older. She's just a kid'

'And you gave her a photo of Sunny?'

He reappeared zipping up a toilet bag. 'I hoped it would be enough for Karen. For a while anyway. I mean, I understood she wanted to know what her daughter looked like and all. She was only seven last time Karen saw her. But I didn't think Sunny was ready for it. I was convinced of it. I'm her dad.'

The statement hung in the air between us. I had to fight to suppress the bile burning into my stomach lining. Yeah, he was her dad, alright. The same dad who, meanwhile, was taking pornographic photos of her. He'd heard it, too, I think, and kept his head down as he pushed the toilet bag into a top pocket of the travel bag. I thought he'd finished and was surprised when he started up again.

'But then, when I talked to Karen, I realised I was wrong. She'd paid her debt for ... what she did. She'd changed. She told me she was going to a Christian commune in the States. I told her to take Sunny with her. Travel a bit. Get to know each other.'

I snorted in disbelief. 'I don't believe you. Why would you go from not wanting them to meet, to suddenly deciding Sunny should go off overseas and live with her.'

There was something he wasn't telling me. He looked at me, his mouth working, but then he clamped it tight and hefted his bag to the floor. The moment had passed. I gave it one more shot.

'Karen hired me to find out if you were molesting Sunny.'

He shrugged himself in a jacket. 'You're lying. I don't believe Karen would ever think that of me.' He seemed surprisingly calm and confident about that.

'Okay, it's true she didn't actually say you were molesting her,' I admitted. 'But she did say she wanted to make sure Sunny was okay — that she was safe.' His eyes flicked from side to side as if he was reading text. 'And she was right; Sunny wasn't safe with you, was she?' A flicker of confusion crossed his face. 'Is that what happened, Justin? Karen threatened to go to the cops and tell them what you were doing? Is that why you killed her?'

He was following his own thoughts and answered me by rote. 'I didn't kill Karen. Even the cops know I didn't kill her. Ask them.'

'Salena said there are other charges pending. It's just a matter of time.'

'That's not about Karen's death. It's more of this shit. They're going to upgrade the charges against me for the photos of Sunny. I've never even seen those photos before. The cops tried to make me look at them but I wouldn't do it. The first one was enough for me. It made me sick. I'd never do anything like that to Sunny. Karen knew that.' I must have been looking at him sceptically. 'I didn't kill Karen and I didn't take those photos of Sunny, but, you know what? I don't care what you think.' He yanked up the bag and carried it to the door.

There was only one other possibility. 'Did you kill Falcon? Is that what Karen had over you?'

He dropped the bag and advanced on me, his face blotchy with rage and didn't stop until his face was right up close to mine. I stood my ground but I was intimidated. 'Every fucking day of my life I miss that little boy. I loved my son more than life itself. Nothing and no one can ever fill the hole Falcon's death left in me.'

We both turned at the sound. It was Neo. He stood in the doorway, mobile phone still clutched in his hand. Justin looked at him. He knew Neo had heard him. I expected him to cross the room to Neo. To put his arms around his son and reassure him that he was the centre of his life. He didn't. Hoisting the bag over his shoulder, Justin pushed past Neo and continued down the hall. We listened to him clatter down the stairs, then heard the front door slam shut. Neo was frozen to the spot, staring in the direction his father had gone.

'Come on.' I put my hand on Neo's shoulder. 'Let's go see Sunny.'

Neo shrugged my hand off his shoulder. 'I want to go with Dad.'

As if in response, Justin's car roared out of the driveway, gravel spitting. In silence we listened to it turn into Jervois Road and then the individual sound of his car accelerating was swallowed up by the noise of the other traffic.

The tears made Neo's eyes look enormous.

'Come on, Neo. Let's go.'

'Why didn't he take me?' he asked plaintively. It was the last thing I expected him to say.

I offered Neo a seat in the front but he said he liked it better in the back. He didn't respond to any of my gambits at conversation but I heard him pulling stuff out of his schoolbag and hoped he was content enough until we got to where Sunny was waiting for him only a short distance down the road.

My phone rang and, where normally I would answer it, the responsibility of having a kid in the back seat made me law-abiding — I'd always wondered what it would take.

Sunny was waiting on the pavement when we pulled up. Ignoring me, she opened the back door for her brother and walked him into the house. A casual arm over his shoulder, she chatted reassuringly to him while I listened to the message on my phone. It was Fanshaw, wanting to know why I had dropped a phone into the police station for him with no message on it.

'Unless, of course, this is some kind of oblique postmodern reference to our relationship,' he quipped. Ha ha, very funny. I must have accidentally erased Karen's message when I unplugged the phone. Stellar work, Diane. Excellent.

Sunny and Neo had set up house in the spare room. Like a weird little couple they squatted on the bed, legs out in front, their backs against the pillows, their heads close together as they studied the iPad.

'Has this place got a network?' Sunny asked without looking up. Before I could answer, Neo traced something on the screen.

'We don't need one,' he said. 'It's got a SIM card.' He frowned at the screen and then tapped it. His face lit up with triumph. 'There you go,' he said, relinquishing the iPad to Sunny.

'You're so clever,' Sunny said and kissed the top of his head.

'Facebook is already loading,' he told her.

'Are you sure this is a good idea, Sunny?' One night in the company of a teenager and already I was sounding like a parent.

She answered without looking away from the screen. 'I need to know what they're saying about me,' she said.

Distraction might work for two-year-olds, but I was pretty sure it wasn't even worth trying on a teenager. Tragically, distraction was the only parenting trick I knew. I was still rummaging around in my memory bank for how to say no to a teenager when something else occurred to me.

'I thought the police took away all your computers?'

'They didn't look in my schoolbag,' Neo said, with barely a glance in my direction. 'I was wearing it.'

Sunny was intently scrolling through her Facebook, a look of horror on her face. She wasn't paying me any interest at all. Neo kept glancing at his sister, his concern deepening.

'Do you synch your iPad with any of the other computers?' I asked.

'Yeah, sure. The C: Drive at the gym. I keep my games there.'

I don't think Neo realised the implications, but Sunny did. Her head shot up. We blinked at each other.

'They're on here, aren't they?' Before I could respond, she hurled the iPad across the room. It smacked against the wall and clattered to the floor. Neo's lower lip curled like a cartoon character about to cry. Sunny clambered off the bed and ushered him towards the door ahead of her. 'Come on, buddy, we're going to Tank. You can have whatever juice you want.' She turned at the door, her neck craning round. 'Get rid of them!' she hissed at me, her lips tight. 'Just delete the shit out of them!'

I called out, 'Don't go far,' as she left the room and was rewarded with an ironic look over her shoulder in response. Clearly, I didn't have the parenting thing sussed yet.

There were thirty-six photos of Sunny. They had all been taken at the same time and in the same place. The shots were angled from a position between Sunny and the full-length mirror she was performing to. It meant there were two images of her in every photo. The camera had been set low and tilted up towards her. Several of the shots revealed the distinctive exposed kauri ceiling crossbeams I had enthused over when I met Sunny and her father in his office. A three-walled screen partition gave some privacy from the rest of the room. Some of the shots were framed either side by draped material, giving them an odd old-fashioned silent movie appearance. Sunny was right. The camera had been hidden among a row of hanging clothes. She had no reason to suspect she was being filmed. These days, high-end security cameras are pretty much invisible unless you know what you're looking for.

The photos weren't all that pornographic. What made the images tragic was that the girl in them was just that — a girl of fourteen and a young fourteen at that — with her skinny little child's body only just beginning to imagine itself as a woman. Soft porn, hard porn — what's the defining line? She was a child rehearsing the gyrations of sex and seduction techniques gleaned from music videos and girlie magazines sold at corner dairies. I certainly didn't view the images as sexy, though no doubt paedophiles would. I felt world-weary as I looked at the photos. It seemed to me Sunny's attempts at sexy were more a poignant parody of sexuality than the real thing. In one photo she mimed masturbation. In another she had pulled her skirt up to her waist to reveal her arse to the mirror. It was all to the mirror. All young girls are narcissists. When they're not loathing their bodies they're adoring them. In the privacy of the room, her relationship with the mirror was everything as she attempted to see herself as men would see her: sexy, provocative and inviting. Her performances should never have been photographed by anyone. But what made the whole thing frightening and truly ghastly was that these very personal moments had been captured by her father. The routines were private, for her eyes only. People talk about feeling dirty when they view pornography, but I didn't feel dirty. I just felt immensely sad that these very innocent adolescent moments had been so cruelly taken from her. By her father. They belonged to her and no one else. Sunny had been dispossessed. One by one I deleted them. When I had finished and they were all gone, I would empty the cache.

A thought occurred to me and I hesitated before deleting the last image. I right-clicked on it and checked the shot information. It had been downloaded on Tuesday 27 November 2012. That was the day I had talked to Sunny at the gym. I cleared the shot information from the screen and forced myself to study the photo forensically; Sunny was wearing the T-shirt I had balked at. The one with 'eat me' written over her crotch. I checked what time the photo had been taken: eight o'clock. That was about an hour and half after I had left the gym. My knee stung as a reminder. Justin had attacked me when I was running in the park. If the time matched, he couldn't have taken the photos. My mind raced. Justin's claims of innocence had sounded convincing but I hadn't paid them much heed. But if these photos were taken and downloaded at the time Justin was attacking me in the park — I needed to check that my memory of the time was accurate. But how to pinpoint it? And then I remembered. Aaron Fanshaw had phoned me minutes after my encounter with Justin as I had limped ignominiously through the park to Richmond Road. My phone was recharging in the bedroom, still attached by its umbilicus to the powerpoint. I had to squat down on the floor to reach it. Carefully, I checked the recent calls and there it was; the call from Fanshaw: 8.48 p.m. Tuesday 27 November 2012. I sat back on my heels. Justin couldn't have taken the photos, he was way too busy attacking me at the time. But Anton had been at the gym. He'd caught me behind the counter while I was checking out Justin's flight to Wellington on the work computer. I pictured Anton's eyes sliding towards Sunny.

Finally the pieces were falling into place. Still on the floor, I rang Arohata Prison and managed to convince the superintendent to let me talk to Vex. I waited impatiently for her to come to the phone. There was a lot of clattering and crashing and echoing sounds at the prison end and a fair bit of me muttering 'come on, come on' at my end but, eventually, Vex picked up the phone.

'What do you want, Diane?'

'I need to ask you a question.'

She didn't answer, but she didn't hang up the phone either. You take what you can get.

'You told me that when Norma and Karen made up, Norma changed her will to make Karen the benefactor.' I heard the door downstairs open and close. Sunny and Neo were back. The clatter of their footsteps on the stairs. I didn't have much time.

'Who did Norma name as benefactor before she changed it to Karen?'

It wasn't Sunny on the stairs. It was Ned and he was standing right behind me.

Vex's voice sounded tinny and far away.

'Her stepson. His name's Ned something, I think.'

CHAPTER 24

I'd agreed to hear Ned out without interruption. My back pressed against the wall, arms crossed over my chest, I sat on the floor and did just that.

'When Dad died two years ago he left everything to Norma,' he began. 'I admit I wasn't happy about it at the time. A good share of the inheritance had come down from my ma's side of the family. It's true Dad and Norma had been together a while, but still, Norma knew the money should rightfully have gone to me.'

The thing about listening to someone but not engaging in the conversation is that you get to study the speaker's body language in more detail. The casual lean of Ned's shoulder against the wall, his louche and seemingly relaxed pose — I wasn't convinced by any of it. I told myself I should shut up more often.

'We had a bit of a chat about it, Norma and I, and she admitted she wasn't comfortable with Arthur leaving everything to her.' He pushed himself off the wall. 'Norma offered, as a sort of compromise, I suppose, that she'd name me sole benefactor of her will. Karen was her only child and after what she did to the children, Norma wanted nothing to do with her at all. Nor Sunny, like I told you. Well, it wasn't ideal but I accepted it. It meant that eventually I'd get the money that was rightfully mine, even if it wasn't until after she died. Norma wasn't a big spender. She'd invested the capital carefully. Like I told you, Norma and I got on just fine and I didn't begrudge her use of the money while she was alive. And to be perfectly frank, I didn't think I'd have too long to wait. Her health hadn't been grand for some years. Norma was a fun person to be around but she wasn't exactly a walking advertisement for longevity.' He grinned at me. 'Often those two things go together, don't you think?'

He waited to see if I was going to respond and when I remained silent, he dropped the smile and began to pace up and down like a court lawyer preparing to deliver final arguments to the jury. He may have been rehearsing for the real thing to come.

'So, Norma died. God rest her,' he added by rote. 'It must be nearly three months ago now. And then, lo and behold, the time comes for her will to be read and I learn that some time back she'd gone and changed it and left the whole caboodle to Karen — a convicted junkie who, just by the way, had murdered her five-year-old son and done her best to murder her little girl!' His head swung back and forth in disbelief. 'Oh sure, there were a couple of little personal things belonging to my da she'd left to me,' he waved a dismissive hand in my direction, 'but not the inheritance. Well, as you can imagine, I was not beamingly happy about it.'

He paused, looking to me again for the usual conversational prods, like a smile or a nod. I gave him nothing and eventually he looked away from me. My silence seemed to unnerve him.

'Anyway, I went to the prison to see Karen. I thought I'd have a bit of a fight on my hands, to tell you the truth, but she proved me wrong. Karen says to me she was as surprised by what Norma did as I was. She and her mother had made peace with each other and that was all that mattered to her. She tells me she doesn't want the inheritance; she's going to some commune where they're not allowed money anyway. She asked if I'd agree to her putting aside a sum in a trust for the little girl, for Sunny, that is, but that I could have the rest of it.'

My disbelief forced a barked response. 'Oh, come on! Are you seriously trying to tell me Karen was going to just hand the bulk of her inheritance over to you?' Too late, I clamped my mouth shut again, regretting my outburst.

'It was my inheritance and she knew it.' His indignation was real enough. 'Norma had next to nothing when she and my da got together. By rights he should have left it to me when he died.' He took some deep breaths, calming himself. This was an argument he'd had in his own head many times. 'But I could understand he wanted to make sure Norma was comfortable,' he said, forcing his tone back to reasonable. 'But the deal was that Norma would leave the money to me when she died. She had no right to change her mind and alter the will so that her daughter got everything, and to do it without even having the decency of talking to me about it. Karen knew it was wrong.'

He waited, willing me to engage. When I didn't, he sighed and picked it up again where he'd left off.

'So Karen was going to keep enough money to get herself to the commune and I was in total agreement with her putting some funds in a trust for Sunny, and that's the truth. I'm not a greedy man.' He threw a glance in my direction, hoping for confirmation of that statement, I think. He gave up pretty quickly when I didn't respond. 'But I'd waited a long time for my inheritance. Dad died over two years ago and I'm coming up to thirty-five, for heaven's sake. Norma was dead. I wanted what was rightfully mine. Karen accepted that. It was all very ...' He hunted for the right word. 'It was all very civilised,' he concluded.

'Until you killed her, that is. That wasn't terribly civilised.'

He stared out the window at the mottled rain clouds threatening to drop their load. He looked at them for a long time without answering. He seemed tired now, bored with having to explain himself. He transferred his look to me. I stared right back at him. Finally he spoke.

'It wasn't like that,' he said. 'I trusted Karen would do as she promised and gift the bulk of the inheritance to me. That's why I waited until she got out of prison. I wanted to give her a chance to sort out her affairs. I believed her. She was a born-again Christian, for fuck's sake. That's why I was so shocked when she suddenly up and changed her mind. Just like her mother did.'

The first pellets of rain skittered against the window like

gravel. We both startled. It reminded me that Sunny and Neo were due to return. The sudden rainstorm would hurry them back. I didn't want them walking in on Ned's confession. Ned was following his own thoughts.

'Karen told me she'd hired you. She was wanting to get things sorted with Sunny before she left the country.' His tone was flat. 'That was all fine. It was nothing to do with me.'

'What was Karen afraid of? For Sunny, I mean. Did she tell you?' It was worth breaking my silence if he could answer this.

Ned's shoulder's relaxed, relieved that I'd spoken. I'm sure that, in his mind, my question made this more like a two-way conversation and less like a confession.

'Well, it's pretty obvious now, isn't it?' he said, amiably. 'Justin was the danger. I had no idea about any of that, and that's the honest to God truth. Maybe he did something to Sunny when she was a wee girl. Or maybe Karen had caught him with some other young girl when they were together. I don't know. I never liked the man at all, to tell you the truth, but God help me, I had no idea he was like that.'

His answer was plausible, but I still wasn't convinced Justin was the danger Karen had been so concerned about. 'So Karen gets out of prison,' I said, pulling him back to his story. I wanted it over with now. Wanted to be somewhere clean and fresh and clear. Somewhere away from him.

'So Karen gets out of prison,' he repeated. 'She's sticking to the plan of selling everything up, cashing it all in before she goes away. That was what we'd agreed on and that's all I cared about.' He was quite animated now, pacing up and down, confident, I think, of his ability to convince me. 'I never doubted Karen would do as she promised and once she'd got everything settled, I'd get my money. But then things went to shite. Suddenly she's decided to keep the inheritance. I couldn't believe it! That money was mine. I'd trusted Norma and she screwed me. Then I trusted Karen and she was about to screw me too! And now here she is saying she's going to take Sunny to the commune with her but that they might not stay there. She was thinking that they might even go away to Europe to live, travel around a bit and see the world. She's going on about what a great life they're going to have together, so I was pretty angry. I've got myself up to my neck with all kinds of financial commitments. I've been counting on that money. And here she is rambling on to me about her and Sunny swanning around Europe together, for fuck's sake. And this from the woman who had tried to kill her!' He'd worked himself up during this rant, spit flying, hands gesticulating. He quietened now, letting go of some of the self-righteousness. 'So, yeah, things got heated.'

'When?' I asked.

He shut his eyes, realising he'd gone too far to pull back now.

'When did things get heated between you and Karen?'

His chest deflated as he let out a deep breath. 'Saturday morning.' He seemed relieved to finally admit the truth. 'I flew down to see Karen early on Saturday morning.'

A memory flashed as bright as a neon: Ned's jacket hanging casually on his bedroom door handle. When I'd passed it on my way out to meet Karen and Sunny that morning, I'd made the stupid assumption he was still in his room.

'You were Karen's visitor,' I said, the realisation only now dawning. 'The one we heard on the phone message. That was you arriving.' No wonder he was so shaken by Karen's phone call to me on the landline. Another piece clunked into place. 'You wiped the phone message from Karen, didn't you?'

He shrugged helplessly. 'What else could I do? With you determined to take the phone to Wellington and hand it over to the police and all.'

'You flew down to Wellington to kill her?'

'It wasn't something I planned,' he said indignantly. 'I'm not a cold-blooded killer. You know me better than that.'

He was wrong. I didn't know him at all.

'I went down to reason with her,' he said. 'That's all. It started off just fine. I told her how I felt, she said she understood.' He paused to moisten his lips with the tip of his tongue. I hadn't noticed before how red and plump his lips were; it was the mouth of an indulged thumb-sucker.

'I was trying to get her to listen to me, but she wouldn't. She was like a little girl getting herself all dressed up for the meeting with Sunny, trying things on and then changing her mind. I had no time for any of it. She wasn't paying any attention to what I was saying. Then she says to me that she's too excited about meeting her daughter to talk to me about the money right now. She wants me to wait and talk about it another time. Well, I'd done with the waiting. I'd been waiting for years. And I'd flown down there to talk to her. Well, like I said, I was angry. Justifiably. But things got more heated than I'd meant them to be. I admit that. You have to understand, I was about to lose everything.' He hunkered down with his back against the wall opposite me. His hands open in front of him in a plaintive gesture, strangely reminiscent of Karen's beseeching hands

233

open in her lap. For one awful moment I thought he was going to reach those long elegant fingers out to touch me. 'She fell, Diane, that's all,' he said quietly. 'She fell down the stairs, awkwardly. Her head must have banged on the step or the banister or something on the way down. I don't know exactly what happened, to tell you the truth. It's all a bit of a blur. All I know is that in the heat of it, she fell. Badly. I was pretty shocked by what had happened and no doubt I wasn't thinking straight when I just up and left her. But she was alive when I left the house. I swear it.'

I looked at his hands, his eyes, his whole body language. I had been attracted to this man. Now I was repelled by him. 'I don't believe you,' I said. 'I think you killed her.'

His knees clicked as he straightened again. He was calm, accepting my accusation seemingly without rancour. 'Well, I can see you've made up your mind about me and no doubt there's nothing I can say that will change your mind.' He stretched his back. Story finished.

'Why then?'

He rolled his shoulder muscle. 'What do you mean?'

'Why did you go to see Karen then? Why Saturday morning? You couldn't have known until you got there that she had changed her mind about the money.'

A flicker of something crossed his face. I couldn't read it. 'You told me,' he said. 'The night before, when we were at the restaurant. After your phone call with Karen, you told me she was going to sell the house. I sensed something wasn't right.' He was lying. That wasn't the catalyst for his sudden flight down to see her. There was more to it. He saw my suspicion and cut back to the main point, determined to have one more try at convincing me. 'It was an accident, Diane.'

I struggled to my feet, flinching from the pain of my lacerated knee. 'Yeah, well you can explain all that to the cops.'

'I can't let you tell them,' he said, staring down placidly at the rain-drenched streets.

'What are you going to do?' I scoffed. 'Stop me?'

No sooner had I said it than I realised what a really stupid question it was. Stopping me was precisely what he intended to do. He looked at me with sympathy, then his arm swung out wide. The lights went out then flickered back on again like an old black and white movie caught in a sprocket. Somewhere a loud church bell tolled. A tsunami of nausea rocked me. As the sound receded I realised there was no church bell, it was in my head — Ned had punched me in the temple. The right side of my brain felt like a painfully expanding balloon in some weird 1950s scientific experiment. At some point it would reach the limit of its expansion and would burst. There was only one thought in my head but it was clear and lucid and terrifying: this is what Ned had done to Karen. My legs gave way and I slumped to the ground, instinctively throwing my hand out for support on the way down. My arm hit against the back of his knees. They folded, unbalancing him and he toppled towards me. My hands flew up to protect myself from his fall. The munted mobile phone was still in my hand. I'd forgotten it was there until it smashed into his cheekbone. The already fractured glass shattered on impact.

Ned screamed. 'My eyes! Fuck! My fucking eyes!'

He was on his knees using both hands to hold his eyelids open, screaming and howling in pain and fear. I pulled myself clear of him and crouched in the corner, clasping my big balloon head between my hands to try and stop it expanding.

Salena was in the doorway. That was odd. My befuddled head couldn't compute what the hell she was doing here.

She dropped to her knees in front of Ned. 'What the fuck? Ned!' Her arm around his shoulder, she crooned reassurances as she helped him crawl along the floor towards the bathroom. Her phone skidded to a halt beside me. 'Call an ambulance,' she yelled. She must have mistaken me for someone who cared if Ned went blind.

He was whimpering. 'Fuck, fuck, fuck ...'

While I waited for the phone to be answered, I watched Salena gently brush the shattered glass from Ned's face. Emergencies create a special kind of closeness between people. But it was obviously more than an accidental closeness with these two. There was familiarity, physical familiarity. I'd even go so far as to call it intimacy. Finally, through the expanding universe of the organ that I had once so casually taken for granted as my working brain, the truth became clear: Ned and Salena were lovers.

Once he knew the ambulance was on its way, Ned's panic subsided enough for him to let Salena pluck the bigger pieces of glass out of his eyes with a pair of tweezers. He ignored me completely. It was as if after delivering that deadly blow to my temple, as far as he was concerned I no longer existed. I think this was probably how Ned dealt with most things that got in his way; if the charm didn't work, he switched seamlessly to violence. In contrast, having taken on the role of nurse, Salena became downright chatty and happily babbled on while I leaned my head against the cool tiled wall and focused on keeping the nausea at bay.

'Justin comes home and tells me Karen has decided to use her mother's money to take Sunny away to Europe with her. I know this money is Ned's money. It is the money we have been waiting for. I ring Ned and I tell him: that bitch isn't going to give you your money. I say to him, what are we going to do? And Ned says not to worry, he'll sort it.'

Well, he'd certainly done that. It occurred to me that if I'd slept with Ned that Friday night, as I'd been sorely tempted to, he'd never have taken the phone call from Salena; he wouldn't have flown to Wellington first thing the next morning to confront Karen; he wouldn't have killed her. On a bad day I could feel I was responsible for Karen's death. On a good day … well, I hadn't had one of those for a while, so I'd just have to wait and see.

'Why did Justin agree Karen could take Sunny away with her?' My voice echoed around the room but I couldn't tell if it was a symptom of the blow to the head or impressive bathroom acoustics. 'Why did he agree to that?'

'I don't know,' Salena said. 'That's the truth!' she added, as if it was a rarity that surprised even her. She spoke to my disbelieving look in the mirror. 'It must have been something big Karen had on him because he would never even let her name be spoken in the house. He didn't want Sunny to have anything to do with her. I don't know what she said to change his mind.'

We all turned at the sound of a siren. The ambulance was only minutes away. I had it all figured out now anyway, but I wanted confirmation. I was hoping this was the last time I'd ever have to see them.

'So Ned caught the red-eye to Wellington on Saturday morning and stuffed up your plans by killing Karen,' I said.

Salena did that European turned-down mouth thing that indicated agreement. 'He said it was an accident,' she said, not even trying to make it sound convincing. She kept her focus on Ned.

'Karen dead meant all the money would go to Sunny,' I continued. 'The only way you two could get your hands on it then was if Justin was out of the way leaving Salena as Sunny's guardian.' I looked from one to the other. 'So which of you two took the photos of Sunny?'

For the first time since he'd hit me Ned acknowledged my existence. 'What do you take me for?' he said. I was pretty sure he already knew the answer to that without me having to spell it out for him.

Salena looked away from us both, caught her image in the mirror and adjusted her hair.

CHAPTER 25

While the two ambulance men attended to Ned, I wandered onto the street to settle my nerves and to keep an eye out for Sunny and Neo. They'd been gone over an hour and I was starting to worry. The pavement steamed from the heavy downpour. Having dumped their load on the city streets, huge grumbling thunder clouds lumbered off towards the Waitakeres. The street was rich with pohutukawa, decked out in their full crimson garb. Soon it would be Christmas with all its accompanying madness. The expanding balloon sensation in my head had been replaced with a high-pitched whistle, like wind moving across the prairie in an old Western movie. I almost expected a tumbleweed to, well, tumble by.

'Things settled down a bit in there, have they?' I'd clocked the wiry, middle-aged man bent over stroking a ginger cat but didn't recognise him until he spoke. Manny made room for me on the concrete fence a few doors down and we sat calmly together for a surprisingly long time, the big ginger cat weaving in and out between our legs. Manny was one of those rare breeds of people that you feel comfortable being quiet with.

'What are you doing here, Manny?'

'I hear that everyone does these slide shows at funerals now,' he said. 'No reason I could think of why Karen shouldn't have one of them as well. I came up to collect some photos.' His eyes slid in my direction without making purchase. 'It's her funeral on Saturday.' The cat leaned itself against his leg, head stretched up in invitation, its eyes narrowed with pleasure. Manny responded with a luxurious stroke of his hand down the length of its body.

'I'll let you into Norma's place when the ambulance is gone, if you like,' I said.

Manny smiled and again ran his hand confidently down the cat's back, fingers expertly massaging the muscular shoulders. It arched its back with pleasure, tail rising like a pump lever. Though he still avoided any eye contact with me, Manny studied the cat with direct and unmistakable liking. It did the same in return.

'No need,' he said. 'I can let myself in.' Somehow he caught my expression. 'I warned Karen about keeping her key under the welcome mat, but she wouldn't be swayed by me. She said she wanted to keep her trust in some things.' He smiled to himself at the memory of their conversation. 'I'll come back for the photos later.' He stood, keeping his eyes averted but otherwise at ease.

'There's no hurry.' He brushed some golden cat hairs off his pants but then bent again to give the insistent cat another full body stroke. Something occurred to me.

'Manny.' I waited until his head tilted in my direction. 'Did Sunny come back? While you were here?'

'Aye,' he said, amiably. 'She turned up here with the wee boy about the same time I did. And if you're going to ask me if I spoke to her, yes, I did. I managed to say what I needed to say to her out of hearing of the lad.' He threw a fleeting glance in my general direct. 'I had a message for Sunny, you see, from Karen. That's what I needed to give her. That's why it had to be me who gave it to her.' I followed the direction of his glance. Salena's car was gone. Manny smiled shyly. 'She needed some time to think.'

The cat startled as my feet hit the gravel. 'You let Sunny drive off in the car? With a six-year-old!'

For the first time he looked ill at ease. 'She didn't steal it, did she? She told me it was her mother's car. She had the keys.'

He'd missed my point entirely. 'Manny, she's fourteen years old, for God's sake!'

'Is that a fact?' he said, unconcerned. 'Well, it's true that I didn't look at her all that closely.' Manny didn't look closely at anything. He didn't look at anything. 'She drove off well enough,' he said. 'It looked to me like she knew what she was doing. She seemed a very capable sort of girl,' he declared confidently.

Clearly, in Manny's world, fourteen-year-old girls driving off with their six-year-old brother in the back seat wasn't something to be too worried about.

'What did you say to her, Manny?'

He waited for the cat to return and worm around his legs again before he answered. 'I didn't know Sunny would be here at her gran's house,' he said, blunt tattooed fingers massaging the cat's neck. 'God must have planned that I'd come across her this way and I'm glad he did.' He gave the cat's back a final stroke. 'I find He usually knows what He's doing,' he added with a shy smile. And then to my surprise, he stretched his hand out and squeezed me reassuringly on the shoulder as if I was just another feline in need of a good stroke. His touch surprised me. 'I'll come back for the photos later. I'll let myself in and be gone before you know it.'

Suddenly he turned and strode quickly off down the road. I was about to call out to him but just then the front door opened. He must have heard them before I did and wanted to make himself scarce. First an ambulance attendant emerged and then Ned on a stretcher. Salena hovered next to him, his hand squeezed tightly in hers.

When I looked back up the road, Manny was gone.

A pad of wet gauze covered Ned's eyes. I gave him a poke so he'd know it was me. 'Just so we're clear, I'm telling the cops what you told me.' His mouth turned down at the sound of my voice but other than that he didn't respond. 'If you want to make it easier on yourself you should give them your version first-hand. It'll go better for you, if you do.' He turned his head away without saying anything and the attendants slid the stretcher into the back of the ambulance. Salena held out her hand for one of the attendants to help her climb in the back. They ignored her.

She turned her attention to me. 'Where's Neo?' she asked, looking me up and down as if I might have him hidden in my clothes somewhere.

'He's with Sunny,' I answered evasively.

Satisfied with that answer, she removed her impossibly high heels and hauled herself up into the back of the ambulance.

'Salena, listen,' I said. 'Ring Justin and tell him to meet me here as soon as possible. It's important.' She hesitated and then reluctantly reached for her phone. The driver closed one of the back doors. I leaned in before the other door was closed. 'And while you're at it, you might want to tell him who took the photos of Sunny.'

The attendant closed the other door before she could respond.

I only had enough time to grab my jacket, splash cold water on my face and take a couple of paracetamol to quieten my whistling-kettle head problem before Justin burst in the door.

'What the fuck's going on? Salena said there's an emergency and then she just hung up on me. Where's the kids?'

I thought it would be wise to start with some good news. 'Justin, you've been cleared of taking the photos of Sunny.'

He stared at me. 'What the fuck?' I saw the hope ignite. 'For real?'

'Yep. The person who took the photos has confessed.'

'You're shitting me.' He lowered himself into a chair, a smile tempting his lips as he processed this piece of information.

'That's the good news,' I added and then mentally started counting to ten.

At the count of five he suddenly shot to his feet. 'Who did it?' Bingo. 'Who took those photos of Sunny? I'll fucking kill him!'

I took a deep breath. 'Salena.'

'What?' It made no sense to him. 'Salena?'

I nodded.

'Bullshit. Why would Salena take dirty photos of Sunny?'

I took an even deeper breath. 'Okay. Well, that's more bad news.' He waited. There was only one way to do this — quickly. 'Salena and Ned have been having an affair. I don't know for how long, but long enough for them to decide to set you up so that you'd be out of the way and they'd have access to Sunny's inheritance.'

'What?' he said again. I didn't think I could repeat it. I was about to say I was sorry but then that unidentifiable bruised organ of mine reminded me it hadn't yet forgiven him for being rammed against the bridge post.

Justin was looking at me like I was some kind of dangerous nutcase, which, given the strange whistling brain event I was still experiencing, might have been a reasonable assessment. 'What have you done with my kids?'

I swallowed. 'Sunny drove off in Salena's car. She has Neo with her.' His face drained of colour. 'But I'm sure she won't have gone far.'

Justin sank to his knees. 'No, no, no!' He rocked back and forth, hands holding his head in an eerie mirror image of me earlier. I knew this was definitely in the bad news category, but his reaction was worse than I had expected.

'She can drive, right? She's a smart girl. She's driven Salena's car before?'

He just stared at me, his face fallen in ashen folds, his mouth open.

'It's an automatic,' I added weakly.

I hadn't been all that worried about Sunny until confronted by her father's all too real panic. He was staring at his mobile.

'Does she know?' He looked up at me. I saw the hope in his eyes. 'Does she know it wasn't me took the photos?'

I shook my head. 'Not yet. But you can tell her.'

'I can't ring her,' he said. 'Not until she knows. She won't answer if she sees it's me'

He was right, of course, but I couldn't help. A good percentage of my mobile was presently speeding towards Auckland Hospital embedded in Ned's face, and Norma's land phone was on Fanshaw's desk in Wellington. Or more likely in Fanshaw's rubbish bin.

'Ring Neo.'

He pressed Neo's speed-dial number and waited. I could hear the ring tone from where I was standing. After just three rings Justin looked close to breaking down. Then he let out a yelp of relief.

'Neo! It's Dad. Where are you? Neo? Neo!' He brought the phone round close to his face, and stared at it. 'She cut me off. She grabbed the phone off him and cut me off.' He dialled again but we both knew it would go to voicemail.

'It's okay, Justin. They'll be okay. We'll find them.' His reaction still seemed disproportionate to me but his fear was infectious.

He turned his face to me. It was bleak and grey. 'We've got to ring the cops,' he said.

'Okay. We can do that.' I took the phone from his hand and prepared to ring them. He seemed to be paralysed, in shock, incapable of doing anything. 'Do you have any idea where they might be?'

He didn't answer. His head dropped into his hands and his body folded in half until his forehead rested on the floor. I didn't know if he was praying or if he'd collapsed. A terrible sob racked his body. His reaction seemed way over the top. Okay, Sunny was only fourteen but heaps of fourteen-year-olds can drive as well as anybody. And then, looking at him, a whole heap of things suddenly became clear.

I knew why Justin was so devastated. And finally, I knew what Karen had told him the night before she died.

CHAPTER 26

APRIL 2005

Sunny

The day Falcon drowned, Mum had the yips really bad. She'd been hanging out for her drugs all day. I hated her when she had her drugs but I hated her even more when she didn't. It was Falcon's birthday and I felt sorry for him that he wasn't having a normal birthday with cakes and party hats and games and other kids. Falcon didn't have any friends. I had friends, but I knew not to bring anyone home. I knew Mum's drugs and her yips weren't what other mothers had and I knew if I said anything about it to anyone, we'd all be in terrible trouble. It was a family secret that was so secret even the family didn't talk about it. I hated the weekend days because it meant we had to spend the whole time trying to keep out of Mum's way. Usually Falcon would just do what I said and I could protect him, but something was funny about him that day. Gran had sent him money for his birthday. He'd never had real money of his own before. He kept hassling Mum about taking us to The Warehouse to buy his present. He kept asking Mum if she was sure he had enough money to buy a PlayStation. How did she know how much it cost without ringing up the shop to ask? When were we going to go and get it? That sort of thing, the sort of thing that would really wind Mum up. It didn't take much to wind her up when she had the yips. And on Falcon's birthday she had the yips worse than I'd ever seen.

When the car was filling up with water Falcon kept saying 'I'm scared, I'm scared', and then he undid the seat belt on his booster seat and put his arms around my neck because I was in the front seat. The car was floating down. It kind of tilted head-first, which made my ears pop like on the plane that I went in once with Dad when we going to see his granddad, or maybe it was his dad.

I told Falcon not to be scared and I sang 'Somewhere Over the Rainbow' to him because that was the song he learnt at kindy. It was his favourite, even though Dad said it's not really a boy's song. Falcon joined in singing with me but then he started to cry again and put his face in my neck. I told him it was okay. I told him he was going to heaven where it would be his birthday every day forever. A real birthday with presents and a cake and party games, not the shit birthday Mum was giving him. I told him that heaven was a bit like Rainbow's End, only better, and that he'd be allowed to go on all the rides. He said he wanted to go to The Warehouse with Mum and get his PlayStation but I knew Mum had spent his birthday money on her drugs and she wasn't going to The Warehouse at all, she had just been saying that to shut him up. And when he cried more, when the water came gushing in from the tops of the windows, I promised him he'd get his very own PlayStation in heaven and it would be far better than any PlayStation Mum could get him. That it was called PlayStation Zillion because it was so flash. I told him we were going to go to heaven together and that I would look after him. And I was — I wanted to. But the man saved me and it ended up that I didn't go with Falcon. I didn't want the man to save me. I wanted to go to heaven with Falcon and get away from Mum forever. That's why I took the handbrake off when she got out of the car to have a cigarette. I knew that when she went into that house with the scary dogs tied up outside and blinds all down, then when she came out again with her eyes looking like the white rabbit in *Alice in Wonderland*, I knew she had used Falcon's birthday money to buy her drugs. I knew we weren't going to The Warehouse to buy Falcon's PlayStation. But he didn't know that.

The man who pulled me out of the car made me sit on the grass next to all the swan poo. He told me to stay where I was and he dived straight back into the water again to try to get Falcon. But his arms came up through all the weed and then his head popped back up out of the water and he was gasping in big gulps of air but he didn't have Falcon with him.

Mum came and put a blanket around me that smelt like a dog and she sat beside me like she didn't notice all the swan poo and we watched all the other people diving into the water. All those people scared the swans away. I heard people say 'She's in shock', but I didn't know if they were talking about me or Mum. And then ages later when the ambulance was there, two men came out of the river with the water pouring off them and one of the men was carrying Falcon in his arms and he had green slime all over him and he was white and very wet. They tried to push the water out of his stomach with their hands.

Afterwards, when I was in the hospital, it was nice. Everyone wore shoes that squeaked on the floor. The nurses were kind to me and gave me green jelly cut up into squares and strawberry ice cream. They wouldn't tell me if Falcon was dead but I knew he was and then later Dad came in with his eyes all red and told me the doctors hadn't been able to save him.

When Mum sat beside me on the grass with all the swan poo and put the smelly dog blanket around me she made me promise never to tell anyone it was me who took the handbrake off. She said I got it wrong. She said I hadn't done that. She said I'd imagined it. Mum said that she had killed Falcon, that it was her fault he was dead. And she was so sure about it. And in a funny way, I believed her.

CHAPTER 27

Despite the cool shuddering breeze that had blown up, all the windows of Salena's BMW were wound down. Had Sunny done that so the car would fill up quicker? So it would sink faster? It wasn't until I was halfway down the street that I could confirm it was indeed Sunny in the driver's seat. Approaching as I was from behind the car, it took longer to identify Neo hunched down in the front passenger seat, his fine, blond curly-haired head coming only halfway up the seat. Four sneakered feet waggled on the dashboard. Both heads were bent over, their attention focused on something below the dashboard. The handbrake? Heart pounding, I slowed my step and listened for their voices above the hum of distant traffic and the plaintive honking of the black swans.

Justin had parked at the top of the street and reluctantly agreed to stay out of sight while I approached Salena's car on foot. He knew it was safer for me to talk to Sunny but he hadn't found it easy to trust me and from where I stood, halfway between his car and Salena's, I could still see him pacing back and forth nervously. It was Justin who had guessed Sunny would come here. That he'd been right about it was a shock to me. I continued to walk slowly towards the car, conscious of the need to keep calm so as not to alarm either of them.

The BMW was parked at the bottom of the dead-end street, the nose of the car parked right over the footpath. A wide muddy lawn directly in front of the car sloped steeply down to the lake. Even from where I stood I could see the lake was alive with waving tendrils of lake weed. A noisy gang of black swans congregated around the car, honking and hissing loudly at each other. A fight broke out as something flew from the driver's window and several of them attacked each other with wings outstretched and necks extended. A couple of pukeko high-stepping across the muddy lawn turned to see what the commotion was all about.

Fear purled in me as I walked slowly towards the passenger window. When I saw Sunny's fist punch out between her and Neo I quickened my step. Was she reaching for the handbrake? As I neared the window, Neo wrapped his hand around her fist and they both laughed. They were playing rock-paper-scissors.

The swans screamed their objections with much flapping and screeching but reluctantly made way for me as I squatted down with one elbow casually on Neo's open window.

'Hey, you two.'

Sunny had spotted me approaching and feigned disinterest. Neo offered his wide open face to me and smiled. A spread of fish and chips lay open across the handbrake between them. That's what their attention had been focused on.

'What happened to your "I only eat white food" thing?' I said, ducking my head to better see Sunny's face.

'Fish and chips are white,' she said, biting the end off a chip and holding it up to me as proof. 'The tomato sauce is for him.' Neo rammed his chip into a blob of blood-red sauce tipped into the middle of the paper and held it up in front of her face mischievously. She mugged back at him. The swans squabbled around my ankles, annoyed with me for getting in the way of their fast food delivery. Keeping an elbow casually angled on the open window I closed my fingers around the door handle. If Sunny let the brake off I'd have the door open and Neo dragged out before the car started its steep pitch to the water's edge.

'Neo, your dad's here,' I said calmly. Neo spun his head around to check out the back window. Keeping to our agreement, Justin was still out of sight. 'He's parked up at the top of the street. How about you go see him. He's worried about you.'

Sunny turned away and disinterestedly threw a chip to the posse of swans gathered beneath her window. They screeched their approval.

'I don't want to see him,' Neo said, studying Sunny's profile for approval. 'Not after what he did to Sunny.'

A swan made a move on my laces. Keeping one palm on the door handle I flung the other arm out to ward off the aggressive bird. The whole gang of them went into hysterics, honking and hissing at me. Sunny and Neo grinned at each other, enjoying my discomfort at being ganged up on by a pack of stroppy oversized birds.

'Sunny.' I waited until she looked directly at me. 'It wasn't your dad.' She went very still. 'Justin didn't take those photos of you.'

She looked at me for a long time and then turned away to watch the pukekos prancing on the lawn. Neo studied her nervously.

'Go on.' She turned back to him with a smile and bundled up the parcel of fish and chips in her hands.

'You can take them,' she said. 'I've had enough.' When he hesitated, she leaned over and pushed the door open for him. It almost toppled me into the raucous gang of swans. 'Go see if Dad wants some.' Still he hesitated. 'Go on!' she said, giving him a shove.

He clambered out of the car and then leaned back in, scattering fish and chips all over the seat, to kiss her awkwardly on the cheek. He nodded at my instructions to stay on the pavement and, gathering his diminished package of chips, meandered off towards where I knew Justin would be waiting for him.

When he was out of hearing Sunny spoke. 'Are you totally sure Dad didn't take those photos?'

'Yes.' I brushed chips off the seat to the screaming crowd of swans, climbed in and slammed the door shut on their delighted shrieks. Sunny had angled the rear-view mirror to watch Neo. She shook her head, smiling as we both watched him drop a chip and bend to pick it up out of the gutter. In the process, the remainder of his chips tumbled out onto his feet. He squatted on his haunches and started gathering them up, one by one.

'Who took them, then?' she asked, her eyes still on the mirror.

'Salena.' I thought it best to leave Ned out of the equation for now.

She turned an incredulous look on me. 'Seriously?'

I nodded. She closed her eyes, taking this in. 'Okay. Well, I'm pleased it wasn't Dad,' she concluded. 'They're totally useless, you know? Parents.' She was watching Neo again through the rear-view mirror. I craned my neck to watch out the back window as Justin approached Neo and shook the regathered chips from his hand. Clearly irritated with the boy's clumsiness, he took the package off him and threw it in the gutter.

'Adults shouldn't have kids.' Sunny said, shaking her head in disgust. 'They're useless at it.'

'This is where it happened, isn't it? Where Falcon drowned.'

She dragged her attention from the mirror and stared down towards the water. 'Yeah. The car went in right there. From here it doesn't look all that deep, but it is.' She pointed to where a duck was settling itself contentedly under a pohutukawa. 'And that's where I sat with Mum while they were trying to get Falcon out of the car.'

The lake looked idyllic. Postcard blue and decorated with the delicate question-mark necks of the black swans. They're horrible birds really but they do look beautiful. A breeze rippled across the water. Only the beckoning fingers of the lake weed looked sinister and that was probably because I'd imagined the rescuer striding from the water with Neo in his arms. The pale, limp little body draped in the possessive slimy lake weed.

'Why'd you bring Neo here, Sunny?'

She shrugged. 'Dad would never bring me here after it happened. But Falcon and me used to love it here. Before he drowned, I mean. We always had such a cool time when we came here. We used to love chasing the swans and we used to pretend this was our very own front lawn; we even pretended that we'd live here in one of those rich people's houses one day — you know, just me and him — and we'd spend all day here, just hanging out with the swans and having picnics and everything. When I was a kid this was the only place where I was happy.' She stopped, embarrassed at having given away so much. 'We didn't have stuff, you know, like toys or a dog or anything like that. I adopted a stray cat once but it wasn't supposed to come inside and Mum wouldn't let me feed it. I don't know what happened to it …' She stared off towards the horizon, remembering. 'We never had any money. It all went on the drugs, I suppose, but I didn't really understand any of that when I was, like, seven.' She looked at me frankly, without guile. 'I just thought Neo would like it here too. Like Falcon and I did.'

'It was you who let the handbrake off, wasn't it? Not Karen.'

She looked out again to where the sky met the water. 'I meant for us both to die. But the guy dragged me out first. Falcon's foot was trapped under my seat. I think it got twisted up in the seat belt. The man went back for him but he was already dead by the time they got him out.'

'Why did Karen take the blame?'

'She told me it was her fault and, I don't know, I just kind of believed it and then after a while, I just, well, I kind of forgot it was me.'

She continued to stare out towards the horizon but her hand hovered near the handbrake. She was reliving that moment seven years ago when she had pulled it towards her and then released it. I looked at the long sloping lawn leading to the lake. The car would have rolled slowly at first and then, gathering speed, it would have rushed headlong down into the lake. I imagined it floating. For how long? Seconds? And then it must have tipped, the weight of the engine tilting it forward, and then silently sunk into the water, claimed by those long waving arms of lake weed.

Sunny's pale skin was even whiter than usual. 'Gran knew,' she said, her eyes blank as she remembered. 'She came round to our place the day after it happened. The day the police took Mum away. When we were alone, Gran said she knew I killed Falcon, but that Mum deserved all she got. She said she wouldn't tell but she never wanted to see me again. She said she'd always loved Falcon more than me.' She shrugged. 'I screamed and screamed at her but I don't blame her for hating me.'

She was surprisingly calm. I reminded myself again that she'd lived with these horrors for most of her life.

'What did Manny say to you? When you saw him outside your gran's place. What did he tell you?'

She smiled to herself before answering. 'He said Mum was frightened for me. That she thought carrying the guilt of killing Falcon and the guilt of her taking the blame for it would eventually, you know, destroy me. She wanted me to tell the truth. To confess.'

I remembered Karen had said something similar to me on the phone the night before I was to meet Sunny and Justin. Something about the importance of taking responsibility. That it was the only way you can forgive yourself. I had assumed she was talking about herself, and maybe she was. But now I realised she had been talking about Sunny, too.

She looked at me directly, her eyes clear and untroubled. 'I don't know if she meant I should confess to, like, a priest or a minister or something. Or if she meant the police. I guess I'll never know that now.' She turned that delicate neck to stare at the horizon again. 'She was going to stand beside me when I did it.'

Suddenly, Sunny's door was flung open. We both startled.

'Get out of the car, Sunny.' Justin was dealing with this situation in the same way he dealt with everything: with anger.

'Leave her alone, Justin. I'll drive her back ...' I stopped myself from saying 'home'. I didn't know where that was any more. Sunny probably didn't either.

He ignored me and bent down to yell in Sunny's face. 'What the fuck did you think you were doing with Neo?'

Her head dropped. She answered calmly but her lips and voice trembled. 'You never see what's really going on, Dad. You never saw it with Falcon and you never saw it with me. You never looked out for us. You're the same with Neo. You and Salena never see what's going on for him. You're all the same; all parents are the same. You only think of yourselves. I just wanted to get him away from that shit for a while.'

She was brave, this girl. I'd thought it the first time I'd met her.

'But why the fuck did you bring him here? Why here?!'

She choked back a sob. 'I would never hurt him, Dad.'

Justin reached in and grabbed her arm. He pulled her out

of the car. She let herself be manhandled by him. I leapt out my side, scattering outraged swans in all directions. Justin stepped back from her, his hands held up. She remained just where he'd put her. Her arms hung loosely at her sides. Sunny's passivity seemed to frustrate him. I lurched around the bonnet towards them just as he leaned forward and yelled right in her face. 'It's where he fucking died!'

I pulled up beside them.

Sunny tilted her face up to him. 'You think I don't know that!'

I hovered nervously, ready to step between them if Justin so much as put a fingertip on her.

'Falcon was the only person in the world who loved me,' she yelled at him. 'You and Mum didn't care about us. And when he died I was completely alone.'

Justin took a step back from her anger.

'I'm going to lose Neo now, too, aren't I? You and Salena are going to break up and I'll never see him!'

Justin opened his mouth to speak and then shut it.

Sunny's anger seemed to dissolve. Her voice broke. 'I've lost you, too, Dad, haven't I?'

I thought he'd put his arms around her. I thought he'd tell her she would never lose him. He didn't. They stood like that, facing each other, not touching. He walked a few steps away and then, before I could do anything, he spun on his heels and walked back. He stood in front of Sunny, shuffling from one foot to the other, trying to find the right words. She waited, her eyes enormous from the tears. When he did speak, it was straight to the point.

'Look, Sunny, I wish I was a bigger person and all. But the fact is, I'm not. I can never forgive you for killing Falcon. That's just how it is. It's better that you know that.' The heat was gone but that just made it all the more devastating. With one final immense shrug that said all the things he was unable to say with words, Justin turned and walked away.

Sunny stared dry-eyed at his departing back. Then she turned her gaze to where a satisfied duck squatted beneath the pohutukawa. It was the same place she had been sat, seven years old, bedraggled, half-drowned, to wait for her brother's body to be lifted to the surface. I put my hands on her arms and pulled her little body towards me. She was even lighter than I imagined. I drew her into my arms and she stayed there. Over her shoulder I could see Neo watching. Justin had his back turned, mobile phone to his ear.

He was calling the police.

CHAPTER 28

Robbie put his arm around Sunny's gaunt shoulders. He's the kind of guy who can do that without thinking too much about it. It was good of him to be there and, even though she'd only met him an hour before, Sunny leaned into his shoulder. I took that as a good omen. Being able to take comfort from someone is a good place to start when it comes to relationships. Sunny hadn't had a great start in life but little signs like this made me optimistic for her.

There were just three of us in the front pew on the family side of the church. Justin had agreed to Sunny attending her mother's funeral, which was something, I guess. Sunny didn't want Neo there and I'm pretty sure Justin wouldn't have let him come anyway. Both Ned and Salena, though nominally family, were otherwise engaged, aka in prison awaiting bail hearings. Ned continued to claim his innocence. He was sticking to his story that Karen's death had been an accident; in the midst of their argument she had fallen down the stairs and had hit her head. Seven years earlier Karen had accepted her penance and served a prison sentence for a crime she hadn't committed. To be killed only hours before she was to begin a new life both for herself and Sunny ... well, that was a crime I hoped wouldn't go unpunished. It would be up to a jury to decide if Ned was telling the truth — or not. As for me, I was in no doubt he had killed her. Whether he had done it hot-bloodedly or in cold-blood made no difference really. Karen was still dead.

Manny was the only occupant of the front row on the friends side of the church. Aaron Fanshaw was sitting in a back pew, probably hoping to make a quiet getaway part-way through proceedings. I counted ten other people in the congregation of mourners but I was pretty sure most of them were ring-ins from the minister or habitual funeral-goers who weren't fussy about whose big day it was. If I'd known there would be so few people I'd have hauled in a few ring-ins of my own, Gemma certainly, and maybe even Smithy, though he may have a code about going to funerals of people he has autopsied. Hard to know with Smithy.

The police were still 'looking into' what they would do with Sunny's confession for Falcon's death seven years earlier. No one wanted to reopen the case. No one wanted to admit they'd been wrong in sending Karen to prison, particularly now that she was dead. As for Sunny, once the truth had surfaced she had refused to back away from it. She'd insisted on giving a straight-up factual statement to the police. Justin had talked her into waiting until he engaged a lawyer for her but, despite the lawyer's advice, Sunny stated categorically that she had known what she was doing when she took the handbrake off: she had intended both her and Falcon to die, but had succeeded in killing only her little brother. No one wanted to prosecute a fourteen-year-old girl for something she did when she was only seven. The criminal age of responsibility being ten, she was too young at the time of the offence to be now charged with murder or homicide, but the authorities were still arguing among themselves over whether she should be punished for not admitting her guilt sooner. And it would involve different authorities to decide whether she comprehended her guilt even now. The arguments would go on for a very long time and without doubt none of those arguments would go to the heart of what Falcon's death had really been about. Things would take their course now but the process would be slow. In the meantime Sunny had booked herself into an exclusive boarding school somewhere in Vermont. The kind of place rich kids are sent to keep them as far away as possible from their parents' lifestyles. It was the kind of place Sunny could go to reinvent herself. With Norma's inheritance now going directly to her, there was no lack of money. Justin made no claims to any of it. He told her she was welcome to come home in the school holidays but they both knew it would be avoided if possible. She wouldn't come back if she could be somewhere else, not for some years to come, anyway. She'd make friends at the school and go to their homes in the breaks. Sunny was, as Manny had reported, a very capable sort of a girl. She had never had the chance to be anything else.

Manny shuffled his way to the front and I readied myself for the big God speech from him. The old 'For everything there is a season, and a time for every matter under heaven: a time to be born, and a time to die; a time to plant, and a time to pluck up what is planted' or some other all-time funeral favourite, but he surprised me. Instead of stepping up to the microphone, Manny stood beside the coffin, one hand resting lightly on it as you do on a friend's shoulder. He spoke simply about Karen and what he said was all the more eloquent because of it. He talked of little things, such as her love of 'sixties television shows, like *Hogan's Heroes* and *Doctor Who*. Sunny squeezed my hand and when I turned to her she whispered, 'I love *Doctor Who*.' Her eyes were bright and it wasn't just the tears. Manny talked of demons, but it wasn't the pitchfork fiery-hell variety; he talked instead of Karen's struggle to overcome the demons of her drug habit and he praised her for her eventual victory over it. He talked of the love she had for her children and how much she had been looking forward to spending time with Sunny again. I glanced at Sunny, expecting to see a sneer but she was looking at the coffin as if it was Karen herself speaking to her and she nodded. Manny was an honest and warm speaker and when he finished we were all smiling. Before walking slowly back to his pew he knocked three times on the lid of the coffin. I don't know if it was a rehearsed gesture or what it meant. It may have been a simple tattoo of farewell or a private superstitious code. It didn't matter. He'd earned the right to farewell his friend as he saw fit.

While we joined the minister in a tragically thin and tuneless version of 'Nearer, My God, to Thee', Manny fumbled with the keyboard of a laptop. Sunny watched him, then pushed past me towards him. Robbie and I exchanged a look but let her go. She leaned across Manny and clicked confidently at the keyboard and then straightened up as an image on a screen at the side of the altar appeared. It was a photo of a young Karen holding a newborn baby, Sunny. Karen's cheeks were flushed, her eyes shining as she held the brand new soft-cheeked being to her face and breathed her love onto her. The photo faded and was replaced with another and then another. I hadn't seen any of the images before. Manny must have found them at Norma's or maybe they were from a personal collection Karen had kept to herself. The hymn petered out and was thankfully replaced by the soundtrack accompanying the photos. It was a version of 'Somewhere Over the Rainbow' that I hadn't heard before. It was perfect. Sunny and Manny exchanged a look; this song was obviously Sunny's choice and they'd organised this tribute of photos and music together. There were early photos of Karen with baby Falcon too; Sunny still a toddler leaning over to kiss his little scrunched-up new baby face. One by one, the images faded to be replaced by another. There were photos of Karen as a young girl. One was of her holding a rabbit almost as big as her; another of her on a three-wheeler bike, her head thrown back in laughter, a gap where her front teeth had once been. Sunny was transfixed by these images. Her mouth partly open, her eyes shining.

Outside the church the ring-ins wandered off. Fanshaw raised two fingers to his temple in salute and threw a grin in my direction. I caught it and gave him a wan smile in response. I stayed back from the hearse and watched as Sunny leant forward to say something to Manny. He nodded and moved away from the coffin to give her privacy. She reached into her pocket and withdrew what looked like, from where I was standing, a small plastic toy robot. She placed it carefully on the coffin and then stepped back as if an important task had been completed. It meant something to her, this toy, but I had no idea what.

I waited until the coffin had been slid into the back of the hearse, then wandered off to join Robbie, waiting for me beneath the big pohutukawa tree smothered in the crimson blooms of summer; New Zealand's Christmas tree. It reminded me of the first time I had spoken with Karen, when she'd phoned me at the swimming pool while I was awkwardly waiting out the two minutes' silence in memory of the anniversary of the dead Pike River miners. The pool had been decorated with the first of the early Christmas decorations and I had been feeling less than festive. As I looked down the street I noticed it was festooned with bells and angels and Santa Clauses. Two weeks had passed since Karen had first called me and I still wasn't feeling all that ho-ho-ho. Mind you, a lot had happened in those couple of weeks.

'You think she'll be okay?' Robbie asked.

I glanced over at Sunny. She was listening to Manny, nodding. One foot was turned in and her head was tilted to the side like a little girl's. She was still very young and the young heal well, I think. 'I hope so,' I said.

'What about you, Di? Will you be okay?'

I looked at him directly. 'I'm sorry, Robbie. Sorry about all of it. I fucked up.'

'Hey, careful. God is just in there, you know,' he said, angling his head towards the church. We exchanged droll looks and then scuffed our feet in the gravel as the silence between us lengthened. Both Detective Inspector Aaron Fanshaw and my ex-husband had used the same phrase to describe Robbie; they'd both said he was a great guy. No argument from me there. Robbie Lather was most definitely a great guy. But even though I would most likely live to regret it, Robbie being a great guy wasn't enough to make me stay.

'Can I come visit Wolf in Auckland? We might even let you join us for a walk, if you wanted.'

'Yeah, definitely. We'd both like that,' I said, and it was true.

He tipped an imaginary hat at me and walked off towards Sunny to say goodbye. And he took that fabulous hitched grin with him. I missed it already.

There's a theory that ghosts aren't apparitions of the dead but echoes of the living. That house hauntings are the memories, thoughts, passions and dreams of past inhabitants. According to the theory, it's the living who haunt as often and as convincingly as the dead. All those dreams where you walk through houses you've lived in; well, that's you haunting the rooms, causing shivers up the spines of the inhabitants. You're the glimpse out of the corner of the eye, the shimmer on the stairs. And the stronger the emotions you experienced when living in a place, the more powerful the haunting. That's how the theory goes anyway. If it's true, then I didn't envy the people who had bought our house; the place Sean and I had bought and lived out our marriage in together. The new owners may have thought they'd got a bargain but, if that theory of hauntings was correct, my guess is that pretty soon they'd be running from the property screaming for ghostbusters. Something about that haunting theory always fitted with me. It seemed right. And my own addition to this theory is the belief that the only way to exorcise those old ghosts is to beat them at their own game; have even more powerful emotions and experiences in the place you inhabit than those ghosts did. Fill it with your own vibrations, inhabit it fully with all the life you can muster. Become your own haunting.

The furniture had been sold. Our belongings finally divided up between us. It was much easier than I think either Sean or I imagined it would be. There were no arguments. No 'That book's yours', 'This one's mine', 'Whose is this?', 'I don't like it anyway so you have it'. The detritus of a relationship, when all said and done, is tragically inconsequential. Our footsteps echoed through the empty rooms, loud on the wooden floorboards, recycled demolition rimu. I'd sanded, Sean had pollied. We kept our voices low out of respect for the ghosts who howled all around us. It was good of Sean to do this, walk through the house with me one last time. But it had the opposite effect to what I thought it would; I felt the distance between us, not the closeness. He'd moved away from me and, with heart sinking into my gut, I finally had to admit I had moved away from him, too. There was no suggestion of anything as crass as a goodbye fuck and we steered clear of any declarations of everlasting or any other kind of love or promises we'd once so willingly made each other. We kissed goodbye and held each other for long enough. Then Sean walked to the door for the last time and closed it quietly behind him. I stood, rooted to the spot, listening to the creaking of the house, the rattle of the loose glass in the frames.

And in that big empty room, I danced. It wasn't something I'd planned to do, which is probably why it was okay. I danced with the ghosts of friends, of family, parties, laughter, tears. I danced with the years that were gone and could never be recovered. I danced with the beauty of what had been the beginning of our love and I danced with the tragedy of it ending. I danced for our imagined children who would now never be born. And I danced to my dead sister, Niki, whose voice still echoed in these empty rooms. I danced to the youthful love Sean and I once had and the mature love we'd lost. And I danced because if I didn't dance, I'd crouch down in the corner by that bit of skirting we'd always said we'd fix but never did, and I'd weep. And this house, our shelter, our home, deserved to be honoured in some way that wasn't about weeping and wasn't about real-estate agents or mortgages or settlements. I danced because it seemed right to dance.

And that dance would undoubtedly haunt the house forever.

And when the dance was ended, I put the keys and a bottle of wine for the new owners on the benchtop, picked up Wolf's smelly old sheepskin and walked quickly out of the house. I drove away with Wolf's familiar breath huffing on my neck and I didn't turn back around. Not once.

ACKNOWLEDGEMENTS

Thanks to my agent, Daniel Myers, for his expert advice and encouragement. Thanks as always to my family for their generosity and kindness, and to Max for his expertise; to Bella Leia for reminding me of the strength of innocence and to Mischa for the importance of humour. And thanks to Ian, my partner in life and crime.